"You have two hours to gather your things and leave our country. I'll send an officer to your hotel to escort you to the airport. Don't ever come back, *comprenden, gringos?*" the police sergeant ordered.

"Si, comprendamos, capi," Gage hastily responded in agreement. He had a butterfly bandage over his left eye and purple bruises under both. He draped Ethan's arm over his shoulder and started down the short flight of steps. "Jesus, Ethan, I don't know why I keep working with you. You look like shit, by the way."

Ethan winced with every step but said nothing. He glanced over his shoulder at the sergeant still scowling at them from the top of the steps.

"Now what do we do?" Gage asked. "They smashed my camera, so we got no video of those fuckers trawling in a protected reserve. They offloaded before we got back to port, so we got no proof of their catch. We ain't got squat, boss. Hell, we got less than squat. You got broke ribs. My nose probably is as well." Gage cringed, touching the bridge of his nose. "Messed up my pretty face, goddammit. Our sponsor fired us, man! We used all our money to get out of jail. We're fucked, man, just plain fucked."

Ethan kept silent while they shuffled on, a dull pain punctuating his every step.

"You got nuthin to say?" Gage said. "Nuthin at all?" Ethan looked over his shoulder again at the sergeant. Figuring they'd gone far enough, he lifted his hand to his mouth and spat something into it. Turning toward Gage, he smiled and winked his right eye—the one not swollen shut.

"The memory stick!" Gage exclaimed. "How did you…? You cagey son of a bitch."

Praise for *VARUNA*

The manuscript was selected as a finalist for best novel in the Thriller category in the 2018 Pacific Northwest Writers Association contest.

Varuna

by

Phillip Vincent

This is a work of fiction. Names, characters, places, and incidents are either the product of the author's imagination or are used fictitiously, and any resemblance to actual persons living or dead, business establishments, events, or locales, is entirely coincidental.

Varuna

Contact Information: info@thewildrosepress.com

Cover Art by *Kristian Norris*

The Wild Rose Press, Inc.
PO Box 708
Adams Basin, NY 14410-0708
Visit us at www.thewildrosepress.com

Publishing History
First Crimson Rose Edition, 2019
Print ISBN 978-1-5092-2771-6
Digital ISBN 978-1-5092-2772-3

Published in the United States of America

Dedication

Dedicated to the memory of Luella and Price,
my mom and dad.
I would like to thank my sisters, Alice and Sherrill,
for their unwavering support.

Chapter 1

Jakarta, Indonesia

The steel door swung open and sunlight spilled onto the concrete floor. A guard reached out and gruffly ushered Malik Bashir inside, then pointed to the far end of the cavernous warehouse where a single light hung from the high ceiling. Malik started across the floor toward the light, when the clang of the heavy door slamming shut behind him stopped him in his tracks.

Malik had bolstered his confidence rehearsing what he would say while on his way to the dank warehouse in the Maura Angke slum on the northern outskirts of Jakarta, but now his courage faltered. Needing more time, he lit a cigarette and paused to let his eyes adjust to the dim light. He took a drag, noticed his hand tremble, then dropped and crushed out the cigarette with the toe of his boat shoe. He set his jaw and started toward a group of men under the light at the far end.

The warehouse smelled of dust and moldy cardboard and was stacked high with boxes and crates. The rubber soles of Malik's shoes squeaked with each step, the sound reverberating down the wide corridor, making him all the more nervous. Approaching the far end, he recognized Anand Priya, the man who'd summoned him. To his left, stood another man with shoulders as broad as he was tall, a long braided beard, and a fierce scowl. There was no mistaking Eko, Anand's ever-present bodyguard and enforcer. A chill ran up Malik's spine. *Courage.*

Another man was seated between the two in a folding metal chair, wearing what appeared to Malik to be a green military jacket. The man's hands were tied behind his back, his knees strapped together with a belt, and his ankles bound to the front legs of the chair. His face was bruised and swollen, and his jacket and shirt ripped open, exposing an undershirt soaked with sweat and stained with blood.

Eko cast a contemptuous glance toward Malik and then poked at a burlap bag on the floor at the man's feet. The bag writhed and twisted in response. The man in the chair saw Malik and struggled at his bindings. "You've come to help me?" he pleaded. "Please! He's insane. Get me out of here."

"Ah, *selamat pagi,* Malik." Anand ignored the man's pleas and greeted Malik in Indonesian as if he'd unexpectedly run into an old acquaintance. He glanced at Eko. "Shut that blubbering fool up while I talk with my old friend, Malik."

Eko picked up a roll of duct tape, tore off a piece, and slapped it across their captive's mouth.

Anand had been a leader of the Black Sea Tigers, a commando unit of the Tamil Tigers, but now his business was gunrunning, smuggling, and hijacking. More recently he'd added running illegal fishing fleets poaching the waters of protected marine reserves. He used the warehouse to store and distribute stolen or smuggled merchandise and to interrogate, torture, or execute his enemies.

"You arrived just in time," Anand said. He walked

behind the seated man and patted his shoulders. Anand was dressed impeccably, as usual: white linen shirt, its sleeves rolled perfectly up to just below the elbows, tailored silk slacks with creases like the features of his face, sharp as a dagger's edge. The patches of gray at his temples softened his otherwise hard features, giving him an air of sophistication, even kindliness. Malik knew better.

"Work before pleasure, though," Anand continued. "I was disappointed I didn't hear directly from you about your new charter."

Malik stumbled for words. "I…I was going to tell you," he lied. *How could Anand already know about my charter?*

"I'm sure you were. You wouldn't intentionally keep information like that from me, would you?"

"No, of course not," he lied again. "Looks like you're busy, Anand," Malik said, with a nod toward the seated man. "Maybe I should come back later."

"Nonsense. I wanted you to see this. Our friend in uniform here readily accepted the generous gifts I offered. All I asked in return was a little cooperation in keeping the authorities away from my trawlers. But then he told me I'd have to pay more, for what he'd already promised. He even threatened to go to my competitors. You know me, Malik. When I make a deal, I keep my end of the bargain. This sort of behavior can't be tolerated. It's bad for business."

The uniformed man struggled to speak, grunting incoherently, his gaze darting back and forth between Anand and Malik.

"I hope he has the sense to tell you what you want to hear." Malik glanced at the terrified man, then averted his gaze, ashamed those feeble words were the only help he could offer.

"And miss the fun? Rest assured, my seafaring friend; he'll give me what I need before we finish here today. Right now, I want to talk about your charter." Anand stepped away from his prisoner and put his arm around Malik's shoulder. "Turns out, the timing of your assignment is perfect. I have some merchandise I want you to deliver."

"Listen, Anand. I've done everything you asked for three years now. I earned you a fortune. I want out."

"I see." Anand frowned and took his arm off Malik's shoulder. He walked to the burlap sack, still writhing on the floor at Eko's feet. Anand squatted, picked up the drawstrings, and carefully spread open the top. "Come look at this."

"Thanks, I'll pass," Malik said, shaking his head.

"It wasn't a request."

Malik inched closer and leaned over to look inside. The head of a large hooded snake rose up struck at him. "Shit!" Malik jerked back, nearly tripping over his own feet.

"Isn't she a beauty?" Anand said, smiling proudly. "Asiatic cobra. Very toxic venom and a nasty temper to boot." Anand pulled the drawstrings tight, picked up the writhing bag and set it on the seated man's thighs. The man wriggled in terror, futilely trying to dump it off his lap.

"Remember what my last pet did to that traitor?" Anand continued. "Watching it was truly a religious experience. He died too quick, though, wouldn't you agree?"

"You're not going to let that thing loose, are you?"

Malik took another step back, his stomach still in his throat.

"Don't be stupid. Eko will put the sack over the colonel's head and tie the drawstrings tight around his neck. Then we'll watch the fun begin. He likes little girls. Let's see how he likes this one."

Anand's favorite pastime was buying exotic animals from poachers at the infamous Yogyakarta Bird Market on Java. He paid top dollar for those that could maim or kill. His previous purchase was a half-starved Sumatran tiger poached from the Tesso Nilo National Park. Anand ordered Malik to sit beside him while Eko shoved a man into a steel cage Anand had his men build for the occasion. Forced to watch, Malik struggled to keep from retching while the tiger killed and devoured the man as Anand sat on the edge of his seat and stared in fascination.

"I think we're ready, Eko." Anand licked his lips in anticipation. "Take the tape off. I want to hear everything."

"I didn't come here for this, Anand," Malik said, swallowing his nausea as memories of Anand's previous demonstrations of cruelty flooded back.

Anand stared intently at Malik. "Need I remind you who saved your life? Do you think you'd be alive today if I hadn't paid off your debt? I own your debt, which means I own you."

There'll be no negotiating with Anand today. Resignation washed over Malik like a bucket of slime. "Give me the details of what you want me to deliver."

"That's more like it, my friend," Anand said, with a grin. He glanced at Eko and gestured toward a nearby stack of crates. Eko brushed the dust off the top of one with the sleeve of his suit coat, and Anand hopped up on it. "Let's get down to business," he said. "Tell me more about your charter."

"I got a call from a dive master working out of Bali," Malik explained. "Her customer intends to film an underwater documentary around the islands of the Nusa Tenggara. The boat she originally chartered for their expedition is no longer available, and they needed another on short notice."

"Indonesians?"

"Americans. She's an expat living in Denpasar. Her name's Addy Lee. She said the guy shooting the film is a journalist—Dayne, I think. Yeah, Ethan Dayne. She came to see my boat, *Varuna*. I convinced her I know the area where they'll be diving, and she hired me."

"Do they need permission from the government?"

"She said they've already secured a permit."

"Perfect! That'll work beautifully." Anand rubbed his hands together like a sadistic child anticipating pulling the wings off a bat.

"What is it you want me to deliver?"

"A hundred kilos of first-grade heroin I recently acquired."

Malik knew from experience "acquired" most likely meant Anand hijacked the heroin from some other criminals and needed to dispose of it quickly.

Anand snapped his fingers, to which Eko immediately responded, going over to Anand's blazer, neatly folded atop a stack of crates. He took a slip of paper from the inside pocket and handed it to Anand. "Here's the contact info for the captain of one of my trawlers. His name is Sumadi. His ship will be in the

Savu Sea. Get in touch with him and agree on a rendezvous point."

"Why can't he just pick up the merchandise himself?"

"The ship has to stay well offshore, out of the jurisdiction of the authorities, where it can process the catch from my trawlers. I've arranged for Sumadi to deliver the heroin to a customer in Macao. Your boat carrying Americans on a government-approved film expedition should slip right past the authorities—or any other parties that might be looking for the heroin."

Malik took off his cap and wiped the sweat forming on his brow. Every encounter with Anand dragged him deeper into the abyss. He shook his head. "I told you before, Anand, I won't have anything to do with your goddamn illegal fishing. I've seen the destruction your bottom trawlers cause, and I want no part of it."

"So, what you're saying is, smuggling heroin is okay with you, but you draw the line at netting a few fucking fish?"

The irony in Anand's words hit home. Malik glanced at the man bound in the chair, then at Anand's hulking bodyguard. *How did I let myself end up here, surrounded by these wretched people?* He knew he had no one to blame but himself for the decisions he'd made that put him in where he was. He closed his eyes and for a fleeting second was at sea again. "None of this is okay with me," he said, staring at the floor.

"And yet, here you are," Anand said. "This has nothing to do with my trawling operations; you're simply making a delivery. Besides, I don't care what you want. This is a new customer. A very important one, so don't fuck this up. Need we discuss what will happen if you fail?"

Malik sighed. "No," he said. *I'll end up staring into the eyes of one of your poacher's latest captures.* He took the paper with the instructions, read it, and stuffed it in his shirt pocket. "What about the money? Am I picking up payment?"

"They've already paid me half as a show of good faith. They'll wire the other half upon confirmation of delivery."

"I'm supposed to do this by myself?"

"I'm sending Raj with you. He's expecting your call. Eko and I will deliver the merchandise to your boat tomorrow."

"Raj? Isn't he a bit young to take on an assignment like this?" Malik asked.

"Would you rather I send Eko?"

"Raj's fine," Malik quickly answered. The thought of Eko on his small ketch made him shudder. Raj was only twenty but had passed as one of his sailors before. Eko couldn't pass for anything other than the murderous thug he was. Malik glanced again at the seated man and then headed toward the door.

"You're not going to stay to watch this?" Anand asked.

"I already know how it ends," Malik answered without looking back. Anand allowed the man to hear the details of what they'd just discussed, which meant the poor fool was good as dead. The sound of tape ripped from the man's mouth, followed by screams, began before Malik reached the door.

After a twenty-minute walk to the nearest taxi stand Malik trusted was safe, Malik climbed into a cab and instructed the driver to stop on the way back to his drab apartment so he could buy a pint of arak. Malik abandoned the spacious house he shared with his wife and child after they were forced to disappear three long years earlier. The sadness of being in the house without them was too much to bear.

Slumped in a folding chair in his tiny kitchen, Malik poured a shot into a plastic cup. Closing his eyes, he raised the arak to his lips. The familiar smell flooded his nostrils. *One drink won't matter.* He resisted the temptation and set it back on the table. He picked up his cell phone and punched in the number for Raj Farran.

"*Selamat pagi,* Malik."

"*Selamat pagi,* Raj," Malik replied. "Anand said you're to accompany me on my charter."

"Yeah, he told me."

"We'll be weighing anchor late tomorrow afternoon."

"I'll be there," Raj said. After a pause, he continued, "It's been a while, Captain. It'll be good to see you again."

"You as well."

Malik hung up and tossed the phone on the table. He liked the young man. Raj was dangerous, but of all the men who worked for Anand, he was the only one with any redeeming qualities, still too young for Anand to have thoroughly corrupted.

Malik worried Raj's presence would complicate the plan taking shape in his mind. *I'll deal with that later.* Taking the wallet from his back pocket, he picked through business cards and crumpled receipts until he found the photo: a faded picture of a smiling young woman holding a child. *One more delivery and I'll be free of Anand and I'll find you again.* He kissed the photo and carefully slipped it back into his wallet. He walked to the sink, poured out the cup, then dumped the rest of the bottle down the drain.

Chapter 2

Punta Arenas, Costa Rica

"Damn, those fuckers already offloaded the catch," Ethan Dayne said, keeping his voice low. He pulled the front of his T-shirt over his nose to mask the overpowering stench of dead fish. He carefully lowered the steel hatch to minimize the creaking of its rusty hinges.

Gage Tucker turned off his video camera and slung the strap over his shoulder "Figures," he said, peeking over the winch on the deck of the trawling ship. "Now let's get the hell outta here before someone spots us."

"Copy that, cowboy," Ethan whispered. "Follow me."

Gage followed him forward along the starboard rail to the gangway, down it, and out onto the pier.

"*Alto, cabrones!*" A voice rang out from behind them.

Ethan glanced over his shoulder. Two men ran toward them. "Run!" he shouted. They sprinted down the pier toward the gate at the far end. Just before reaching the it, two more armed men stepped in front of the gate, blocking their escape. One of the men pointed an automatic rifle, the other a handgun. The other men from the ship caught up, grabbed Ethan and Gage, and pinned their arms behind them.

The man with the handgun holstered it. "What were you doing on my ship?" the captain of the trawler demanded.

"Sightseeing," Gage blurted out. "We're just dumb American tourists, you know. Just out—"

"Cállate, pinche gringo," the captain said, ordering him to shut up. He yanked the strap holding Gage's video camera from his shoulder. "What were you taking pictures of?"

"Listen, *señor,*" Ethan said, "like my friend said, we're just tourists. We meant no harm."

"Mentiroso," the captain said, calling Ethan a liar. "I recognize you. I saw you two days ago off the shore of Cocos. You were with those park rangers chasing my ship. You were taking pictures then as well."

"So, you admit you were trawling off the coast of Cocos Island? You must also know it's a protected marine reserve and illegal to fish there. Give me back that camera. We'll call the authorities and straighten this whole thing out."

"This camera?" The captain held out the camera, as if to hand it to Ethan, then hurled it to the ground. The lens popped off and rolled away in a slow lopsided curve. The captain kicked the housing soccer style, sending it skittering across the pier and over the edge. The housing landed in the water with a plop. The captain turned to his man holding the rifle. *"Golpéelo,"* he ordered, and the man hit Ethan in the gut with the butt of the rifle.

"Argh." Ethan collapsed to his knees, and doubled over holding his belly.

"Yes, *amigo*, we are going to call the authorities. My men and I caught you two trying to steal my ship.

We'll tell them you attacked us and left us no choice but to defend ourselves."

"I'm a journalist," Ethan said, getting back to his feet. "If you kill us, you'll have an army of reporters swarming all over these docks and your ship."

"Kill you? Why would I kill you when I can just have you thrown in jail for attempting to steal my ship?" He sneered. "Besides, asshole, I doubt anyone gives a shit where you are." The captain gestured to his men. *"Pégales y después llama a la policía,"* he said, giving the order for his men to beat them and then call the police.

****

"You're fortunate *Capitan* Ramirez chose to drop the trespassing and theft charges," the sergeant said, walking Ethan and Gage out of the police station in San José five days later. "You have two hours to gather your things and leave our country. I'll send an officer to your hotel to escort you to the airport. Don't ever come back, *comprenden, gringos?*" the police sergeant ordered.

"Si, comprendamos, Capi," Gage hastily responded in agreement. He had a butterfly bandage over his left eye and purple bruises under both. He draped Ethan's arm over his shoulder and started down the short flight of steps. "Jesus, Ethan, I don't know why I keep working with you. You look like shit, by the way."

Ethan winced with every step but said nothing. He glanced over his shoulder at the sergeant still scowling at them from the top of the steps.

"Now what do we do?" Gage asked. "They smashed my camera, so we got no video of those fuckers trawling in a protected reserve. They offloaded before we got back to port, so we got no proof of their catch. We ain't got squat, boss. Hell, we got less than squat. You got broke ribs. My nose probably is as well." Gage cringed, touching the bridge of his nose. "Messed up my pretty face, goddammit. Our sponsor fired us, man! We used all our money to get out of jail. We're fucked, man, just plain fucked."

Ethan kept silent while they shuffled on, a dull pain punctuating his every step.

"You got nuthin to say?" Gage said. "Nuthin at all?"

Ethan looked over his shoulder again at the sergeant. Figuring they'd gone far enough, he lifted his hand to his mouth and spat something into it. Turning toward Gage, he smiled and winked his right eye—the one not swollen shut.

"The memory stick!" Gage exclaimed. "How did you…? You cagey son of a bitch."

****

"Hi Addy, it's Ethan." He sat on the edge of the bed in a hotel room in San Jose, Costa Rica, cradling his cell phone to his ear with his shoulder. He grimaced, adjusting the bandage around his ribs.

"Ethan! I'm relieved to hear your voice," Addy Lee answered from the office of her dive shop opposite Sanur beach in Denpasar, Bali. "Your assistant told me you and Gage got arrested and beat up. Are you guys okay?"

"Yeah, we're fine," he looked over and winked at his cameraman, who was hurriedly packing his clothes, but stopped long enough to shoot Ethan the finger. "We're catching a flight back to the States in a few hours. Did you find us a new charter boat for our expedition?"

"Yes, I did. It's a refurbished ketch. It's smaller than the original boat we hired before you lost your funding, but I'm sure it will meet our needs. The captain's familiar with the area where we'll be diving. It wasn't easy to find someone willing to take on a month-long expedition on such short notice."

The boat Addy originally chartered was a steel-hulled research vessel, fully outfitted for dive operations. That was before Ethan's sponsor, The World Biodiversity Organization, abandoned the project. Already concerned about Ethan's take-no-prisoners reputation to getting a story, the incident in Costa Rica was the last straw, and they dropped his project like a hot rock. "There'll be fewer of us now, so smaller is okay assuming there's room for our crew and equipment. Tell me about it."

"The ship's name is *Varuna*. It's a phinisi, the Indonesian version of a two-masted wooden ketch. While the design isn't exactly ideal for diving, the captain agreed to make the modifications I requested to support our expedition. It's got a newly rebuilt diesel engine. The cabins are small but clean and comfortable. Everyone will have to double up; otherwise, I think *Varuna* will work just fine."

"What did you tell the captain about our expedition?"

"Not much. I told him we were filming a documentary about the pristine reefs of the Nusa Tenggara region. I thought it best to be vague. It's hard to know which of these charter boat captains might be tied up somehow with illegal fishing in the area."

"Great. I trust your judgment, Addy."

"Sorry to raise a sore subject, but since your sponsor backed out, where are you going to get the money?"

"I've got some other contacts I can turn to for funding." Ethan put his phone on speaker and set it on the bed. He carefully packed his Nikonos V underwater camera and strobe into its hard-sided case and snapped it shut.

"So…if you don't mind my asking, what exactly happened to you guys?"

Ethan turned off the speaker and picked up the phone. "Gage and I were sitting in this little hut on an island, three hundred miles off the Costa Rican coast, interviewing these two park rangers. The waters off the island are an important ecological marine reserve."

"Cocos Island?"

"Yes, you know it?"

"I dove there years ago," Addy said. "Spectacular place. Lots of sharks."

"Exactly, but they are still under threat from illegal netting. The Rangers were explaining to Gage and me how outgunned and outmanned they are by pirate fishing fleets raiding the reserve when we saw a blip appear on their radar screen. Suspecting it was a trawler, they ran to their skiff to go out and identify it. We followed and asked to go along. It was dark, but we spotted a trawler running with no lights, so they chased after it. Gage captured video of the trawler dragging nets right next to the island. The bastards were illegally netting sharks. The Rangers called out with a bullhorn and fired warning flares. But the trawler ignored us."

Ethan paced back and forth in the tiny hotel room.

"I convinced the rangers to get me close enough to attach a magnet to the ship with a GPS." He looked over at Gage and laughed. "I thought Gage was gonna shit his pants when they turned the water cannons on us. But we did it. We tracked those fuckers all the way back to Punta Arenas."

"That's where you ran into trouble?"

"Yeah. The ship arrived back in Punta Arenas ahead of us. It's a thirty-six-hour boat ride, you know. We snuck aboard, but they'd already unloaded the catch offshore to one of those goddamned floating fish processing factories. Someone spotted us, and we made a run for it. But they caught us."

"And they arrested you just for that?"

"No. The captain of the ship knew we saw them dragging nets. He had his men rough us up a bit. Then he called the cops, made up this bullshit story we were trying to steal their ship. I'm pretty sure he paid the cops to arrest us."

"Damn. Your assistant said they did more than just rough you up."

"I've had worse," Ethan said, glancing again at Gage, who gave him the finger with both hands this time. "We documented those fuckers raiding the reserve right under the noses of the authorities. Cocos Island is one of the most important marine reserves in the world, and the government doesn't devote enough resources to protect it adequately. I think they didn't want me tarnishing their ecotourism reputation. But we got great footage of the whole thing."

"Tell her those thugs smashed my camera," Gage mumbled. "That was my favorite camera."

"Sorry, did Gage say something?" Addy asked.

"Nope, he didn't say anything. We're off to a good start, Addy. I can't wait to continue our project in Indonesia. I plan to be there with our scientists and film crew by the end of next week."

"Great. I'll have all our dive equipment ready by the time you get here. Good luck, and for God's sake, be careful!"

Ethan hung up and resumed packing.

"Seriously?" Gage asked. "You call what we just endured a good start? I hope I'm not along on what you consider a bad one."

"What are you talking about? It was a small setback. We've documented pirate fishing fleets in Mexico, Belize, Honduras, and Panama, and we've barely gotten started."

"You know I believe in your cause, Ethan," Gage said. "But after what just happened, there's no way Lacy is going to let me turn around and head off to the far side of the world."

"Why not? We're not even halfway through shooting. We still have Indonesia and New Guinea left. Don't quit on me now, cowboy. What's more important than documenting illegal fishing in marine reserves? The world's oceans are overfished to the brink of collapse. Marine reserves are becoming the only places left where fish can find refuge and reproduce. If those continue to be ransacked, a tipping point will be passed from which they can't recover."

"Not important enough to get killed over." Gage grabbed a pair of jeans draped over the back of a chair and stuffed them into his duffel.

Ethan threw up his arms. "Don't exaggerate."

"It's easy for you, Ethan. You're not married."

Gage picked up the bloodstained shirt he'd been wearing for the last five days and started to stuff it in the duffel, but instead tossed it on the floor. "Don't need Lacy seeing that."

"I'll talk to her," Ethan said. "You're the best underwater videographer I ever worked with, man. I need you."

"Don't be blowin smoke up my ass. I don't think you get it. Lacy was against me working with you even *before* we got arrested and beat up. She said you have a reputation for getting the people around you hurt. Or worse." Gage paused. "What happened to us is only gonna make her more dead-set against me going."

"Let me talk to her, Gage. I'll assure her we won't be chasing after pirate trawlers. We'll primarily be supporting Richard Ross's scientific project and documenting pelagic fish migration patterns on this next leg anyway. This is the kind of assignment you told me you've dreamed about filming."

When Ethan wanted his way, half-truths rolled off his tongue and gathered momentum like a snowball down a mountain. He had a talent for reading people and knowing what motivated them. Gage was too important to his project. Although different as two people could be, Ethan had come to rely on his new cameraman and wouldn't allow himself to entertain the thought Gage might not be as committed to his most recent cause as he. Gage embraced technology and could spend hours behind a screen. Ethan wanted no part of that. He cared only for adventure. He needed to be outside, in the mix.

Gage zipped his duffel shut. "You are one silver-tongued devil. Have at it. If you can convince her, I'm in."

"Fantastic. You won't regret it, cowboy. I promise."

Ethan stood at the mirror and studied his face. The swelling had gone down, but he still had a black eye. He was already plotting the meeting he'd arranged with a movie producer in Los Angeles to persuade him to bankroll the rest of his documentary and wondered whether the purple-and-yellow bruises under his eye would sway the guy for or against providing the money he needed.

"Oh, one more thing," Ethan said. "Call Richard and assure him the project's still a go. I'm worried his research partner, Nils, will be trying to talk him out of it. Nils might even have been who convinced the WBO to drop us. I wouldn't be surprised if that fucker is trying to get Richard to do the project without me. Let me know right away if there's a problem."

"You're insane," Gage muttered. He reached in his pocket for his cell phone when someone banged on the door. The police had arrived to escort them to the airport in San Jose. They'd been ordered to leave the country, and the authorities were taking no chances they might try to stay.

"Sounds like our limo is here," Ethan said, sounding suddenly upbeat. "Let's not keep them waiting."

Chapter 3

Port of Sape, Sumbawa Island, Indonesia

Malik stood on *Varuna's* bridge thumbing through rolls of sea charts in the small cabinet under the transom until he found the one of the area around Komodo National Park. He unfurled the chart on the counter and laid a metal ashtray on one side to hold it. He traced his finger across the route he and Addy plotted a few days earlier, re-familiarizing himself with the water depths, shoals, and reefs in the area. One of *Varuna's* ancient mahogany deck planks creaked, and Malik spun around.

"*Selamat pagi,* Malik." Anand stood just inside the narrow doorway. He had the uncanny ability to appear, seemingly out of nowhere, a skill he'd perfected during his years leading guerrilla fighters.

"How did you...?" Malik stepped around Anand and looked over the rail. A narrow white panga with a silver outboard engine was tied up alongside *Varuna's* starboard beam. Eko stood inside the panga, one foot resting atop a large black trunk.

"You're late, Anand," Malik remarked, trying to remain stoic. *Am I going deaf? Was I that lost in thought?* Then he saw the oars stowed inside the gunwales. *Damn! I let the bastard sneak up on me.* Malik scanned the area around his yacht to see if anyone else noticed Anand come aboard. "The rest of my crew and passengers will be arriving any moment. I'd hate to have to explain who you are and what you're doing on my boat."

"You meant to say *our* boat, right, Captain? I hope you'll take better care when my merchandise is on board. If I'd been a pirate, I could've slit your throat."

You are a pirate. "Did you bring the merchandise?"

"Of course I brought it. I've got better things to do than pay social calls to fat captains." Although Malik was stout, he was strong with a solid build. Anand cast insults like seeds to sow his image of superiority. "I don't suppose you bothered to check out who hired you for this little excursion?"

"I told you, she's a well-known local dive guide. I asked around. She's legit."

"Not her. The guy who hired her. The one you said is making a nature film."

"No, Anand, I didn't see the need, but obviously you did. So who is he?"

Anand retreated down the ladder from the bridge to the main deck. Malik followed. "If you'd done a little checking," Anand continued, "you'd have learned he's a fucking war correspondent. Afghanistan, Iraq, Africa, even East Timor. Tell me, Malik, why is a war correspondent making a film about a bunch of goddamn reefs?"

"I don't know, and I don't care, Anand. They hired me and my boat to take them to the remote islands. That's where the reefs are they want to film, and I intend to plot a rendezvous point with your buyer somewhere along the way. You don't like the plan, find yourself another boat."

"It's too late to find another boat," Anand fretted. "I already made arrangements. My gut tells me something's not right about this situation, and my gut is rarely wrong. You damn well better keep them far away from my trawlers."

"I have no say in where they intend to dive. Just keep your goddamn trawlers out of the area."

Raj climbed up through the hatch leading below deck.

"And where the fuck were you?" Anand demanded. "You're not giving me a lot of confidence you're up for this job."

"I'm up for it," Raj answered. "I was below preparing a secure spot for your merchandise."

"I don't care to hear excuses. Maybe this job's too big for you."

"You shouldn't send a boy to do a man's job," Eko sneered from down in the panga.

"I see you brought fat monkey along, boss," Raj said, nodding down toward Eko. Raj leaned over *Varuna*'s rail. "Hey, gorilla man, how'd you gather the courage to get in that little boat? And what, no life jacket? I guess they don't make size ten-x, do they, fat monkey?"

"You little rat," Eko shouted up at Raj. "Let's see you come down here and say that."

"Both of you, shut the fuck up," Anand said. "You two can tickle each other's balls later. We have work to do." He glared at Malik. "What are you waiting for? Get your ass down there, and drag those trunks aboard this…boat, ship, or whatever you call this creaky piece of shit."

Malik had learned to tolerate Anand's personal insults, but he bristled at the insult to his beloved *Varuna*, the only remaining possession he still cared about.

"I'll do it," Raj said, putting his hand on Malik's chest. Instead of turning to climb down the rope ladder to the panga, he hopped up on *Varuna*'s rail, balanced on the teakwood beam long enough to make sure he had Eko's attention and then stepped off the side.

Raj landed on the panga's nearside gunwale causing the narrow boat to list abruptly and send Eko tumbling against *Varuna*'s hull, his head smacking against it with a hollow thud.

Furious and cursing, Eko staggered to his feet, his knees wobbling. He clumsily fumbled for the .45 automatic holstered inside his suit jacket. Just as his hand closed on the grip, Raj leaped to the opposite gunwale. The narrow panga tipped the other way, sending Eko tumbling again to the hull of the panga. He extended his arm to arrest his fall, but his arm slipped over the side, drenching it up to his chest.

Raj burst out laughing, but Anand quickly cut him off. "Goddamnit!" he shouted down at the two. "If you morons kill each other, who's going to load my merchandise?" He took a silk handkerchief from his tailored linen blazer, pretended to wipe his forehead, and shrugged. "I'm surrounded by morons."

A knife already in his hand, at the ready to fend off the anticipated attack, Raj returned the dagger to the sheath tucked in the small of his back. "Relax and tend to that nasty bruise on your fat head, Eko, while this *boy* loads Anand's merchandise," Raj sneered. He grabbed one after another of the four fifty-pound trunks, and swung each one over his head and up to Malik.

His hand still tightly gripping his .45, Eko stared up, beseeching Anand to allow him to take revenge on the boy who just mocked and shamed him. Anand firmly shook his head, forcing Eko to stand powerless, seething with rage, while Raj winked at him and smirked.

"If the coast guard catches us, you know we'll be shot," Malik said, dragging the last heroin-filled trunk over the rail. "Are you sure your guy's gonna show? I don't want this on my boat any longer than necessary."

"He'll show. Just make the delivery as instructed, or you'll beg to be shot before I'm done with you." Anand climbed down the ladder into the panga. "Anything goes wrong, don't be thinking I'll go easy on you," Anand said, poking Raj in the chest. "I'll hold you just as responsible as that sullen captain." He turned and barked an order to Eko. "Untie the rope and get me out of here."

Raj untied the knot himself, and shoved the panga away with his foot and stepped up on the rope ladder.

Eko yanked the cord, starting the outboard engine. Glaring at Raj, a sinister smile crept across his face. He pointed at Raj, then made a slicing motion across his throat. He twisted the throttle handle to full and sped the panga away from *Varuna* in a wide arc, and headed toward shore. They passed two Zodiacs approaching from the docks carrying Ethan, Addy, and the rest of the crew and passengers bound for *Varuna*.

"Damn it, Raj!" Malik said. "You want to get yourself killed, that's your business. Personally, I'd like to live a while longer. Anand may have led you to believe you're his protégé, but don't bet your life on it, son. That bearded monster is a psychopath. You haven't seen the things I've seen him do. Why would you taunt him like that?"

"I've seen what he does," Raj said, his gaze locked on the panga motoring away. "He held me down with his foot on my neck while he shot my friends. I was too young to fight back then, but his day is coming. Someday, I will kill him."

Malik paused midway up the ladder leading to the bridge. "Sorry. I didn't know. Must have been horrible." He looked out and saw the two Zodiacs approaching. "Hurry and get those trunks below decks before the rest of the crew and passengers arrive. And put that goddamn knife away. You can't be wearing a knife when the passengers are on board."

"Okay, Captain." Raj grabbed the handles of two of the trunks and dragged them toward the hatch leading down to the engine room.

Malik continued up the ladder and stood at the helm. *Stay focused. I may never have another chance like this. No turning back, Malik. This plan has got to work.*

Chapter 4

Bima, Sumbawa Island, Indonesia

Addy stomped the brake and spun the steering wheel, barely missing a motorbike that swerved in front of her. *"Awas, bodoh!"* (Watch out, fool), she shouted out the window in Indonesian, as she leaned on the horn of the old converted school bus. A woman carrying an infant and sitting sidesaddle behind the driver stared blankly back at her as the moped sped away, belching smoke, and weaving through traffic. The rickety bus Addy drove was the only vehicle she could find large enough to carry the passengers and equipment she was picking up. Her assistant hadn't shown up to help her load the scuba tanks and diving gear she'd shipped from Denpasar the day before, and she was running late. It wasn't the first time her assistant proved to be unreliable, but she swore under her breath; it would be his last.

She stepped on the clutch and ground the gearshift down into second, hit the gas, and made a sweeping turn onto the esplanade leading to the tiny airport in Bima. Looking past the tall chain-link fence, an Indo Air 707 taxied toward the terminal. "Dammit! He already landed."

Addy screeched up to the curb and yanked the emergency brake. She made her way to the baggage claim area, squeezed through the crowd, and stood next to the glass inside the terminal in time to see Ethan pause at the top of the gangplank. *He's taller than I expected.* She was glad to see it. At just over six feet herself, and with the lean build of a swimmer, her stature sometimes intimidated her clients, especially the male ones.

Six months before, Addy returned to her dive shop late one afternoon after taking a group of divers to the sunken wrecks at Tulamben on the northeast coast of Bali. While her assistant unloaded scuba tanks from their van, she stepped into her office to check for messages on her answering machine. Her spirits soared listening to Ethan Dayne introduce himself and describe the project he was leading. He was looking for a dive master to guide him and his team on a three-week expedition to the remote reefs of the Nusa Tenggara region of Southeast Indonesia.

She did some quick research and found he was a well-known freelance journalist. Most of his recent work was as a war correspondent, and controversy often surrounded him. Rather than raise alarm bells, it intrigued her. *He's not just another soft-spoken environmentalist,* she thought. *Maybe this guy can actually accomplish something.*

The opportunity sounded too good to let pass. She called him back, saying she was intimately familiar with the area, having dived there several times before. In addition to her experience as a dive guide, she told him she'd studied marine biology in college then worked as a research assistant before becoming a dive guide. She hoped her background might set her apart from the other guides she assumed he was interviewing.

It worked. Ethan hired her, and over the next few months, they communicated weekly via email and Skype, mapping out the expedition.

"You're finally here." Addy brushed past Ethan's extended hand and instead hugged him.

"Great to see you, Addy," Ethan said. Thanks for hanging in there with me."

"Never doubted you for a second." She thought Ethan looked remarkably relaxed standing there in khaki trousers and a polo shirt, considering he'd just traveled halfway across the world and only a week earlier was languishing in a Central American jail. His height wasn't his only Scandinavian feature. He had bright blue eyes, the left with a still-visible bruise under it. His light-brown hair was combed straight back and hung loosely to just above his broad shoulders. He was darker than she'd expected. All that time in the Middle Eastern deserts, she supposed. "The other members of your crew arrived yesterday."

"Lounging by the hotel pool drinking Mai Tais, I imagine."

Addy laughed. "Probably. We'll swing by, pick them up, and then head straight for Sape seaport. The captain I told you about is waiting for us on his boat. He says he'll be ready to sail upon our arrival. We'll make the crossing of the Sumbawa Strait tonight and be at our first dive site off the north coast of Komodo Island before sunrise."

"Great. Have you spent any time getting to know my crew?"

"A little. Gage is funny. Love that Texas drawl. Fab's nice too. I was surprised you'd have someone so young on your crew. When I first saw her, I thought maybe you brought her along for a fashion shoot," she joked.

"The guy I turned to for money, after the WBO dropped the project, is a film producer. He had a few stipulations before agreeing to pick up the financing of my project. One was that I hire his daughter as part of my crew and teach her videography and film editing. He wants her to learn the movie business. Just not the kind he makes. To my surprise, she's turned out to be a quick learner and has a great attitude. What do you think of our two marine fisheries experts, Richard and Nils?"

"They arrived later, so I only had a chance to say hello."

"Richard and I have been friends for a long time. I think you'll hit it off. You share a passion for the undersea world. He's scary smart but with a great sense of humor and fun to be around. He was an astrophysicist before becoming a marine biologist. He'll be testing his new algorithm for estimating fish populations. I'm lucky to have him on this project."

"Can't wait to hear more about his work." She picked up one of Ethan's bags, a large hard-sided camera case. "I've rented us an old bus for the trip to the harbor at Sape. The hotel is on the way. I'll apologize in advance for the cushion-less benches. It'll be a bumpy ride."

"No problem. Let's get this expedition underway."

****

After meeting Ethan's film crew and the two scientists at their hotel, they loaded their gear and headed out. The drive to the seaport took an hour and a half and wound through dense forest, lush rice fields, and finally a coastal plain with acres of salt evaporation ponds. Arriving at the harbor, Addy's assistant, Nate, was sitting atop a pylon on a decaying wooden pier. He was wearing flip-flops, a torn T-shirt, and board shorts. Two sailors in crisp sailor whites stood nearby in front of a couple of Zodiacs tied alongside the pier.

Fabiola, sitting in the first bench behind the driver's seat, leaned up and whispered to Addy, "OMG, check out the tattooed Adonis on the pier."

"That's no Adonis," Addy replied, her gaze narrowing. "He's my assistant."

"Wow. What a tough life you lead, Addy," Fabiola joked. "You live in Bali, scuba dive every day in a paradise, and you have *that* guy as your gofer.

Addy started to reply but instead kept her attention, and ire, directed at her assistant, and sometimes boyfriend, Nate. *What was I thinking?* Addy asked herself. Seeing him there on the pier reminded her of everything she was growing to regret in her life. This expedition was the type of thing she'd dreamed about being a part of when she decided to study marine biology. *This guy, Ethan, is trying to save the oceans. What does Nate care about, other than catching the perfect wave and mooching off me?* And she'd been allowing it. She decided right then, the opportunity this expedition presented, to be a part of something meaningful, was too important to risk having Nate fuck it up. Addy drove up to the pier, hit the brakes, and skidded to a stop. She cranked the lever, opening the bus door, jumped out, and strode briskly across the gravel parking area and onto the wooden planks of the pier. "Where the hell were you this morning?"

"Sorry. Perfect swells and onshore winds this

morning at Uluwatu. Guess I lost track of time."

Addy shook her head. "Again. I'm tired of this, Nate. Get the fuck out of here."

"Oh, come on. Chill. I'm here now." He started toward the bus to unload the gear.

"No." She grabbed him firmly by the arm. "You knew how important this assignment was to me. I had to load all the gear by myself and was late picking up my clients. You're fired. Leave. Now."

"You're not serious. You can't handle this project by yourself."

"The hell I can't." She brushed past him over to the two sailors waiting to greet her.

"Nice to see you again, Miss Addy," one of the sailors said. He looked the part of an experienced sailor, in his early thirties with an easy smile, rail thin, and short, well-groomed black hair.

"*Selamat pagi,* Sanjeev," Addy greeted him in Indonesian. "I hope you are doing well. Sorry we're late. I had an unexpected delay." She glanced over to see Nate sling his duffel over his shoulder and walk past her clients, who by then had gotten off the bus. She waved at Ethan to come over. "This is Sanjeev, first mate on *Varuna*," Addy said. "Sanjeev, meet Ethan Dayne, the leader of our expedition."

"On behalf of our captain, I bid you and your team welcome, Mr. Dayne. This is Talib, our bosuns mate."

"Selamat pagi," Talib said, greeting Ethan with a slight bow. He appeared to be a good ten years older than Sanjeev and at least forty pounds heavier.

"*Varuna*'s moored out in the harbor," Sanjeev continued. "The captain's awaiting your arrival. If you and your team will please climb aboard the Zodiacs,

Talib and I will load your gear and luggage, and then we will be on our way."

"Everything okay?" Ethan asked Addy after the two sailors left to load the gear.

"Just fine. Sorry you had to hear that."

"So he's not going with us?"

"I know I told you I'd have an assistant, but I can handle everything," Addy quickly asserted. "I promise it won't be a problem."

Ethan turned to see Addy's assistant climb into a beat-up Nissan taxi. "If you say so. Seems like a lot to handle by yourself."

"Don't worry a bit, Mr. Dayne," Sanjeev said, coming to Addy's rescue. "When I'm not working on *Varuna*, I crew on dive boats and fishing charters and have for many years. I assure you my crew and I will give Addy all the support she needs to make your expedition successful. Now shall we get your gear loaded?"

Addy flashed Sanjeev a grateful *I owe you one* smile and then headed back toward the bus to help collect the gear and luggage.

Once everyone was aboard, the two sailors started the outboard motors and steered the Zodiacs out into the harbor, maneuvering past anchored fishing boats, small cargo ships, and long white pangas, the inexpensive to build, preferred style of fishing boat favored by indigenous fishermen across the tropics.

"There she is," Addy said, sitting on the starboard side tubing, toward the bow. She pointed to a two-masted ketch with furled canvas sails moored at the outer edge of the harbor, a hundred yards out. It rested broadside to them, her white-planked wood hull casting a mirror image against the still-as-glass water of the bay. Teak rails ran the length of her sides, from her raised square aft, to her rakish upswept prow. Nothing lay behind the yacht but the rolling surf of the breakwater, and beyond, the open sea.

A postcard image, Addy thought, feeling pride in finding this beautiful ship on short notice. Her excitement grew knowing they'd soon be weighing anchor and starting the long-anticipated expedition. She loved her guiding business but was becoming frustrated her clients didn't seem to share her sense of wonder or her passion for protecting the pristine places she took them to see. This would be her chance to do something genuinely worthwhile.

"You've got to be kidding me," Nils said to Richard, loud enough for everyone on the Zodiac to hear. "You turned down the WBO for this? We went from a fully outfitted research vessel to that antique? Are we here for a research project or a barefoot cruise?"

"I know *Varuna*'s not like our previous charter, Dr. Gedron," Addy said, her hackles rising. "The captain and crew spent all last week outfitting her to my specifications. We might feel a bit cramped, but I think you'll find she'll meet our needs."

"I think it's awesome," Ethan reassured her.

Addy breathed a sigh of relief. Finding a boat willing to take on an extended expedition on such short notice was challenging to say the least. Especially given the severely diminished budget she had to work with after Ethan's sponsor bailed. She'd been on the docks looking for potential boats to hire and was about to give up when she spotted *Varuna* motoring into port. She'd waited for the captain to disembark, and after a conversation over a cup of tea, became convinced he was a seasoned pilot who knew his way around the islands.

Once the two Zodiacs carrying Addy, Ethan, and his crew, maneuvered alongside, a rope ladder dropped over *Varuna*'s rail. A stout man in a blue captain's cap pushed back on his forehead, barely covering a thick shock of jet-black hair, appeared at the gunwale and looked over the side. "Hello. I'm your captain, Malik Bashir." He leaned over and extended a hand to Fabiola, the first passenger on the ladder, and helped her step up onto *Varuna*'s deck.

After helping the other passengers aboard, Malik continued, "Welcome aboard *Varuna*. Addy's told me a bit about your expedition, and I'm looking forward to piloting you to the reefs and islands she's mapped out. I'm confident we will have a memorable journey." Malik wore a short-sleeved white cotton shirt with the word *Varuna* underlined by a set of blue waves stitched over the left front pocket. He had wide expressive eyes and a warm smile, and although slightly overweight, had stately features that demonstrated an air of authority of someone comfortable being in command.

His welcome speech was interrupted when a tall young Indonesian man climbed down from the bridge and stood beside the captain. He was shirtless and barefoot, and his cargo pants rolled up to just below his knees. His dark hair hung loosely over well-muscled shoulders. His arms and chiseled torso were covered in intricate tattoos, the most pronounced of which was a griffon with an eagle's head and talons, the mane of a lion, and a long dragon-like tail. Flames shot out of its curved beak and extended down to the fingertips of his right hand.

Malik gestured toward the young man and sighed. “This is our second mate, Raj Farran.”

Raj hadn’t been onboard the first time Addy met the captain to check out his yacht. Shaking the young man’s hand, Addy had doubts whether he was in fact even a sailor. He had a firm grip, but his hand wasn’t calloused like she’d expect to find with anyone who made their living on a ship handling rope and cargo. He had a handsome, boyish face, but his piercing eyes lacked the innocence of boyhood. The intricate tattoos covered small pockmark scars dotting his chest and arms. Addy speculated they were meant to disguise cigarette burns. A twinge of concern crept over her as she realized she knew nothing about the young man they were about to spend several weeks with on an expedition.

“Hello,” Raj greeted the passengers with feigned interest.

“Hi, Raj. My friends call me Fab,” She shot out her hand. Nice tats.”

“I beg your pardon?” Raj said, taken aback, his swagger suddenly rattled. His brooding façade morphed into a full-on blush.

“Your tattoos. I like them.”

“Uh, thank you.” Raj awkwardly averted his gaze. Then, glancing at Ethan and Gage, some of his swagger returned. “Were you two in some kind of accident?”

“Car crash. Back in the States,” Gage fumbled to respond. “We’re okay though. Thanks for asking.”

Raj raised an eyebrow and shot a glance toward Malik.

“Please excuse my staff’s forwardness,” Malik

said, annoyed by Raj's boldness. He addressed his new passengers again. "I hope you'll find *Varuna* comfortable. Rest assured, my crew and I will do all we can to make your expedition a success. Feel free to go anywhere on the ship, except the engine room, if you please. We all speak English, so let us know of any needs you may have."

"*Terima kasih,* Captain," Ethan said, thanking the captain. "Can you tell us a little about *Varuna*? She's beautiful. Like something from a bygone era."

"It's called a phinisi. Her design is ancient Dutch with local influence. She was most likely built on Sulawesi over a hundred years ago. I was piloting a freighter when I spotted her foundered on the rocks a few years back. Whatever crew may have been aboard had disappeared, so I patched her hull and towed her to a salvage yard. I've been restoring her in my spare time."

Ethan looked around, admiring *Varuna*'s meticulously finished brass hardware, varnished hardwood decks and rails, and her squarely set rigging. "I wonder what terrible circumstances occurred to have led a captain and crew to to abandon such a boat."

"I've often wondered the same thing," Malik said. "She looked nothing like she does today when I found her. She had a gaping hole in her side and was encrusted with barnacles. Of course, I thought it strange no one had claimed or salvaged her, but then I never wanted to overly question my good fortune."

"You've done an incredible job. She's a beautiful ship," Ethan said. "I can see why they say builders of wooden boats are true lovers of the sea."

"You can feel the sea on a wooden ship," Malik

said. "If you know how to listen, she will speak to you. Most people want their legs planted firmly on solid ground. Me, I'd rather face an angry squall than have to spend a day in the city."

"It seems we've found a kindred spirit in you, then, Captain," Richard said. "We're not sailors, but we also love the sea. I've dedicated my life to doing all I can to save it. Ethan's taking a break from chasing pirate fishing fleets around the globe to help Nils and me test the program I've developed to predict migration routes and estimate populations of the ocean's largest fish."

"I'm here to do what I can to help make your expedition a success," Malik said.

"The name of your boat, *Varuna*, sounds Hindu," Richard said. "What does it mean?"

"The name was on her hull when I found her," Malik replied. "*Varuna* is one of the eight principal Veda, and god of the celestial sea. The stars are said to be his eyes, watching over the lives of men at sea, snaring and punishing liars and fools."

"Hear that?" Gage nudged Ethan in the ribs. "Liars and fools. Hittin' a little close to home, don't you think?"

Chapter 5

After Malik's crew stowed his passengers' gear and showed them to their cabins, he climbed the ladder to the bridge and ordered Sanjeev to cast off the bowline and raise the stern anchor. Malik engaged the engine. A shudder ran through the ship as *Varuna*'s diesel engine groaned to life. He idled *Varuna* into the narrow channel leading toward the mouth of the harbor. Reaching the breakwater, he powered her to half-full and nosed her into the surf. Malik smiled as a squadron of pelicans soared across the bow and dipped low, surfing the air currents coming off the waves. *A good omen*, he thought.

Clearing the last breaker, Malik steered *Varuna* out to sea. He charted a heading that would take them north of the island of Komodo. He intended to sail through the night and arrive just before dawn at a tiny isolated group of islands Addy chose for Ethan's crew to make their check-out dive and test their equipment.

The smell of the salt air and warm ocean breeze blowing across his face lifted his spirits and helped him forget, if only for a moment, how his life had veered off course. The bright turquoise of the shallows changed to cobalt as *Varuna*'s bow sliced through the swells into the deeper waters of the strait. Ahead was the open ocean—the only place his demons left him at peace. The one place he still felt he belonged.

An old wooden crate lying in the corner caught his eye, and the memories overtook him. "Can I steer her?" He remembered his young son asking. It was the last time Malik's wife and son had been aboard, only a week before they'd been forced into hiding, their lives shattered, put at risk because of his own weakness. He'd dragged the crate over so his son could reach the teak batons of the steering wheel. "All ahead full!" his son squealed, standing on his tiptoes. "Look, Mama, I'm steering *Varuna*."

"Where are we headed, little one?" Malik could still hear his wife's laugh.

"Swimming, Mama. We're going swimming!"

They'd gone to a tiny atoll with a protected beach for a weekend vacation. It was three years ago, but Malik kept the crate, still sitting empty in the corner. The creak of the door to the bridge returned Malik to the present.

"It's a beautiful day, sir," Sanjeev said, stepping inside the small bridge and gazing out over the bow. "Not a cloud in the sky."

Malik gathered his composure. "It is a beautiful day. A perfect day to be on the water."

"I'll take the helm if you'd like to join the passengers on the foredeck, Captain."

"Thanks, I think I will." He looked out across the wide blue expanse. No boats were in sight, and the ocean was calm. "There shouldn't be much activity on the water this evening. I'll come back up in an hour or so. Are you clear on the route we'll be following?"

"Yes, sir, I'll be watching for the landmarks and obstacles you pointed out, as well. Captain?"

"Yes, Sanjeev?"

"When we were ferrying the passengers to *Varuna* in our Zodiacs, we passed two men in a panga headed away from *Varuna*. One of them was huge. The scowl he gave me sent chills up my spine. May I ask what they wanted?"

"To charter *Varuna*. I told them we'd already been hired out."

"That's a relief. Not sure I'd want to be anywhere near that guy. One more thing, sir, if I may."

"Sure. What is it?"

"What am I to do with Raj? He doesn't know the basic tasks of a sailor, and frankly, sir, he scares me."

"You shouldn't be frightened of Raj. He's a good kid. At heart, at least. I know he's inexperienced, but he's one of the crew on this voyage, so teach him what you can and assign him tasks you think best. He'll catch on."

"Yes, sir," Sanjeev answered. "If he chooses to."

Raj accompanied them at sea once before when Malik was piloting a freighter, but this was his first time on *Varuna*. During an earlier assignment, Sanjeev questioned Malik why he would hire someone so inexperienced. Malik replied Raj was the adopted son of an associate he owed a favor to. Malik made every effort to conceal his dealings with Anand from Sanjeev. His first mate had strong moral principles and would quit if he ever learned of Malik's smuggling. More importantly, he feared the loss of Sanjeev's respect.

Sanjeev took over the wheel, and Malik climbed down the ladder and walked along the narrow passage between the galley and starboard rail toward the bow. His passengers were relaxing on the benches lining both sides of the foredeck.

"Care for a cold one, Captain?" Gage reached into the ice-filled bucket Talib brought out for them and offered Malik a beer.

"Thank you. I don't drink anymore." Seeing the cold beer made Malik's mouth water, so he changed the subject. "I know your cabins are spartan, but I hope you found them acceptable."

"They're just fine," Ethan said. He was seated next to Addy. "I have to confess I had concerns when I first saw *Varuna*," he continued. "But now I'm intrigued. I think the ship will add an interesting dimension to our film. Do you plan to unfurl the sails at some point? I'd love to see her under full sail."

"Assuming we find favorable winds and currents, and your schedule permits," Malik responded.

"We should have time. I know you and Addy went over our itinerary at length. Any thoughts or concerns?"

"Now that you ask, I do have some questions. Your route takes us through some narrow straits between islands where the tidal currents can be tricky to navigate. I'm curious why you chose those areas."

"Those currents are why we chose those locations," Richard answered. "The strong tidal currents bring cold, nutrient-rich water up from the deep which attracts baitfish, and baitfish attract pelagics."

"Pelagics?" Malik asked.

"Big fish. Sharks, rays, tuna, etcetera. The fate of the ocean's biggest fish is the focus of my work. Did you know ninety percent of the ocean's largest fish have already been lost? Gone forever."

"I know there's overfishing, but I didn't know it was to that extent," Malik answered. "I guess I shouldn't be surprised, given the evidence I've seen sailing these waters. You intend to dive in those waters with tricky currents?"

Addy answered, "Yes, we do. That's where we're most likely to encounter the largest fish. As long as we pay attention to the tides, we'll be fine."

"And what about getting to and from those sites through those straits? *Varuna*'s engine has plenty of power, but the whirlpools that form there have been known to swallow boats," Malik said, only half joking.

"With your permission of course," Addy said, "I thought we could anchor *Varuna* in calmer water and use the Zodiacs to ferry the divers to and from the dive sites each day."

"Yes, I suppose that would work," Malik said, scratching his two-day beard stubble. "The route also takes us to some remote areas. I'm sure you're aware there are diving spots less problematic and more popular for divers." *And where we're less likely to come across one of Anand's pirate trawlers. That complication is the last thing I need right now.*

"We purposely intend to go to areas with the least contact with divers. Areas that fall along deep-sea ledges," Ethan said. "Which naturally means they'll be more remote and difficult to dive. That's why we needed an experienced captain like you."

Malik understood he and his boat weren't their first choice, but he didn't care. It was a paid assignment on his beloved *Varuna*, and the route would take them close to where he intended to rendezvous with Anand's buyer. Once the delivery was made, he would make his escape, and go in search in of his wife and son. "If you and your team are brave enough to dive those waters"—he wanted to say *foolish* enough—"I assure you, I can pilot us through them."

"Do you normally hire out *Varuna* for dive trips, Captain?" Richard asked.

"I wish that were the case, but I don't have enough charter business yet. I mainly pilot cargo ships ferrying goods between the islands. Mostly to and from Java and Bali, as well as Singapore and Malaysia. I know *Varuna*'s design isn't as functional for diving as newer boats, but I made several modifications and outfitted her according to Addy's instructions. She's got a sound engine and will get us everywhere you need to go. I grew up sailing these waters and know all the routes and obstacles. I assure you I'll do everything I can to make your project a success."

"That's good to hear, Captain. Thank you," Richard replied.

"Just one more question," Malik said, thinking ahead to the delivery of Anand's merchandise, "Your schedule shows us navigating to a spot off the southeastern coast of Flores, correct?"

"Yes," Addy answered. "That will be the easternmost point of our diving."

"And your itinerary shows us being there on the twenty-fourth?"

"That sounds about right. Why do you ask?"

"I just want to make sure I do my part to keep us on schedule."

Chapter 6

The Flores Sea, off the north coast of Komodo Island

Ethan clipped the last of the negatives from the photos he'd shot the night before onto the line strung across the makeshift darkroom, which Malik allowed him to set up in a small storage area in the hold. Gage made fun of him for not going digital, but developing the negatives helped Ethan feel closer to the subjects of his photos. The time spent in the darkroom was his private time to reflect and plan. His father had taught him, and using and developing film was his way of honoring his father's memory.

He jotted the last of his notes, ducked through the hatch, and climbed the varnished ladder to the main deck. The sun was well above the horizon when Ethan stepped out onto the aft deck. His crew was already preparing for their check-out dive. They'd sailed through the night and anchored in a small cove a hundred yards off a rocky beach lined with palm trees.

"Good morning," Addy said. Standing at the whiteboard hung on the outside of the aft galley wall, she was updating the map she'd sketched of the topographical features of the undersea area they were about to dive. She picked up a thermos of coffee from the small table next to her and poured Ethan a cup.

"Just what I needed, thanks," Ethan said, and he breathed in the steam rising off the cup. He walked to the rail and took in the tranquil beauty of the idyllic cove. The trees and rocks lining the crescent-shaped beach blocked the winds, and the early-morning sun glinted off the smooth-as-glass turquoise water. He looked over the side and could see the tops of coral heads directly below through the crystalline water. "Nice spot for a dive."

"Thought you'd like it," Addy said. The top of her wetsuit hung loosely around her waist. She wore a yellow one-piece swimsuit, and her sun-bleached auburn hair hung just past her freckled shoulders in a long braid. A white stripe of zinc sunblock covered the bridge of her nose. "I chose this site as a tranquil and easy spot to start our dives. It's one of my favorite dive sites."

Ethan walked the few steps of the small aft deck and looked over the rail. Gage was already floating on the surface of the water holding the wooden platform off *Varuna*'s stern.

"Here you are, sir," Sanjeev said, kneeling on the slatted platform and handing down Gage's bulky camera and housing. The housing had a long arm extending from either side, each with a strobe at the end. Gage took the camera gear, then sank below the surface, a tornado of tiny silversides swirled around him as he descended.

"Glad you finally decided to join us," Richard said. He walked up next to Ethan and put a hand on his shoulder. He was already in his wetsuit; his face mask pulled up on his forehead. "How are things in the nineteenth century?"

"Make all the fun you want. Even with all your fancy equipment, I'll still be the one getting the best shots with my plain old thirty-five-millimeter Nikonos. Need some help getting into your gear, old man?"

"I can manage, thank you very much. Come over to my laptop and have a look," Richard said, motioning Ethan to follow him to the Astroturf-covered table in the middle of the aft deck. "I've got my algorithm set up and ready for testing. I'll record data from our first couple of dives, and then we'll analyze the output to make sure the kinks are worked out. If so, we'll set the program up on our network, and everyone can begin inputting observations."

Richard's algorithm was the basis of a multimillion-dollar grant Richard and Nils sought from the NOAA. The algorithm used visual and photographic observations to mathematically predict the number and type of species present in a given marine ecosystem. When compared to a baseline in a healthy ecosystem, the output could be used to judge its state of health according to ratios of certain bellwether species. Richard believed the program had far-reaching implications for reducing the human impact on ocean ecosystems. Ethan planned to showcase Richard and his algorithm in the documentary to demonstrate the dire effects of reckless overfishing of the world's oceans.

"Sounds great," Ethan said. "We'll all meet each evening after the last dive of the day to review the day's film footage. Let's plan on analyzing the video then. What do you think, Nils?"

"Richard and I can accurately record everything we observe during a dive," Nils said, "but frankly, I'm not convinced input from amateurs can be scientifically valid."

"Nils, we've gone over this before," Richard said, exasperated. "Once we develop a training program and certification, we'll be able to collect exponentially more observations. Otherwise, it's just a theoretical exercise."

Deciding not to get in the middle of another argument between the two, Ethan turned to check on Fabiola. Out of the corner of his eye, he'd seen her climb down the stern ladder to the dive platform. He followed and sat beside her, dangling his feet in the balmy, eighty-two-degree water. Fabiola already had on her fins and wetsuit. She was watching Gage, still visible in the crystalline water thirty feet below.

"You doin okay, Fab?" Ethan asked.

"Absolutely. Can't wait to get in. Thanks again for giving me the opportunity to work with you, Ethan. I know my dad pressured you to bring me along."

"I'm happy to have you here. By the time we complete our film, you'll be an expert videographer, just like he wanted. If you can film underwater in the conditions we'll be shooting, you can film anywhere."

Raj carried Fabiola's buoyancy compensator with its scuba tank and regulator already attached, down the ladder in one hand, her weight belt in the other. Ethan got up to help.

"I got it, thanks," Raj said. He sidestepped Ethan and handed Fabiola her weight belt.

"Give her the BC and tank first," Ethan said. "The weight belt's always the last thing on." Ethan knew by the way Raj handled the gear; he'd never been around diving equipment. "That way, if she needs to ditch her gear in an emergency, it will fall away clean and not get caught on something."

"Thanks." Raj set the equipment against her back and helped her into it.

"Raj, how do you say thank you in Indonesian, again?" Fabiola asked.

"Terima kasih."

"*Terima kasih,* Raj. Would you mind getting my camera and strobe? It's up on the table."

"Yes, ma'am." Raj turned toward the ladder.

"Seriously? Ma'am? I told you before, call me Fab."

"Okay, Fab," he said, his grin a mile wide.

Ethan chuckled. "Looks like you're in good hands, Fab. Stay here, Raj. I'll get the camera and hand it down to you." He climbed back up onto the deck, retrieved the video camera and strobe, handed it down to Raj, and then went over to where Addy sat on a bench slipping on a pair of three-feet-long skin-diving fins. He stripped off his T-shirt, grabbed his wetsuit from the nylon clothesline strung above the port rail, and started pulling it on. "You're going to free dive?"

"Yep. This shallow bay may be my only opportunity to skin dive on this trip, so I'm going to take full advantage."

"The water here's fifty feet deep," Malik said. He'd come down from the bridge and was leaning against the port rail, his arms crossed over his chest, watching the crew prepare for the dive. "That's shallow to you?"

"Oh yeah. Most of our dives will be at a hundred to a hundred and fifty feet."

"Goodness." Malik took off his cap and scratched his head. "I consider anything over my head deep water."

Addy laughed. "We'll have to change that perception and get you in the water sometime then."

"That'll be the day. I'm staying dry on this trip, thank you."

"You don't know what you're missing." Addy pulled up the top half of her wetsuit, reached behind her to grab the long strap, and zipped the suit up to her neck. She buckled her weight belt tight around her waist and then picked up her mask and snorkel. She shuffled backward on her long, awkward fins to the starboard beam, then turned and dove, arcing over the rail and torpedoed into the water.

She popped to the surface, looked up at Ethan and teased, "You gonna stand there drinking coffee, or you gonna come diving?" She pulled her mask over her face, took three long relaxed breaths to ventilate her lungs, and then dove below the surface, her long fins thrusting into the air like the fluke of a whale starting a deep dive.

Ethan grabbed his scuba gear and climbed down to the aft platform, pulled on his BC and tank, buckled his weight belt, and jumped in, holding his mask and fins in his hands. He put them on as he sank, squeezing his nose to force air into his sinuses every few feet of descent to equalize the pressure. At twenty feet, he pushed the button on his octopus rig, shooting air into his BC to slow his descent and neutralize his buoyancy. A shadow passed overhead. He looked up to see the mottled gray and white underbelly of a huge manta ray. Another, with a ten-foot wingspan from tip to tip, gracefully glided by below.

Ethan swam to where Gage was focusing his

camera on a pair of clownfish darting in and out among the tentacles of a giant snow anemone. Fabiola was a few feet to his left holding her camera in one hand and trying to gently coax an octopus out of its hiding place with her other. Something tugged on his tank, and he looked up. Addy waved and smiled, her emerald eyes sparkling through her mask. With a few kicks of her long undulating fins, she glided into the path of an approaching manta and rolled over as they passed each other belly to belly.

Over the next hour, Addy swam among the scuba divers, surfacing every two to three minutes to take a few breaths before diving down again. Completely at ease underwater, as if she had a kinship with the ocean, Addy swayed with the current, drifting back and forth across the reef with the natural rhythm of the sea. Twice during the hour-long dive, she swam down fifty feet to retrieve Richard, who kept drifting into deeper water, lost in his observations.

One by one, the divers exhausted their air supply and climbed back aboard *Varuna*. Ethan and Addy were the last two in the water. "That was impressive," Ethan said, grabbing the lip of the platform. "I timed you at four minutes between breaths a couple of times. I didn't know you were a free diver. I keep learning new things about you."

"I used to compete," Addy said. "That was many years ago, though. I don't get much chance anymore. I hope you didn't mind. I doubt I'll skin dive again during our trip." Addy took off her weight belt and fins and tossed them up on the platform. With a big kick, she sprang out of the water and sat on the platform in one smooth motion.

"Not at all." Ethan unbuckled his BC and tank and let them float next to the platform. Addy lifted them onto the platform and then gave Ethan a hand up. Richard was sitting on the other side of the platform struggling to get out of his gear.

"Here, let me help you." Addy popped loose the chest buckle on his buoyancy compensator and scuba tank and helped him out of it.

"Thank you, my dear," Richard said.

"How was your dive?" she asked.

"Fantastic. What a spot. Several varieties of colorful nudibranchs. Tiny creatures but a significant marker of the health of the ecosystem." Then he leaned in and said, "By the way, dear, you don't have to hold your breath, you know. They've invented something called scuba. You should try it."

Addy laughed. "I'll keep that in mind."

"Ethan tells me you're a marine biologist."

"Was. I didn't have the discipline for the lab work. The sea kept calling me."

"I'm glad you answered. It put you here with us today. But I do hope this guiding business is only an interlude. We need all the bright minds we can get."

"Thank you, but I've been away from the science too long. I doubt I'd be able to catch up."

"Au contraire, mon chéri. I found some of the papers you wrote online. I'm most impressed. I'd like your input on the algorithm we are developing."

"You're very kind, Richard. I'm looking forward to it." Addy turned to Nils, who'd just rinsed off the salt water under the showerhead set up over the platform and was eavesdropping on their conversation. "What about you, Nils? Have a nice dive?"

"I'm not here to have a nice dive. I'm here to work. I thought that dive was a waste of time."

"I'm sorry you feel that way," Addy responded. "It's always a good idea to start a series of dives in a shallow, calm spot to give you a chance to check out your equipment."

"My equipment's just fine. I'm not here for a vacation."

"Of course not. I do need to reiterate, however, Dr. Gedron, we'll be using the buddy system on all our dives, and since Richard *is* your dive buddy, I'd appreciate if you guys stay together while diving. I noticed him stray off by himself a couple of times."

Nils rolled his eyes. "Richard can take care of himself."

"Christ, Nils, a little cooperation, please," Ethan intervened. He shook his head, then stepped over to the showerhead and pulled the cord. He stripped off his wetsuit under a shower of warm fresh water.

Addy stepped under the spray next to Ethan after Nils and Richard climbed the ladder up to the main deck. "What put the bee up his butt?"

"Sorry. Nils can be a bit of an ass. He's been arguing with Richard about the grant they're working on since we left LA." Ethan glanced up to make sure no one else was close enough to hear. "I didn't think I needed Nils, but Richard thought it would cause him problems if I didn't ask him to be a part of this."

"Too bad. Richard seems like a sweet guy. I'm looking forward to learning more about his research." She leaned in to let the warm water wash over her face and hair, pulled down the long zipper chord on the back of her wetsuit, and stepped out of it. "Nothing like a warm shower after a dive, right?"

"Yeah, nothing like it," he said, mesmerized by the sight of the water cascading down the hollow of her back. Suddenly feeling awkward, he grabbed a towel, wrapped it around his waist, and climbed the ladder to the deck.

"Everything's functioning perfectly, and I'm ready to rock and roll, boss," Gage said. "Where to next?"

"From here, we'll head southeast toward Komodo," Addy answered. She'd followed Ethan up the ladder. She rubbed her hair with her towel then wrapped it around her, tucking it just above her breasts. "We'll thread our way along the west coast of the island and make several dives off the coast as we head south."

"Komodo. Awesome," Gage said excitedly. "Any chance we'll get to see some dragons?"

Chapter 7

Savu Sea, south of Komodo Island

The fourth day into the expedition, *Varuna* lay at anchor in a small bay at the southernmost islet of an archipelago off the southeastern coast of Komodo. The sun was low on the horizon when Ethan and his crew gathered on the foredeck to review the day's film footage. Like the previous three days, they'd made four dives that day and were relaxing after another great dinner prepared by the ship's cook, Talib.

"Don't start the video just yet," Fabiola said. Moments earlier, Gage put a disk from his video camera into the laptop propped open on a folding chair. "Let's enjoy the sunset." The late-afternoon sun was beginning to dip behind the rock outcropping to the west. Ocean swells rolled in and crashed against them, sending plumes of white foam high into the air silhouetted against the fading orange sun. After the last sliver melted below the horizon, Gage pressed play.

"Mind if we join you?" Malik asked, stepping out onto the foredeck through the galley door followed by Raj. "Raj told me you were kind enough to let him sit with you last night while you reviewed your camera footage, and he said it was quite amazing. We won't be weighing anchor for a couple more hours, so I thought we might join you. If you don't mind, of course."

"Not at all. Pull yourselves up a cushion," Ethan replied.

"It's a world I never imagined existed," Raj exclaimed, his voice animated. "The brilliant colors. And the sounds! You'd think the reef would be silent, but it's alive with strange sounds. Clicks and chirps and squeaks. Amazing." Raj, usually silent and standoffish from the other crew and passengers, now gushed like a kid describing his first trip to an amusement park.

"I saved you a place, Raj," Fabiola said, picking up her jacket from the cushion next to her.

Even though the divers experienced the reef with their own eyes only an hour earlier, they were again mesmerized by the stunning beauty displayed on the screen of the laptop. Swirling clouds of rainbow runners shifted back and forth across the tops of the reef as if directed by a single thought. Intricate soft corals swayed with the current. Nimble clownfish darted through the poisonous tentacles of giant purple anemone. Octopus danced over the coral, their color morphing to each variety of color, on the lookout for prey and to confuse their mortal enemy, the moray eel, hiding in the nooks and crannies.

A pair of pulsating cuttlefish glided by several bump-head parrot fish bouncing their razor-sharp beaks against the coral, breaking off tiny chunks, digesting it, and excreting sand. Napoleon wrasse, some three feet long, swam around the enormous sponges in the deeper areas of the reef. Deeper still, the camera panned out, and dozens of hammerhead sharks appeared, gliding like ghostly shadows patrolling the undersea ridges.

"Impressive," Malik said once the video ended. "I've been sailing over this for years oblivious to what lies below. Maybe I *will* put on that gear and see for myself someday."

"I'd be honored to teach you," Addy replied. "I promise you'll love it."

"Sounds as if you're at sea, often, Captain," Richard said. "Do you have a family?"

"Yes, a wife and son."

"How do they deal with your long absences? My kids are grown, but my wife still gives me a hard time about being gone so much."

"They're far away now," Malik said. He averted his face and looked toward the horizon.

"Forgive me," Richard said. "It wasn't my intent to pry."

Ethan spoke up. "Gage, we're getting great footage of healthy reefs, but we also need topside narrative of Richard discussing his algorithm. Make sure to get him explaining his work before our first dive tomorrow morning."

"Aye, aye, chief."

"Fab, I'd like you to shoot Addy at her predive briefing at the whiteboard tomorrow morning."

"What about me?" Nils asked.

"What about you?" Ethan said.

"You said to make sure to get Richard on film discussing his work. Richard and I are partners. I feel as if I'm being excluded."

"I don't know what you're talking about, Nils, but, sure," Ethan said. He looked at Gage. "Get some footage of Nils as well." Ethan didn't want Nils's ill manner and deadpan delivery included in his film but figured he could edit him out later.

"Congratulations to you all on your work," Malik

said, standing. "Very impressive. However, if you will please excuse us, we need to prepare to get underway if we are to reach tomorrow's dive sites by daybreak."

"Can you stay, Raj? The footage I shot is next," Fabiola said, touching Raj's arm.

"Sure," Raj said, without looking at Malik for permission.

****

"I was wondering where you went," Ethan said. He'd walked to the aft deck after they'd finished reviewing the day's footage. He found Addy leaning against the rail and gazing down at the water. It was a moonless night, and the reflection of the milky way shone brightly on the surface.

"I never get tired of this view," she said, watching the phosphorescence around the ship light up like blue runway lights as sharks streaked by, chasing baitfish. "Ever since I left my marine research position and started my guiding business, I've worried I wasn't doing enough to protect the wonders of this incredible place. Thanks for including me on this project. I feel I'm a part of something worthwhile."

Ethan stood beside her and rested his arms on the rail. "None of this could've happened without your contribution. I'm happy you're here. And not just because of your guiding."

"What's next for you? After this project." Addy asked. She tucked a loose strand of hair behind her ear. The temperature dropped after sundown, and she wore a thin jacket and cotton bell-bottoms.

"It's hard to see beyond it right now. I'll tell you one thing. I'm not going back to what I did before. I've seen enough death and destruction to last a lifetime.

Nothing I've done has made an iota of difference. And I got friends and coworkers hurt. And some killed."

"I'm sure it wasn't your fault."

"That's what I told myself. I convinced myself I was doing the right thing. That I was showing the horror of war. In reality, though, I got caught up in the thrill of it all and ended up glorifying it. No wonder the army brass loved me and let me go wherever I wanted. By showing the bravado of young soldiers, the sophisticated weapons, and the adrenaline rush of combat, my reporting convinced young people to enlist. The more recognition I got, the more I sought the most dangerous assignments. To make it worse, I convinced people to follow me."

"It was still their choice."

"I suppose. After my cameraman was killed, I went into a depression. I quit reporting. I pretty much quit everything. It was Richard that brought me out of it and gave me purpose. He convinced me to do this project. He told me men would always fight wars, but we have a limited time to protect the oceans. He said if I truly wanted to make a difference, it'll be with projects like this one."

"What you're doing will make a difference," Addy said. "I want to stay involved with you." She blushed. "With your project, I meant."

"I'd like that."

"So what do you think of *Varuna* and her crew so far?" Addy asked.

"It's all great. I can see why Malik loves this boat. It feels like it's alive with the way it creaks and moans in concert with the motion of the wind and waves. I'm glad things turned out the way they did, I can't imagine being on anything else. Sanjeev's also been a huge help. Super good guy and clearly has a lot of experience with diving operations. He's always there to help, and always with a smile."

Addy nodded her agreement. "Wish we could say the same about Raj. There's something about him that makes me uneasy. I should speak to Malik about it."

"Don't worry about it. We're managing just fine," Ethan reassured her. "He's making sure Fab is well taken care of," he chuckled. He glanced at Addy and saw her eyes had narrowed and she was staring intently into the darkness beyond him. He straightened and followed her gaze toward the gap in the rocks forming the little bay where they were anchored. "Did you see something?"

She shook her head. "Did you hear that?"

"Hear what?"

"Listen. Can you hear that low rumble?"

Ethan cocked his ears and stared into the darkness, listening. "I don't hear anything."

She stepped up onto the rail and grabbed the line running from the mizzenmast to steady herself. She pointed beyond the mouth of the bay. "There! A ship running without lights. I bet it's a fucking trawler!" She jumped down and raced past him to the hatch leading down to the berths.

Ethan scoured the dark horizon. Then he saw it: the faint outline of a shape moving past the opening of the bay. The low thump, thump, thump, of a ship's diesel engines rumbled across the water. Addy burst back through the hatch carrying her dive flashlight, a hand radio, and her camera.

She tossed Ethan the flashlight. "You coming?"

"Hell yes."

Reaching the stern, Addy vaulted over the aft rail and landed on the wooden platform. She grabbed the line holding one of the Zodiacs, pulled it up close, and climbed in. Ethan followed, untied the line, and jumped in with her. He shoved the Zodiac away from the platform while Addy yanked the cord starting the Zodiac's outboard engine. Out of the corner of his eye, Ethan saw Malik run out onto the aft deck. He turned to tell Addy to wait, but before he could get a word out, she gunned the engine and sped away from *Varuna* and toward the dark shape, drowning out Malik's shouts.

Ethan held tight to the line with one hand and flipped on the flashlight with his other as they steered out of the bay into open water. The Zodiac bounced over the rolling ocean swells and rapidly closed the distance between them and what Ethan could now see was the stern of a ship. Addy steered to the right, away from the ship's churning wash. They crossed the ship's wake and ran the Zodiac alongside the ship's starboard beam. Ethan swept the light from stern to bow, searching for the ship's name and its flag. The ship displayed neither. Ethan swept the light back toward the stern "Look at those," he said. The beam illuminated two large cranes. Long steel cables extended from the top of the cranes out into the churning water behind.

"It's a bottom trawler," Addy shouted over the high-pitched whine of the Zodiac's outboard. "Can you see any markings?" She pointed her video camera with one hand while holding the throttle and steering handle with the other.

"No. It's not flying a flag either," Ethan shouted back. "It's a pirate trawler all right."

Addy kept the Zodiac running parallel to the ship, matching the trawler's speed. Several men gathered along the starboard rail, looking down and pointing. She shouted up at them, "These are protected waters. What's the name of your ship? What is your flag?" Realizing they couldn't hear a word she was saying over the whine of the outboard and the chugging of the ship's diesel engines, she motioned to Ethan, "Here, take the throttle."

Ethan climbed to the back and took the throttle while Addy turned the dial on the handheld radio to a channel monitored by the Indonesian coast guard.

"Coast guard! Come in coast guard," Addy shouted into the radio.

Ethan's head was reeling. Only a few moments earlier, he was relaxing on *Varuna*'s deck, gazing into Addy's green eyes. Now he steered a tiny inflatable boat in the pitch dark alongside a ship ten times its size. He pointed the flashlight up again at the line of men. A man shoved his way to the rail. Suddenly, the ship lit up from the bright star-shaped staccato burst of an automatic weapon. The water around the Zodiac erupted as bullets zipped past.

"Get down!" Ethan shouted. He dropped the flashlight to the bottom of the boat like a hot rock, twisted the throttle wide open, and jerked the steering handle hard to the left.

The sudden swerve caused Addy to lose her balance. Tumbling over the side, she grabbed for the rope running along the top of the inflatable, just catching it with her right arm. Her legs careened off the boat and bounced across the water. She struggled up on top of the tube, straddled it, and held tight.

Ethan looked back over his shoulder as another burst of light erupted from the ship. Sparks flew as bullets ricocheted off the Zodiac's engine. Ethan dropped to the bottom of the boat but held tight to the throttle while bullets zipped past.

"The running lights! Turn off the lights!" Addy shouted.

"Oh shit!" Ethan switched off the lights, and they sped away into the darkness as fast as the little boat would carry them. Ethan looked back again. The ship was no longer in sight. He slowed the craft to an idle. "Are you okay?"

"I think so," She swung her feet into the boat. "Those motherfuckers intended to kill us." She picked up the radio, submerged under four inches of water. "This is done for," she exclaimed, holding the dripping radio and clicking the talk button futilely. "You better hit the gas, Ethan. We're sinking."

****

"Was that gunfire?" Malik shouted as the Zodiac motored up to the platform on *Varuna*'s stern. "What happened? What did you do to my boat?" The tubing surrounding the Zodiac's fiberglass hull had entirely deflated, and water sloshed over the sides. He tossed a line into the Zodiac. "Loop this around the engine," he ordered Ethan, then he waved toward Sanjeev, "Secure the bow."

Sanjeev quickly tied the bowline to *Varuna*'s stern, and Ethan looped the other line around the transom of the outboard. The two sailors pulled the lines taut and kept the Zodiac from continuing to sink.

"It was a pirate trawler, Malik," Addy said, taking Sanjeev's hand and climbing out of the boat onto the platform. "They fired on us! We were only able to stay afloat by running at full throttle. We were trying to chase it away. Or at least identify it."

Malik felt the blood drain from his head. "You challenged a ship in one of my Zodiacs?" He climbed down from the deck and onto the platform. "How dare you take one of my boats without my permission!"

"That ship was illegally trawling in a marine reserve and destroying the reef," Ethan said, stepping to the front of the boat and then climbing out. "We tried to capture them on camera but the SOBs started shooting at us!"

"Get them on camera? You filmed it? You're here to film sea life, not fishing vessels."

"Didn't you hear, Malik?" Addy said. "They fired on us. Not to scare us, but to kill us. They knew they were fishing in a protected reserve. I was calling the coast guard on my radio when they started shooting at us."

Malik's face turned even paler. "Did you identify our position or the name of our boat?"

"No, my radio fell in the water before I could relay that information," Addy said.

Malik breathed a sigh of relief.

"We need to get to your radio," Addy said, "to report their position before they get too far away." Addy stepped up on the ladder, but Malik grabbed her arm.

"Hold on. I'm the captain of this vessel. Any communication to the authorities will be made by me. Don't ever commandeer one of my Zodiacs again without my permission." He brushed past her and climbed off the platform up to the main deck. At the top of the ladder, he turned and barked another order to Sanjeev: “Winch up that Zodiac, then prepare to weigh anchor.”

Ethan followed Malik up to the deck. “Wait just a minute, Captain. We’re not leaving. We have to stay here so we can go out tomorrow and film where the ship passed.”

“What? The schedule was to leave tonight and head south to your next dive site. That’s what was agreed.”

“That was before this happened.”

“Why would this make any difference? If anything, we should press on.”

“I need to film the destruction caused by that trawler.”

“What does that have to do with your film? We’ll continue according to the schedule.”

“Look, Malik, if it’s a matter of cost, I’ll pick up the overage. If it’s time, we’ll cut short the other sites we had planned, but we’re not leaving until after we’ve documented the damage caused by that ship.”

“Malik, this is our chance to do something right,” Addy pleaded. “We can’t waste this opportunity.”

“I want nothing to do with it. It will just invite trouble,” Malik insisted. He turned again to head up to the bridge.

“You abandon this site now, and I’ll show you trouble,” Ethan warned. “Don’t forget I’m a journalist. I’ll make sure the authorities and everyone else knows you hindered us. That you knew of illegal activity occurring and did nothing. Let’s see what kind of charter business you have after the light I cast you in.”

Malik hesitated, his mind racing. “You two follow

me up to the bridge."

"What are you doing, Malik?" Raj demanded. He was listening intently to their exchange. "You're not actually going to call the authorities?"

"I'll handle this," Malik shot back. "You go help Sanjeev."

Once they were up to the bridge with the door shut, Ethan said, "Why would Raj say that? You do intend to notify the authorities about what we saw, don't you?"

"First, explain to me the intent of your film. You led me to believe you were filming a documentary about large fish migration patterns."

Ethan glanced at Addy and then back to Malik before saying, "These pirates are not only destroying critical habitats, but they're also stealing food from the mouths of hungry families. Local families. It's great that countries like yours have the foresight to set aside reserves and put limits on hauls. But these criminals know they don't have the resources to protect them adequately. These criminals don't respect haul limits. They don't care about the impact. They only care about making money."

Malik leaned back against the helm. "You're making a documentary about illegal fishing in protected reserves by organized crime."

Ethan nodded. "It wasn't what we set out to do in this leg of our expedition, but yes, it is a major focus of my project."

"Why didn't you tell me that when you hired me?"

"We didn't know who we could trust. It's no secret some charter boat captains share information with these criminals."

"I may be a lot of things, but I don't provide

information to those goddamned poachers." In Malik's mind, it was one thing to be a smuggler but completely another to be a poacher, despite Anand's repeated demands. "All right. We'll stay here one more day. So you can film. We'll cut the expedition short by a day to make up for it."

"We can do that," Ethan agreed.

"Now can we call the coast guard?" Addy asked, nodding toward the satellite phone on the console.

"Yes. I'll call them."

Addy and Ethan waited for Malik to pick up the phone.

Malik picked up the receiver. "I'll let you know what they say."

"They may want to talk with us," Addy said.

"I'll let you know if they do. Now, if you please, get off my bridge."

Raj waited until Ethan and Addy stepped off the ladder and then raced up to the bridge and inside the small cabin. "You didn't call the authorities, did you?"

"Of course not." Malik set the receiver back in its base. "But they don't know that."

"You know that could have been one of Anand's trawlers. You're going to allow them to film the area where the trawler passed?"

"It will cause us more trouble if I don't. Making the rendezvous on time is my only priority."

"We damn well better. For your sake. And mine." Raj left the bridge.

A smile crept across Malik's face. *What a fitting parting gift this film will make. I think I'll ask Ethan for an autographed copy...to leave for Anand.*

Chapter 8

"I am amazed neither of you got hit last night," Sanjeev said. He handed the last of the scuba gear to Ethan. "And very happy you didn't."

"Thanks, Sanjeev, me too. We were lucky that's for sure." Ethan set the BC and tank in the hull of the Zodiac. He looked over at the boat hanging from the winch just off the port stern. A line of round black epoxy splotches ran along the length of the bottom.

"It was more than luck. The gods protected you," Sanjeev said. "I patched twenty-five bullet holes in that boat." He untied the bowline and climbed into the Zodiac.

"The visibility will be poor," Fabiola said, looking down from *Varuna*'s stern rail. "You guys be careful."

All the divers and their gear wouldn't fit in one boat, so only Ethan, Addy, Richard, and Gage were going out to the reef. Ethan told Fabiola and Nils they would have to stay behind on *Varuna* until the epoxy patches on the other Zodiac had time to set.

"Thanks. We will." Addy shoved the Zodiac clear of *Varuna*'s stern.

Sanjeev started the engine and steered the four divers out toward the mouth of the bay.

"This is bullshit," Nils said to Fabiola. I'm the one who should be going. What's the point sending that cameraman if there's no visibility?"

"Ethan knows what he's doing," Fabiola said. "Besides, he said we'd go out on the afternoon dives."

"Humph. Let's go over to the table. I need you to enter some data on my laptop."

"Yeah, maybe later, Nils." She glanced past him toward Raj, who stood leaning against the mizzenmast, watching her. She walked past Raj without making eye contact and then glanced back over her shoulder. "Wanna join me for breakfast? Or do you have work to do?"

"It can wait." Raj followed her into the galley.

****

"Let's stop here," Addy said to Sanjeev, once the Zodiac was about a half mile offshore. "The trawler passed right along this line," she said, motioning with her arm. "We'll enter the water here and drift down current. Stay with us, following our bubbles," she instructed him.

"Will do, Addy." Sanjeev switched off the engine.

The divers pulled on their fins and buckled on their scuba gear in somber silence. The only sounds were the water lapping against the sides of the boat and the occasional call of a lone seagull circling above.

Ethan made eye contact with each of his team. "This won't be pleasant, but let's remember this is the reason we're here. Film everything you can. The trawler will have churned up the sand, and it'll be murky, so stay together. That means you too, Richard. Try not to stray." He glanced at Addy. She nodded her understanding to keep a close eye on Richard. He pulled his mask over his eyes and nose. "Let's get this over with."

Gripping their regulators in their teeth, the four

divers tumbled backward into the water and sank below the surface. Six feet down, Ethan pinched the nose of his mask and blew to equalize the pressure in his ears. Turning his gaze downward, he caught his breath. The devastation was overpowering. He flashed back to Iraq and the war zones he'd witnessed. Tears welled, blurring his vision. What before was a vibrant ecosystem teeming with life was now a jumbled graveyard of broken coral and toppled sponges. Grainy particulate dredged up the night before still hung in the water, lowering the visibility to less than twenty feet. The day before, it was more than a hundred.

Two long parallel trenches scarred the bottom. They looked like a semi had driven over the reef. But he had no doubt what made them. He'd seen photos while researching his film. Giant rubber wheels weighted by heavy steel plates supporting bottom-trawling nets the size of a football field gouged these trenches. Vast sections of coral ripped loose from the rock shelf lay scattered along the bottom. Little remained undamaged. The giant sponges, intricate fan coral, and colorful anemones they'd marveled at the day before lay smashed and broken. The day before the reef teemed with thousands of fish. Now, only a disoriented handful drifted above the ruins.

The divers proceeded with the miserable job of documenting the destruction. During their morning briefing, Ethan told Gage and Richard he wanted to repeat the prior day's dive plan to get an accurate before-and-after comparison.

I've got proof of a ship trawling under cover of darkness in a protected reserve, Ethan said to himself while snapping photos. *We captured them firing live rounds at us and I have images of the Zodiac full of bullet holes.*" He sensed something above and looked up. Addy hovered above him, floating like an angel, backlit against the rays of sunlight filtering through the churned-up particulate. Tears streamed down her face, visible even through the lens of her mask. Before their first dive, she'd told him this reef was a special place to her, and how she marveled in awe at its beauty.

He squeezed her hand gently, then resumed snapping photos. He crept along the bottom getting close-ups of broken shards of coral and shorn pieces of giant anemone. Exhausting all but three hundred psi of his air supply, Ethan drifted toward the surface, snapping the last of his roll of film, capturing shots of the few remaining fish which had escaped the net.

****

After the last dive of the day, the team gathered around the camera table on the aft deck. Richard and Nils had taken numerous water samples, marking each vial with an underwater pen. Richard also directed Gage to exact locations of specific corals he'd remembered from the day before to make sure they had the side-by-side comparisons Ethan wanted.

"What do you say we put off reviewing this footage?" Gage said. "We'll be sailing most of the day tomorrow. Couldn't we do it then? I think we deserve a break, boss."

"I could go for that," Ethan said. "Hell, let's get drunk." He went inside the galley, then returned with a bucket filled with bottles of beer. After handing a few out, he popped his open and drained half the bottle. "You know, I got so caught up in all the beauty we've observed since we arrived, I almost forgot why we're here. I just wasn't ready for what we saw today."

"Goddamn bastards," Richard said. He gulped his beer, tipping it too fast. Foam shot out his nose, and everyone exploded in laughter.

"That's so cute," Fabiola said with a smile. "I think that was the first time I've heard Richard curse."

"Really professional, Richard," Nils said. "I can't believe you people think it's appropriate to laugh and drink amid all this. If you decide to do some work, I'll be in my berth. Unless you're too drunk, that is."

"Wait a second, Nils. Come on. Sit down," Richard said. "I've been waiting for the right time to tell you all this, and since we're in need of some happier news, I have an announcement to make." A smile beamed across his face.

Nils sat back down. He stared at Richard with his eyebrows pinched in an ugly scowl.

"You waitin for a drumroll or what, Richard?" Gage said. "Let's hear it."

"You know that grant we applied for from the NOAA? Well," he paused for dramatic effect, "we got it."

"What?" Nils bolted to his feet. "When did you find out?"

"I got the letter right before we left. I've been waiting for the right time to announce it."

"And you never told me?" Nils said, looking incredulous. "I'm your partner. Why would you keep that from me?"

"I needed to take a little time to think about it. About how we'll use the money."

"That's a decision we need to make together."

"I've already decided. We all hope Ethan's film

will expose the issue of pirate fleets raiding under-protected marine reserves, destroying sensitive habitat, and depleting young fish vital for breeding. But we also need to propose solutions. To do that we have to be able to better estimate fish populations and migration patterns."

"They already know what our algorithm does, Richard. Get to the point."

"Yes, of course, that's the purpose of the beta testing. But to be able to make a truly scientific assessment of the state of the world's pelagic populations, we'll need to gather a tremendous amount of data. Once we have the data, the program can provide a basis for international treaties to protect our oceans. And our food supply. Time is of the essence."

"How long do you think it would take to gather enough observations to make the assessment?" Addy asked.

"No more than two years, I hope," Richard answered.

"That would require an army of researchers and use all our grant money," Nils said. "We need to talk about this, Richard."

"That is what the grant money was for, Nils. Trust me, it's possible."

"This calls for a toast," Ethan said, standing up and raising his beer. "Congratulations, Richard. That is exciting news. It couldn't have happened to a more deserving and capable guy."

"Here, here!" Addy said, clinking bottles with everyone except Nils, who sat in sullen silence.

"I also have a follow-up announcement," Richard added.

"Don't keep us waiting," Fabiola said, "what is it?"

"The team of researchers will need a leader," Richard announced. "Someone who understands the science behind what we are doing but who is also skilled at organizing and leading groups of divers. I've become impressed with her knowledge of the marine environment, and I can think of no one more passionate about saving our oceans." He flashed a smile at Addy and winked. "So what do you think, young lady? Are you up to the challenge?"

"I…I don't know what to say, Richard. Your confidence humbles me, but I need to be on the ocean. I learned a long time ago lab work is not for me."

"Perfect. Leave the lab work to me. I need you in the field. You have the background and training for it. Not only do you possess a trained eye, but you've also retained a sense of wonder I think is vital to this work. You're a natural-born leader, and you made it obvious you believe in the cause by chasing down a pirate trawler in the dark."

"He's right, Addy. You're perfect for the job," Ethan said.

Addy took a deep breath. Her eyes lit up, and she beamed. "I'd be honored, Richard. Thank you."

"This is not acceptable, Richard," Nils pleaded. "Can we talk about this in private?"

"Later, Nils. You'll see. This is what we need to do."

"I can't believe this is happening. You didn't even discuss it with me. Fuck you, Richard. Fuck you all." He turned and stormed away.

"Aw, come on, Nils," Gage mocked. "Don't leave mad." Then under his breath mumbled, "Just leave."

"Take it easy on him, Gage. Can't you see he's feeling hurt?" Addy said.

"Gage is right, Addy," Fabiola said. "Nils is always complaining, and he's rude. Why's he so mad? He won a huge grant; you'd think he'd be happy about it."

"We've never agreed on how the money would best be spent," Richard said, shaking his head. "He wants to use it to reimburse us for the work we've done to date and to live on while we continue to do research. I fear if we take that long, fisheries will collapse, and none of this will matter. I didn't think he'd react this way, though. I wanted this to be a good surprise for him as well. Guess I got that wrong."

"It's obvious even to a redneck like me, the science has passed him by," Gage continued. "He's just hanging on your coattails. He hasn't contributed anything to this project."

"Geez, dude, that's a little harsh," Ethan said.

"I'm just sayin' everyone needs to carry their weight. Literally. Have you seen how he makes the crew carry all his shit? Like he's some kind of fucking royalty."

"I thought you said we were going to get drunk," Fabiola said. "If you guys keep talking about Nils, I'm going to my room."

"You are absolutely right, my lovely young friend," Richard said. He took another gulp and his face contorted in a pucker. "How much of this vile brew do I have to drink to accomplish that?"

"Just keep up with me and you'll get there," Gage said, clinking his bottle to Richard's.

"Good lord, don't do that," Ethan said. "Gage has already lost too many brain cells. You're the only genius on this crew, Richard. We need to make sure you keep yours."

"You guys are such bummers," Fabiola said. She took two bottles from the bucket. "I'm going to my room." Instead of heading through the galley toward the hatch leading below decks, she strolled past it toward the foredeck.

"Think someone should tell her she walked right past the door to the cabins?" Gage said.

"She took two beers," Addy said with a wry smile. "I don't think she's going to her room."

Chapter 9

"Captain Sumadi here."

"I have the shipment for you from Anand," Malik said, speaking into the satellite phone. Raj stood next to him on *Varuna*'s bridge.

"It's about time you called," Sumadi growled.

"I'm southwest of Komodo Island, sailing east toward Rinca," Malik said. "Where are you?"

"South of Flores, heading west. Where are we going to meet?"

Malik studied the chart spread out on the small table. "There's a small island southeast of Rinca called Gili Motang. Do you know it?"

"Yes, I see it on my chart," Sumadi answered. I can't risk steering my ship that far north."

"I can't sail much farther south without raising the suspicions of my passengers," Malik responded. "If you can come northward far enough to launch a small craft from your ship, I can bring the merchandise in a Zodiac. We can plot a GPS coordinate and meet twenty kilometers due south of the island."

There was a pause on the line. "That could work. Give me the GPS coordinates."

Malik slid a ruler along the chart and plotted the coordinates. "Let's meet at 8 degrees, 51 minutes south by 119 degrees, 47 minutes east. We can be there at 02:00, the day after tomorrow. The weather's projected to be calm and clear. We'll turn on our running lights. You shouldn't have any trouble finding us."

"All right. You better be there."

"We'll be there," Malik said. "When you see our lights, flash yours three times. We'll respond with the same. "

"We'll find you," Sumadi said gruffly.

"If you don't show, the merchandise is going over the side." Malik pressed the end-call button and fumbled to set the phone back in its cradle, his hand shaking.

Raj took the phone from his hand and hung it up. "Nice bluff, Captain. Anand would be proud."

"Not something I aspire to." Malik took his hat off and wiped the beads of sweat from his forehead. "I don't like this, Raj. We'll be exposed on the open sea. They'll likely have us outmanned and outgunned. What if this is part of a plan Anand has to get rid of me?"

"You worry too much. Why would he want to get rid of you? Anyway, I'll be with you. Anand wouldn't do anything like that with me along."

"Worry keeps me alive. You trust him too much for your own good." Malik pointed to a spot on the map. "We're right here. After the film crew's last dive tomorrow, we'll weigh anchor and sail toward the south coast of Rinca. I told Addy and Ethan about a secluded spot they should check out. The dive site is directly on the route to our rendezvous." Malik dragged his finger to another spot on the chart. "We'll anchor somewhere along here." He ran his finger along the north coast of Gili Motang. "I'll put you on watch at 23:00, and tell Sanjeev to relieve you at 05:30. I'll come up at midnight and pull one of the Zodiacs alongside while you go down and get the trunks. We'll paddle far enough from *Varuna* so no one will hear us start the engine."

"Will that give us time to make the exchange?" Raj asked.

"I figure it'll take us an hour and a half to get to the rendezvous point. It should only take a few minutes to make the exchange, but let's say half an hour, to be safe. Another hour and a half to get back. Should be plenty of time. Make sure the Zodiac is gassed up and it's not the one with the patched bullet holes. Don't want to risk a leak out in the middle of the sea."

"Will do."

"Did you bring weapons?" Malik asked.

"Of course I did. Three Glocks. Two for me, one for you."

"You keep the guns. I wouldn't be much help anyway. I've never shot anyone."

"They try anything; I'll kill 'em all."

"Don't be overconfident. I don't like the way that Sumadi fellow sounded." Malik fretted.

"Like I said, you worry too much. It'll be fine." Raj took out a pack of smokes and offered one to Malik. "What will you do next?"

"With luck, we'll be safely back on board before anyone knows we're gone and breathe a long sigh of relief."

"I meant, what will you do once we're back in port? Anand told me to watch you. He doesn't trust you. He said you wanted out after this shipment."

Malik hesitated. He liked Raj. He could see he enjoyed being at sea and was learning to embrace his role. Raj had once saved his life. Malik wanted to trust him, but he was Anand's protégé, and Malik dared not confide his plans in detail.

"I never told you the full story about the casino mob Anand paid off, did I?" Malik sat on the edge of the tall stool in front of the ship's spoked wooden wheel at the helm.

"You said they cheated you. I remember those three guys kicking the shit out of you in that alley. I didn't like those odds."

"I'm sure those three will never forget the beating you gave them," Malik said. "I'd be dead if you hadn't come along."

Although gambling is illegal in Indonesia, the local mafia ran several underground casinos and brothels in Jakarta. Raj happened to be in one of those casinos and walked out into the alley to make a call when he saw three men viciously beating someone. He'd grown up fighting for his life on the streets of Jakarta, and rose to be the leader of his street gang. After recruiting him, Anand sent him to learn jiujitsu and Muay Thai. Not the kind taught in your local martial arts studio. The kind that taught to maim and to kill.

Raj intervened and left the three thugs in a crumpled heap of broken bones and shattered teeth. Afterward, Malik mentioned he was a charter boat captain. Thinking Anand might find Malik useful in his smuggling business; Raj offered to introduce Malik to someone who might be able to help. Anand paid off the debt, and Malik found himself in the thrall of an even more dangerous criminal organization.

"I figured if you wanted me to know more, you'd tell me," Raj said.

"I had a drinking and gambling problem then,"

Malik continued. "I was on a big winning streak one night when the casino boss had a woman slip a drug in my drink. I woke in a room with two prostitutes. When I got home, two men from the casino were waiting for me. My wife was huddled in a corner with my young son. Photographs of me with those two women were scattered on the floor in front of her. I'll never forget the look on her face." Malik closed his eyes and let the warm, humid air blowing across his face take away the painful memories.

Recovering his composure, he continued. "They claimed I lost thirty thousand dollars gambling and they wanted their money. They told me I had a week to get them the money. If I didn't pay, they'd come back for my wife and son and make them work in their brothels to pay off my debt."

"What did you do?" Raj asked.

"I took my wife and son to the port that very day. I gave her all the money I had left and told her to get as far away as they could. I told her I'd find them once it was safe. Standing on the pier watching their boat sail away was the worst moment of my life. I died inside that day. That was the last time I saw them."

"I'm sorry. Where are they now?"

"I wouldn't tell you even if I knew. I haven't looked for them. Yet. I've been afraid Anand would have me followed. If I found them, so would he. I don't want to risk their lives again."

"I don't tell Anand everything. He doesn't own me."

"Anand believes everyone who works for him is his property. You can become more than what he's turning you into. You have your whole life ahead of you."

"I grew up an orphan on the streets. I fought for my life every day. It was the only life I knew until Anand took me in."

"He took you from the streets," Malik said, "but you're still fighting. Do you want to spend your life robbing and killing until Anand decides you're a threat and has you killed? You have a choice, Raj. You can get away. I know you love being a sailor. I've seen it in your eyes. I can help you get a new start. I can help you go where Anand will never find you."

"Where?"

"I'll tell you when you decide you're ready to break away."

"Why would I? Anand treats me like his son. I have money and power."

"Only what he gives you. How old were you when he took you in?"

"Fourteen. My friends and I broke into this warehouse and stole a truckload of electronics. Turns out it was one of Anand's. Eko caught us and killed two of my friends. He was about to kill me. Anand stopped him. He took me in."

"To train you to kill. He may have spared your life, but he didn't save it. Just like me, you were an opportunity to exploit."

Raj ran his hand over the sea chart and gazed at the myriad of islands, shoals, currents, and water depths. "Do you think I could've been a good sailor?"

"You are becoming a good sailor."

"I appreciate you treating me like one of your crew. Sanjeev's been very kind to me as well. Before Anand began assigning me to accompany you on deliveries, I'd never even been on the ocean."

"You can have a better life. You just have to decide to go after it."

Raj shook his head. "You make it sound so easy. He'd never give up looking for me. You know how vengeful he is. He'd come after you too. Especially if he suspected you convinced me to leave."

Malik squeezed Raj's shoulder and smiled. "I won't deny it'd be a risk. I know a way to protect us from him if you decide to come with me." He decided to place a little trust in Raj. "Either way, once we've made this delivery, I'm out. I'm going to disappear."

"Why would you tell me that? He could send me after you."

"I'm telling you because I think you can have a better future. You're young enough to change. I don't think you'd hurt me. Anand may be pissed if I disappear, but I will have made his delivery. I'm hoping that will take some of the sting out of his anger."

"You shouldn't bet your life on it."

Chapter 10

Gage rushed to the open window of *Varuna*'s bridge, leaned out, and vomited. "Damn, I'm sorry. I usually don't get seasick."

"Don't worry about it," Malik said, chuckling. "The next wave will wash it away. I warned you last night when you asked if we had anything stronger than beer aboard. Arak can cause quite a hangover."

A fog lay along the horizon and shrouded the morning sun. Except for the distant gray outline of an island to the northwest, there was nothing but open water in every direction. The ship cruised smoothly overnight heading southeast over rolling ocean swells but now *Varuna* rocked and lurched as they sailed into an area of strong currents, creating choppy standing waves.

"I should've listened. My head's still pounding."

"You're a picture of beauty this morning, Addy," Malik said. "You must have heeded my advice."

"I'm familiar with the local liquor, Captain. I didn't need reminding," Addy said. She squeezed into *Varuna*'s small bridge alongside the captain, Ethan, Sanjeev, and Gage.

"Where are we headed?" Ethan asked, taking a deep breath, trying to will away the nausea brought on by the lurching and pitching of *Varuna* on the turbulent water. And too many beers the night before.

"Ask him," Addy said, nodding toward Malik. "He says he knows a place few have ever seen. He thinks no divers have ever been there. No fishing boats either."

"Dead ahead. See it?" Malik pointed straight out in front of them.

"I don't see a thing," Ethan said.

"I think I see it," Sanjeev said. "It looks like the head of a sea monster rising out of the mist."

"I call it the Kraken," Malik said.

Sanjeev looked over the side at the angry, churning swell. "I guess no diving today?"

Addy held onto the rail with one hand and took a sip of her coffee with her other, not spilling a drop, her sea legs effortlessly absorbing the movement of the pitching deck. "I don't see how in this choppy water, but the waters are supposed to be calm up ahead, according to Malik. He says we're in for a real treat, and I'm becoming more intrigued by the moment."

A tall craggy spire appeared in the distance. Sailing closer, two smaller white-capped jagged spires on either side also appeared. The three rose out of the sea like the head and shoulders of a giant monster.

"The islands of the Nusa Tenggara are separated from the Asian mainland by deep sea beds," Malik said, pointing toward the spires. "When the tides change, the sea surges through the gaps between these small islands, producing massive currents and standing waves."

The group on the bridge braced themselves as *Varuna* plowed into a wave and climbed its face. Her diesel engine whined as its propeller cavitated free of the water at the crest. Then *Varuna*'s bow tipped, and she ran down the wave and plunged into the backwash.

Water gushed over the rails surrounding the main deck. The engine bogged, and *Varuna* shuddered as her propeller caught purchase and powered the boat out of the trough and into the next wave. Water spilled off the deck as *Varuna*'s bow rose up onto the face of the next wave.

Dozens of screeching seabirds circled the guano-covered tops of the spires. The lower sections were craggy and broken from the constant buffeting of the raging current and ocean swells smashing onto the rocks. The water around the spires was churned into a frothy, translucent aquamarine, a blue so intense it beckoned like a siren's song.

"Be careful, Captain. We'll be caught in the surge!" Sanjeev shouted over the cacophony of the shrill calls of the seabirds, *Varuna*'s diesel struggling through the chop, and the thunder of the waves crashing against the rocks. His hands gripped the rail so tightly his knuckles turned white.

"I know what I'm doing, Sanjeev. Keep your nerve." Malik idled and waited for the powerful surge of a massive wave to bounce off the rocks, and then he spun the wheel to port and shoved the throttle to full. The retreating wave carried *Varuna* away from the rocks; then the current sucked her into the gap on the left of the tall center spire. Suddenly they were inside a deep canyon, surrounded on both sides by tall jagged cliffs. The waters calmed, Malik pulled back on the throttle, cutting the power, and *Varuna* idled into the canyon. She drifted next to a sheer flat wall on the lee side of the middle spire. The water continued to rage around the edges, but the area inside the three surrounding spires was as calm and indigo blue as a deep swimming pool.

"Amazing. I've never seen anything like it," Addy exclaimed in wonderment, staring up at the canyon wall.

"I thought you might like it," Malik said, a broad smile creeping across his face.

The rest of the passengers rushed out onto the main deck through the galley door and stood along the rail. "Spectacular!" Richard looked up toward the bridge. "Bravo, Captain. This is a true wonder."

"These rocks are the summit of a large seamount," Malik said. "The peak's been eroded and broken into these three spires. You said you were looking for places with deep-sea currents. The seafloor here drops to the abyss. I've seen the upwelling of currents, matching what you said you were searching for. I believe along this wall the water should be calm enough to dive."

"How did you learn about this spot, Captain?" Ethan asked.

"Let's just say I've needed to become invisible from time to time."

"This does look like the perfect hiding spot, so I won't ask any more questions," Addy said with a laugh. "It looks fantastic. Can you anchor here? I'd like to grab my mask and fins and jump in for a quick peek at the topography."

"There's nothing to anchor to. But go ahead. I can keep *Varuna* centered for a bit. If you decide to make more dives here, I know a spot about ten miles from here where we can drop anchor. We can ferry back and forth in the Zodiacs."

"We're going to navigate those huge waves in those tiny Zodiacs?" Gage asked. "That oughta be quite a rodeo."

Malik laughed. "Yes, it'll be a bumpy ride, that's what those boats are designed to handle." He turned to Ethan. "Assuming Addy says it's a go, how many dives will you make here?"

"If she says it's safe, I'd like to make three today, if possible, and a couple more tomorrow," he answered.

"I'll plan on anchoring in the bay overnight, then."

"Sounds great."

Malik nodded. *Perfect. I'll be in position to make the delivery tomorrow night.*

****

Addy surfaced from her dive, took a deep, gasping breath, and yanked off her mask. Carried away with the grandeur of the place, she'd swam down seventy-five feet. That depth would've been easy for her fifteen years ago, but she was out of practice, and her lung capacity wasn't what it once was. After several more recovery breaths, she looked up at the boat. A mile-wide smile beamed across her face. She shot both arms out of the water, gave two thumbs up, and whooped. "It's fantastic!" She swam to the platform, tossed her fins up, and with one big kick, leaped onto the platform. She hurried up the ladder to the aft deck where the rest of the crew and passengers were eagerly awaiting her report.

"All I can say is, wow." She gushed, still catching her breath. "It's a sheer wall that drops off into a deep blue void. But it's not featureless," she exclaimed, still breathless. "There are ledges blanketed with sponges and corals, and the entire wall's pockmarked with caves and crevices. The whole thing is teeming with life." She waved up at Malik on the bridge and gave him the thumbs-up sign again.

Malik responded with an informal salute, then steered *Varuna* out through the narrow canyon and back into the current.

"You dove seventy-five feet? On a single breath?" Sanjeev said, worry lines appearing on his face. "You take too many risks." He took the mask and fins she'd handed him and placed them in her bin.

Ethan nodded his agreement. "He's right. Next time you want to dive that deep, one of us should be in the water in full gear to keep an eye on you."

"Yeah, sorry. I got distracted by the majesty of the place."

"Okay then, dish it out, sister. What'd you see? What's it teeming with?" Gage asked impatiently.

"Oh, not much…Dozens of sharks: whitetips, silkies, a shitload of hammerheads. A school of giant bluefin cruising past, lots of giant grouper, amberjack, and wrasse…and—hold on to your panties, boys—a mola mola."

"You saw an ocean sunfish?" Gage exclaimed. "No effing way!"

"Yes, way. The thing must have been ten feet long and just as wide. I can't wait to come back and for all of you to see for yourselves. I followed it down the wall, and before I knew it, I looked at my depth gauge and was at seventy-five feet."

Malik piloted *Varuna* back out through the currents and standing waves, and an hour later they dropped anchor inside a small bay on the nearby islet.

At her pre-dive briefing a few minutes later, Addy stood at the whiteboard where she'd made a crude drawing of the major features of the dive site. She pointed to the left side of her sketch.

"We'll motor the Zodiacs around to the west side of the wall, gear up, and drop down to a about a hundred feet. The wall drops off into the abyss, so monitor your depth gauges carefully. Stay above a hundred-ten feet, or it will limit your bottom time for subsequent dives. We'll keep the wall on our right shoulders and work our way east. I can't stress this enough: stay inside the protected area along the wall. The tug of the current increases dramatically when you near the edge of the wall."

"It sounds dicey. Are you sure it's safe?" Fabiola asked.

"I swam the length of the wall. There's no current until you near the edge. As long as we stay sharp and follow the plan, we stay safe. But pay attention to where you are at all times. The water is calm to only about thirty feet out away from the wall, so stay in close."

"What if we do get caught in the current?" Gage asked, nodding toward Richard.

"You all saw the size of those standing waves outside the protected area. If you get sucked out and swept beyond the wall, the Zodiac drivers will have a difficult time spotting you in the churning water. So don't. The currents are running about six knots. If you find yourself out there, inflate your orange emergency tubes." Addy winked. "If we can't find you, at least you'll have something to look at while you float toward China."

Following the briefing, the divers boarded the Zodiacs. Raj and Sanjeev ferried them across the turbulent currents back to the Kraken. Arriving at the leeward side, they steered the two inflatables to within a few feet of one another and killed the engines. The divers geared up, rolled backward into the water, and started their descent. The shallower depths along the wall were rich with myriad varieties of small fish. Sinking deeper, giant trevally, Napoleon wrasse, and grouper roamed along the wall. Great schools of amberjack and bluefin swam by below them. Away from the wall, great oceangoing reef sharks patrolled, silhouetted against the deep blue of the open ocean. Schools of hammerheads and barracuda crisscrossed the wall at the edge of sight, far below.

At the end of their first dive, Addy surfaced beside Richard and pushed her mask up on her forehead. "Let me give you a hand," she said, helping him duck out of his gear. She then shoved it up over the side into the Zodiac.

"How was it?" she asked, after giving Richard a boost up onto the side of the boat.

"Even beyond what I imagined. An astounding variety of life. Can't wait to go down again. Healthy corals; lots of colorful micro-life along the wall…and I've never seen such healthy populations of pelagics. Very encouraging."

"Me neither. It's truly breathtaking." She swam over to where Nils just surfaced. "You doing okay, Nils? Thanks for staying with your buddy, by the way."

"It wasn't easy. He was up and down that wall like a yo-yo." Nils swam past her over to the Zodiac. Sanjeev helped him out of his gear and into the boat.

Addy pulled her mask over her eyes again and looked down. She counted the streams of bubbles rising. Seeing all the others were on their way up, she made a big kick with her fins and hopped up onto the side of the boat, gear and all, landing beside Richard and almost bouncing him off the Zodiac.

"Whoa!" he said with a laugh, "A mermaid!"

"Tail and all." Addy kicked her fins, undulating them like a dolphin.

"And here comes Poseidon!" he said, watching Ethan surface next to the boat.

Gage launched himself up on the side of the Zodiac and laughed. "I think our man Richard's been sipping a bit too much nitrogen."

"Just enjoying the moment, my dear lad. With so much of the ocean's largest fish already extinct, it warms my heart to see a place where they can still find refuge. Did you get lots of video?"

"Absolutely. Fab and I both did. I think we got some of the best footage to date."

"Great. I'd like you to erase it all. Especially any footage you took topside as we approached."

"Haha. Wait, you're serious?"

"I'm afraid so. It would be a crime if fishermen or even tourists discovered this magical place."

Gage stared wide-eyed at Ethan. "Tell me it ain't so, boss."

Ethan shrugged his shoulders. He glanced over at Addy, who nodded her agreement. "Damn. Okay then. Once we've reviewed it all and recorded the data we need, we'll erase it."

****

"It's a beautiful night," Raj said. He stood next to Sanjeev on the bridge. Sanjeev had offered to teach Raj some basics of piloting while they lay at anchor. "I've never seen so many stars. It's rare to see them at all in

Jakarta."

"It's nights like these I like to practice navigating by the stars," Sanjeev said. "That's when I feel the closest bond with the sea and a connection to the sailors of days past."

"I've never felt connected to anything. Except for Myra, maybe."

"Myra?"

"She was my friend when we were orphans living on the streets. We had nothing and were always on the run from the cops, thugs, or perverts. That's when I felt most alive and happy. She was a free spirit. Always smiling and making me laugh. She wasn't afraid of anything, so neither was I. She could steal the dark from the night." Raj's smile faded, and his eyes flashed with anger. "But she was taken from me by a monster."

"I'm sorry, Raj." Sanjeev looked down and shuffled his feet. Then he looked up at the sky and pointed. "You know those, right?"

Raj looked up. "The four bright ones?"

"Yes. The Southern Cross. The long axis always points south."

"I appreciate you taking the time to teach me these things, Sanjeev." Raj ran his hands over the spokes of the polished teak wheel. "I would like to learn to sail one day."

"You are learning. Just keep working at it. You'll get there. Tomorrow we can get out the charts. I'll show you how to read them if you'd like."

"Very much, thanks."

"Okay, good night then. I'm going to my bunk. It's been a long day." Sanjeev went out through the louvered door and down the ladder. He passed Fabiola, standing by the rail, near the bottom of the ladder.

She looked up at the stars and pretended not to notice Sanjeev. After waiting for Sanjeev to pass through the galley door, she climbed the ladder to the bridge. “I thought he’d never leave,” she said, one foot still on the ladder, the other on the doorway, her open sarong exposing her bare leg.

Raj spun around. “Fab!”

“Permission to come aboard, sir.”

“Of course.” Raj took her hand. “Sorry, I didn’t hear you come up the ladder.”

“Would you mind a little company?” she asked, coyly.

“I’d love your company.”

“You’re out of uniform, sailor,” she said, running her finger along his tattoo, from his chest down to his waist.

Raj reached for his shirt, hanging over the back of the chair, but Fabiola grabbed for it first and tossed it aside. She touched one of the small round scars on his chest and asked, “What are these from?”

“Cigarettes. Some people get their kicks hurting others.”

Fabiola shuddered. “I’m sorry. Who did it?”

“It doesn’t matter. He’s dead.”

Fabiola thought it better not to ask how the man died. “I heard what you told, Sanjeev. I didn’t mean to eavesdrop. I was waiting for him to leave and overheard you say you were an orphan. What happened? I mean, if you don’t mind me asking.”

“My mother died when I was five or six. I ran away from my father a couple of years later. He made me work on the streets and took any money I made.

One day I realized I didn't need him for anything, so I left."

"How'd you survive?"

"Running and stealing, mostly. I did what I had to."

Steering the conversation in a happier direction, she untied her sarong and let it drop to the floor, "Like my new swimsuit?" She asked, doing a quick twirl. "I was looking for the right opportunity to wear it, but there's a bit of a chill in the air tonight. Don't you think?"

Feels pretty warm to me, Raj thought. Then he got it. He slid his arms around the small of her back and pulled her close.

Fabiola laid her head against his chest. Then abruptly turned around, pushing her hips tight against his. "Have you learned to sail this ship?"

"Not yet. But Sanjeev and the captain are teaching me."

"Hmm. How'd you end up here, anyway? On this boat, I mean. It's obvious you're not a sailor." Fabiola's father owned a yacht and started teaching her to sail it when she was still a child. By the time she was a teenager, she was sailing up and down the Pacific coast from Baja to Vancouver Island.

"Why is it so obvious I'm not a sailor?"

She laughed. "First of all, Sanjeev has to show you how to do everything. Second, you don't look like any of the rest of them. You carry yourself differently. Confident. Aloof. Even though you're much younger, and the low man on the depth chart, Sanjeev and Talib give you a wide berth. It's obvious they're all scared of you. Except for the captain, maybe. What do you really do?"

"You don't want to know." Raj glanced out at the stars and the glint of the moon on the bay where they were anchored.

"Going to play the mystery man, huh? Okay then, sailor boy, teach me how to sail."

"Now you're making fun of me."

Fabiola turned and pressed her chest against his. "Is Sanjeev or the captain coming back up here anytime soon?"

"No. Sanjeev went to his bunk, and Malik is in his cabin." Her hair was still damp from the shower and smelled of honeysuckle.

Fabiola stood on her tiptoes, slid her arms around his neck, and kissed him on the lips. Wrapping his arms around the small of her back, Raj lifted her off the floor and returned her kiss. Fabiola wrapped her legs around his torso, pulled loose the string of her bikini top and let it drop. She pressed her bare breasts against his chest, ran her fingers through Raj's long hair, and gazed into his dark eyes.

Raj lowered Fabiola to the floor and lay on top of her. He pulled the string on the side of her bikini bottom and tossed it aside as their legs entwined.

Fab arched her back and let him push inside. "You going to get in trouble fraternizing with the passengers?" she whispered.

"Do you think I care?"

Chapter 11

Ethan's team made two more dives at the Kraken the following morning, descending to almost a hundred fifty feet, nearing their no-decompression limits, observing the larger fish that roamed the deep. They could only stay at that depth for less than a minute to keep from accumulating too much nitrogen and risk having to make decompression stops on the way up. Too complicated and dangerous to manage given their remote location.

After a lunch break back on *Varuna* followed by a two-hour surface interval to off-gas nitrogen built up in their bloodstreams, the crew boarded the Zodiacs for the bumpy ride back to the wall for the last dive of the day. Since they'd already made the two deeper dives in the morning, Addy instructed them to stay above a depth of eighty feet.

Halfway through the dive, the group was spread out across the wall. The first two dives of the day had gone without incident, and conditions remained excellent. Ethan was at a depth of about sixty feet exploring the underside of a rock shelf when Addy pinged her tank. He swam up to forty feet where Addy was floating next to Fabiola. Fabiola pointed to her right ear and shook her head. Addy pointed toward Fabiola and then toward the surface.

Ethan nodded he understood Fabiola was having a

problem clearing her ears and Addy was going to swim with her to the surface. He turned and swam down to where he'd left the others. He saw Gage but no sign of Richard or Nils. Ethan thought little of it, knowing Richard preferred to stay away from Gage's bright strobes. He swam over and tapped Gage on the shoulder. Taking out his regulator, he mouthed with a stream of bubbles. "You seen Richard?"

Gage shook his head.

Ethan took another breath from his regulator, then took it out again and pointed with it. "Going to "—he took another breath—"look for him."

Gage nodded, gave Ethan the okay sign, and went back to his work.

Figuring he'd find Nils and Richard poking around inside a crevice or under a ledge somewhere along the wall, Ethan swam back east. Nearing the edge and feeling the sharp tug of the current, he grabbed a rock ledge and walked himself hand over hand back safely out of the current. Visibility was excellent, so he was confident he hadn't passed them.

Where the hell are those guys?

Ethan checked his depth gauge and the air pressure in his tank. His depth was sixty feet. His tank still had 700 psi. *Enough to keep searching.* He sank another thirty feet. He'd traveled halfway back across the face of the wall when he spotted a stream of bubbles rising. His gaze followed them down to identify their source. Nils swam horizontally along the wall. He appeared oblivious of Ethan, so Ethan pinged his tank to get his attention. Nils glanced up, then quickly looked away and continued swimming.

Ethan's gaze drifted in the direction from which

Nils just swam. Someone was coming up fast. It was Richard, kicking furiously and flailing his arms in a full-on panic. Ethan swam hard to intercept him, kicking his powerful legs with all his strength, in an upward angle to cut Richard off. Ethan stretched out his arm but missed grabbing a fin by mere inches as Richard rocketed past, his buoyancy compensator vest fully inflated. The regulator dropped from his mouth, and Richard stop kicking. A few seconds later, Richard bobbed to the surface.

****

"You doin okay, Fab?" Addy asked after the two surfaced.

"Yeah, thanks. I couldn't clear my ears. It was too painful."

"Don't worry, it happens." Addy helped her out of her gear and up onto the side of the Zodiac.

Raj noticed Fabiola surface, so he waved off Sanjeev in the other Zodiac, steered the boat closer to her, and killed the engine.

Addy helped Fab out of her gear and up onto the side of the Zodiac. "If you're sure you're okay, I'll leave you here with Raj and go back down," Addy said.

"I'll be fine. Raj will take care of me," Fabiola said as Raj grabbed a warm towel out of the water-tight chest and draped it over her shoulders. "*Terima kasih,* Raj."

Addy pulled her mask back over her eyes, gave the okay sign, and sank below the surface. She glanced up through the translucent water. Raj sat next to Fabiola and put his arm around her. *What have we got developing here?* Addy swam down and spotted Gage but didn't see any sign of Ethan, Richard, or Nils. She swam deeper and traversed the wall westward when several rapid pings caught her attention. She looked down and spotted Ethan banging on his tank, pointing toward the surface.

Addy looked up. Richard floated on the surface, facedown, his eyes wide open in a blank stare, his regulator floating uselessly in the current. Addy immediately swam up, surfaced next to him and lifted his face out of the water. She spat out her regulator, waved her arms and shouted toward the Zodiac, "Over here! Over here!"

Sanjeev started the engine and raced toward them. Arriving, he killed the engine, then rushed to help lift Richard into the boat. Addy shed her gear and launched herself up onto the side.

"Get him out of his gear!" she ordered. "We need to lay him on his stomach over the side."

They unbuckled his scuba gear and then laid Richard facedown on the side of the Zodiac. Addy stood over him and pumped the back of his rib cage to expel the water from his lungs. Then they laid him in the hull of the boat and felt for a pulse. Not finding one, she started CPR. Three breaths and several chest compressions later, a flood of water erupted from Richard's mouth. Addy turned him on his side. Richard vomited, then took a heaving breath. He coughed and spit out more water, had another coughing fit, then took a deep rasping breath. A pinkish froth dribbled down his chin.

****

Ethan looked at the dive computer on his wrist. The gauge indicated his level of nitrogen saturation was too high to descend farther without exceeding his no-decompression limit. He looked at his tank's pressure gauge. It read fifty psi; almost empty. He'd used his remaining air in his desperate attempt to catch Richard. He pinged his tank to get Gage's attention and signaled him to head to the surface. Scanning the ocean below him, Ethan saw Nils swimming slowly upward. He appeared to be fine, so Ethan surfaced and quickly ducked out of his gear.

"Gage and Nils are on their way up," Ethan shouted, frantically. He grabbed the side of Raj's Zodiac. "Once they surface, pick them up, then radio the captain to tell him there's been an accident, and we're heading back to *Varuna*. Tell him to have oxygen ready for Richard when we arrive." Ethan turned and swam hard to the other Zodiac, leaped up on the side and swung his legs over.

Once Ethan was inside, Sanjeev headed for *Varuna* at full speed. Richard's head lay on Addy's lap, his chest heaving, a rasping, gurgling sound accompanying each breath. Ethan helped Addy sit him up, unzip, and loosen the top of his wetsuit.

"Richard, can you hear me?" Ethan said.

"Ran out of air," Richard said weakly, then erupted into another coughing fit. Addy grabbed a towel and wiped bloody spittle from his chin.

"Do you know what happened?" Addy looked at Ethan and asked.

Ethan shook his head. "He came up in a panic. I couldn't reach him in time to stop his rapid ascent."

Addy leaned to inspect Richard's tank and BC. The lead weights had been jettisoned, the CO2 cartridge expelled, and his BC fully inflated. She picked up the hose holding Richard's air pressure gauge, then showed it to Ethan. "There's still 1,000 psi. Plenty to have lasted several more minutes."

Ethan picked up Richard's regulator, put it in his mouth, and took a breath. The air flowed fine. Ethan handed her the regulator, and she tried a breath. Nothing came out.

"What the hell?" Addy checked the valve at the top of the tank. It closed in less than a quarter turn. "His tank valve was barely open!"

"How's that possible?" Ethan asked. "He'd been diving for more than half an hour without any problem."

"I don't know." She took another breath from the regulator, but this time while watching the pressure gauge. Once again, the air flowed fine, but the pressure gauge dropped to zero. Five seconds passed before the pressure was high enough to take another breath.

"He must have thought he was running out of air and panicked," she said.

"Have you ever seen that happen during a dive?" Ethan asked.

"At the beginning of a dive, yes. Halfway through? Never."

****

"We'll take him into the galley," Malik said, standing on platform on *Varuna's* stern. He grabbed the line Sanjeev tossed him and tied it to the rail. "Talib's set up a place for him there." He helped Ethan lift Richard out of the Zodiac and carry him up the ladder to the main deck. "What happened?" Malik asked while he slipped an oxygen mask over Richard's face. Richard had another coughing fit, splattering blood on the inside of it.

"We're not exactly sure, yet," Ethan said.

He and Malik carried Richard into the galley and laid him on a stack of blankets Talib had spread over one of the dining tables. Addy stripped off Richard's wetsuit, spread a blanket over him, and tucked a pillow under his head.

"Something happened to his air supply," Ethan said. "He dropped his weights and made a beeline for the surface. Addy resuscitated him in the Zodiac. We think he has an air embolism, so he likely held his breath on the way up. He might have the bends as well."

"I have little experience with this kind of accident," Malik said. "What can we do?"

"We need to stabilize him, take his vitals, and call the hospital on Bali," Addy said. "They have a hyperbaric chamber and a doctor who specializes in treating diving accidents." She took a blood pressure monitor from the first-aid box beside the makeshift bed and wrapped the cuff around Richard's arm.

"Is he alive?" Nils rushed in from the aft deck through the galley door, the other Zodiac carrying him, Fabiola, Gage, and Raj having just arrived. "Did he say anything?"

"Say anything? Like what, Nils?" Ethan said.

"Like what happened?"

"Not yet," Addy said. She wrote Richard's blood pressure on her palm with a pen.

Ethan put his hand on Richard's arm and leaned in closer to his face. "Richard, can you hear me?"

Richard's eyes fluttered open. His breathing was shallow and raspy; each exhale ending with a gurgle. He winced with pain. "Hurts. My back hurts."

Addy squeezed Richard's hand. "We are going to get you to a doctor." She turned to Malik. "Can we use your satellite phone?"

"Of course. It's up on the bridge. I'll go with you." Malik gestured for Addy to lead the way, and the two hurried out of the galley.

"Addy's calling a doctor, Richard," Ethan said. "What can we do to make you comfortable?

Richard said something too faint for Ethan to understand and then had another coughing fit and drifted off again.

"Can you look after him for a couple of minutes and make sure he doesn't take off his oxygen mask?" Ethan asked Fabiola. "I need to talk to Nils."

"Sure, go ahead." Fabiola adjusted the pillow under Richard's head and pulled the blanket up around his shoulders.

Ethan took Nils by the arm and led him out through the galley door onto the aft deck. "What happened down there?"

"I don't know. Why are you asking me?"

"You're his dive buddy. You two were supposed to stay together."

"We got separated."

"Where were you when you last saw him?"

"I don't know, somewhere along the wall."

"That doesn't tell me anything, Nils. How deep were you?"

"About eighty feet, I think."

"You had to be deeper than that, at least a hundred feet, or I would have seen you earlier. Why were you so down so far? Addy was clear about staying above eighty feet."

"Richard wanted to show me something. He motioned to me."

"What was it?"

"I don't know. I didn't follow him."

"Was he below you? To the right? Left?"

"I don't remember for sure. Why are you giving me the third degree?"

"How can you not remember whether he was below or above you?"

"Below. He was below me."

"Did you see him struggling to breathe?"

"No. Why? Did he run out of air?"

"His tank valve was almost closed. Do you have any idea how that could have happened?"

"How would I know? He's always bumping into things. Every time he comes up, he's got stuff sticking to him. Maybe he bumped it against the wall."

"It takes several turns to close a tank valve. That can't happen just bumping into a wall."

"I don't know. The ship's crew is responsible for filling the tanks between dives, have you asked them? That guy Raj doesn't look like he knows what he's doing. And where was Addy? She's supposed to be watching us."

"Fab had a problem with her ears, and Addy followed her to the surface. Did you check each other's equipment before the dive?"

"I have my own equipment to pay attention to. I don't like your tone, and I don't appreciate all these questions." He took a step to leave but Ethan cut him off.

"I'm just trying to figure out what happened," Ethan said, his face only inches from Nils'. "You were the nearest to him when it happened."

"Don't try to blame me for something that happened because of your carelessness. This isn't the first time someone working with you has been seriously injured or killed, is it?" Nils yanked his arm away from Ethan and went back inside the galley.

When Addy returned from up on the bridge, Ethan was waiting for them outside the galley door.

"I spoke to the doctor at the hospital in Bali," she said. "Based on the circumstances of the accident, he said Richard needs treatment in their compression chamber. He said to keep him on oxygen and get to Bali ASAP. He wants us to call in every two hours and report his condition."

"We're more than five hundred kilometers from Bali," Malik said. He'd lingered briefly on the bridge, trying to process the whirlwind turn of events, before following Addy down to the deck. "It'll take more than thirty hours to get to Bali. We'd have to refuel in Bima, which will add several more hours. There must be an airstrip closer to here."

Addy shook her head. "The lower pressure on an airplane would make his condition dangerously worse. You need to set a course for Bima right away."

Malik felt the floor drop out from underneath. "Hold on. Let's not set out in haste. What about a helicopter?"

"It's a possibility, but Bima is the nearest place where there might be one. In any event, we need to start heading in that direction."

"I'm sure we can find a doctor nearer than Bali. I'll look at my maps and get on the radio and see what I can find." He turned to walk away, but Addy caught his arm.

"He has to be transported to a chamber, Malik. Some local doctor won't help. Bali is the only place within hundreds of miles with a compression chamber. Every minute will be critical."

"I can't," Malik stumbled for words. "We can't…Your mission, the project…"

"I don't care about that right now, Captain," Ethan said. "I only care about saving Richard."

Fabiola stuck her head out of the galley door. "Ethan, Richard's asking for you."

"I'll be right there," Ethan said. He turned back to Malik. "We have to set sail for Bali immediately." He followed Fabiola inside the galley and over to the table where Richard was struggling to sit up.

"Can't feel my legs," Richard said, his voice weak and raspy. He lifted his mask and spat blood into the gauze Fabiola put in his hand. He clutched Ethan's arm. "Am I going to die?"

"Of course not! You're too ornery to die, old friend. We're taking you to a hospital. They have a compression chamber. We'll get you there, and you'll be fine."

"Oh God. I have the bends."

"We don't know that for sure. We're just not taking any chances. Try to relax. Keep this oxygen mask on." Ethan put the oxygen mask back over Richard's nose and mouth.

Richard pulled it off again. "Regulator stopped working. Nothing came out. Nils…" He attempted to sit upright but fell limply back against the pillows.

"Nils? Richard, was Nils with you when you ran out of air?"

Richard nodded. "He swam away. Tried to get his attention. I needed help." Richard coughed up more blood. "Don't let me die. I'm not ready to die." Richard slipped back into unconsciousness.

Ethan squeezed his hand. "I won't, old friend." Ethan stood and turned to Gage. "Can you stay beside him for a few minutes while I go out to talk with Addy and Sanjeev?"

"Of course." Gage grabbed a folding chair and pulled it up beside Richard.

Ethan motioned to Sanjeev to follow him out of the galley to the aft deck.

"Are we heading for Bali?" Ethan asked.

"I assume the captain's preparing to depart," Sanjeev replied, "but he hasn't told me anything yet. He called for Raj, and they went up on the bridge and closed the door."

Ethan nodded. "Follow me." He walked to the stern and climbed down the ladder and into the Zodiac. Addy and Sanjeev followed. Ethan sat on the side of the inflatable and lifted the BC and tank onto his lap. "Sanjeev, tell us your exact process for filling the scuba tanks and loading them into the Zodiacs."

"Yes, sir. We check every tank before each dive." Sanjeev sat across from Ethan and Addy. "I've crewed on dive boats many times before and have filled hundreds of scuba tanks. I know lives depend on doing things right. After filling the tanks, I connect the regulator to the tank and crank the valve open to make sure everything's working properly. Then I close the valve until it's time for the next dive. When we load the equipment into the Zodiacs, I crank the valve on each tank open all the way again and then back it off a quarter turn. Just the way I was taught. I recheck the pressure gauge to make sure there's at least 2,000 psi. Finally, I do a quick inspection to look and listen for leaks."

"What about Raj? Could he have opened Richard's tank valve less than all the way?" Ethan asked.

"No, sir. I check each one myself."

"Thanks, Sanjeev," Ethan said, staring down at the equipment in his lap.

"I'm sorry for your friend. It's a terrible thing to happen to anybody." Sanjeev got up and climbed back aboard *Varuna*.

"Any ideas?" Ethan asked Addy.

She leaned over and inspected the tank and BC again. "I suppose it's possible Richard checked the valve before the dive, while he was still in the Zodiac. Maybe he somehow thought it was closed and turned it the wrong way."

"Ever seen that happen?"

"At the beginning of a dive, yes. If it was only open a half turn or so at the start of his dive, I suppose it's possible he could've bumped into something during the dive that moved it another quarter turn."

"Or someone."

"Someone? You mean bumped into someone?"

"What if someone closed it during the dive?" Ethan said.

"You mean closed it on purpose?"

"Just before I spotted Richard swimming in a panic toward the surface, I saw Nils swimming away from where Richard must have been moments before. There was something strange about the way he looked at me."

"Strange how?"

Ethan shook his head. "I can't say for sure."

"Come on. Nils already said he got separated from Richard. He should have stayed closer to him, for sure, but Richard *was* often oblivious to where everyone else was. It's my fault. I lost track of them when I took Fab to the surface."

Ethan put his hand on hers and gently squeezed it. "It wasn't your fault. Fab needed your help. You did what you were supposed to do. It happened when you and I were distracted."

"I still feel responsible."

"You're not. When I asked Nils about what happened, he was vague and defensive. The water visibility was excellent. How could he claim to not to know where Richard was?"

"What are you saying? That Nils did it on purpose?"

"After we carried Richard into the galley, the first thing Nils asked was, did Richard say anything, and was he alive."

"So? By then he knew Richard was gravely injured."

"You don't think it's strange? Wouldn't a normal person ask how he is?"

"I agree it's strange, but you and I both know Nils is a strange guy. That doesn't mean he'd try to kill his partner. What possible reason would he have?"

"I don't know, but I'm telling you, it doesn't add up."

"I understand you're upset about Richard. We all are, but it's too early to jump to that kind of a conclusion."

****

"How's he doing?" Fabiola asked Gage. She pulled up a chair.

"He's still coughing up blood. He goes in and out of consciousness. I don't know what to do for him."

A gurgling sound accompanied each of Richard's breaths. It at least reassured them Richard was still breathing. Addy had given him acetaminophen for the growing pain in his back, and it helped to calm him a little.

"I don't think there's anything we can do, other than keep him on oxygen, and get to a chamber ASAP," Fabiola said.

"It's not fair. Richard's a great guy. He doesn't deserve this. I don't understand how this could have happened."

"Me neither. Ethan and Addy are trying to figure it out."

"What they're doing is trying to blame me," Nils said. He was sitting at a table across from them in the galley. "It was Addy's responsibility. That's why she was hired. Your boss should never have let Richard dive here. It's too dangerous. He's the one who should be held accountable for this, and I intend to see that he is."

"Why don't you shut the fuck up?" Gage said. "No one's trying to blame you. Show a little empathy, for God's sake. Richard's your friend and partner."

"Yeah, what's up with that?" Fabiola said. "Richard's struggling for his life. Why aren't you over here with him, instead of skulking in the corner?"

"I don't have to explain anything to you people." Nils stood and walked out of the galley.

He headed straight to the berth he shared with

Richard. He grabbed Richard's laptop, opened it, and typed in the password Richard unwittingly provided him weeks earlier. He copied all the files containing details of Richard's algorithmic formulas, observations on populations and ratios, critical ocean zones, and migration patterns, to a thumb drive. Once he'd transferred everything he wanted, Nils disconnected the thumb drive and slipped it in his pocket. He grabbed Richard's briefcase and rifled through his handwritten notes, taking the ones he considered might be of import and stuffed them in his own briefcase.

Satisfied he had everything he was looking for he closed the lid of the laptop and set it back on the bedside table. He shoved the briefcases back under their respective bunks and laid back, crossed his legs, and interlocked his fingers behind his head. He gazed up at the ceiling and smiled.

Chapter 12

Malik stood on the bridge and leaned back against his captain's chair. He lit a cigarette and gazed out the window as the last vestige of the afternoon sun disappeared below the horizon. "I was almost home free. Only a few more hours, and it would have been done."

"What are you talking about?" Raj said. "We have to make that delivery tonight!"

"Bali's the opposite direction from our rendezvous point."

"It's only a few more hours, Malik. We can head to Bali in the morning. *After* we've returned from making the delivery."

"Did you see that man? If we delay, he could die."

"Nothing's more important right now than this delivery," Raj insisted.

"I won't have his death on my conscience."

"Your conscious won't matter for shit if you're dead. We've got five million dollars of Anand's heroin onboard. You fail to deliver it, and he'll kill you."

"We'll have to tell Anand what happened. He'll need to make other arrangements." Malik took a sea chart from under the transom and spread it on the counter.

Raj yanked the chart away and tossed it to the deck. "Are you insane? He'll order me to take over your boat and do it myself. Come on, Malik. Get your priorities straight. We have to stay long enough to make the delivery."

"For the first time in a long while, I have my priorities straight. Believe me. I wanted nothing more than to make this delivery and be done with Anand and this wretched life I fell into. But we're weighing anchor and heading for Bali."

"There's no fucking way I'm allowing you to do that."

"What are you going to do? Hijack my boat and hold all the passengers and crew at gunpoint?" Malik leaned out the open window and shouted down, "Sanjeev, raise the bow anchor and prepare for departure. We're heading for Bali."

"Yes, sir. Right away." Sanjeev saluted and headed toward the bow.

"Shit." Raj ran his fingers through his hair and paced back and forth in the tiny bridge cabin. "I can't let you do this."

Malik ignored him and pressed the button to start the engine. He checked all the gauges while Sanjeev cranked up the anchor. He looked over his shoulder at Raj. "I'll tell Anand it was my decision. I'll take all the responsibility."

Sanjeev waved from the bow, giving the captain the signal the anchor had been raised and stowed. Malik slipped the gearshift into forward. Easing the throttle to one-third power, he nosed her out of the bay and turned west. He picked up the chart from off the deck and spread it out again.

Raj shook his head. "It won't make any difference to Anand that you took responsibility. Failure is failure."

"Listen, son," Malik said, turning to face Raj, "You're young, and I know you had a difficult life. Anand preyed on that and twisted your mind. But a good man lies injured down there. A man who cares about this world and is doing great things for it. I can't…No. I won't make up some bullshit story to delay our departure. I can't sit in that Zodiac carrying drugs out to a bunch of fucking criminals when every minute counts. We're not letting that man die."

"Then get away from the wheel."

Malik turned back around and put his hands on the wheel.

"I don't want to have to hurt you, Malik."

"Then don't."

Raj paced, looking down at the deck, his mind racing. The hum of *Varuna*'s diesel grew louder and louder until it was like a freight train running through his head.

"I'm sorry." Raj shoved Malik away from the helm and sent him sprawling against the far wall of the bridge.

Malik struggled to his feet and rushed at the young man. "Get away from the controls of my boat."

Raj anticipated Malik's charge and used Malik's momentum to hurl him against the opposite wall again. Malik fell against the wooden crate he kept for his son's step stool, shattering it to pieces.

Malik leaped to his feet and rushed Raj again, tackling Raj before he could sidestep the move and they crashed to the deck. Raj immediately rolled Malik off him and pinned him down. He grabbed Malik's right arm, swung a leg across his neck then hooked it with his other leg and squeezed. Malik struggled in vain to get loose, but Raj had Malik's neck and arm clamped between his legs like a vise.

Raj momentarily loosened his grip enough to turn Malik's head slightly to make sure he didn't crush his windpipe and then squeezed again, choking off the air and blood flow to his brain. Seconds later, Malik went limp.

Raj released the pressure and rolled Malik on his back. He put his head to Malik's chest to make sure he was breathing, then got up and went to the helm. He turned the wheel around slowly, so the other crew and passengers wouldn't notice the boat coming about. He held the turn until the compass on the console read due east, toward Gili Motang.

****

Malik woke and dragged himself to the wall. He rubbed his neck and blinked several times to clear his head. Raj stood at the helm. Malik knew *Varuna* inside and out. He felt every creak like they were in his bones. Even in the dark, he could tell whether she was running with or against the wind or current. If *Varuna* were sailing westward, toward Bali, she would have been cutting into the waves, her engine chugging against the swell. Instead, she was quartering with it, her motor humming at full speed.

"How long have I been out?"

"A while."

"Think this through, Raj," Malik said, still rubbing his sore neck. "What are you going to do when Sanjeev and the passengers realize we've turned around? Are you going to fight them all?"

"If I have to."

"Even if I gave you the coordinates of the rendezvous point, which I won't, you don't know how to navigate to get there."

"I heard you say twenty kilometers due south of Gili Motang. I'll find it."

"You know you can't. You don't know the currents. You don't know how to track twenty kilometers. You'll just get lost."

Malik was right; Raj just hadn't been ready to accept it. His shoulders slumped. "We can't take the heroin back to port, Malik."

"Maybe there's another option," Malik said, an idea taking shape. One that might still save him, and his plan for escape. "If you'll let us turn around and head west again, I'll steer us near the southern coast of Komodo. We could load the merchandise in one of the Zodiacs, and you can take it there. It's sparsely populated, and you'll be able to stay of out sight until I come back."

"Anand won't go for it."

"I'll wait to call him until after you're ashore. I'll explain it was the only way to protect his merchandise."

"He'll still kill you."

"Not before he gets his merchandise. Not before I've gotten that man to the hospital."

Sanjeev burst through the door and shouted, "Rocks off the starboard bow!"

The islands of the Nusa Tenggara sit like a dam separating the waters of the Pacific Ocean from those of the Indian. The levels between the two oceans can vary by as much as six inches, creating some of the strongest and most unpredictable tidal currents on Earth. Trillion of gallons surge through the straits as the tides change.

That night, the western currents were still receding while those of the eastern side flowed stronger, creating a powerful eddy several miles wide.

If Malik been at the helm, he would have noticed the currents had changed. But he wasn't. Raj only knew to keep the compass needle heading due east toward the agreed rendezvous point. It was pitch dark, and he was too inexperienced to realize the eddy was sweeping *Varuna* southward.

A long, thin stretch of land once jutted from the southern shore of one of the Lesser Sunda Islands, but constant battering by the sea over eons had broken and eroded the land, marooning the outermost section. The soil washed away, nothing remained but a long finger of stalwart rocks, visible only during the troughs of the ocean swells at low tide. Malik knew to steer clear of such hazards, to stay out in the channel where the waters were deep. But the eddy had doubled *Varuna*'s speed and swept her far off course.

Malik sprang to his feet and spun *Varuna*'s wheel hard to starboard. Too late. A violent jolt rocked *Varuna* as it slammed into the rock ledge. A sickening screech followed as *Varuna* lurched up on the rock and her bow rose high out of the water. The impact sent Malik and Raj tumbling against the bulkhead, and catapulted Sanjeev off the ladder and onto the main deck.

Varuna's hardwood siding held at first, but the force of her weight against the sharp rocks was too strong, and her hull buckled with a deafening crack.

The jagged rock punctured her port beam and *Varuna*'s bow crashed down, tipping her bowsprit into the water. The force of the rushing water held her there, pinned against the rocks, quivering in the raging current.

Chapter 13

"What the hell just happened?" Ethan picked himself up from the floor of the galley. "Are you okay?"

"I'm fine," Addy replied, rubbing the knot forming on her head from being slammed against the galley wall. "We've hit something. Feels like we've run aground."

Ethan hurried across the shuddering deck to Richard, who'd been thrown from his makeshift bed atop a dining table and lay crumpled against the wall.

Piercing screams echoed up from below decks. "I'll take care of Richard," Addy shouted as Ethan helped her carry him back to the table. "Go check on the others!"

Ethan rushed out of the galley and slid down the ladder leading to the cabins. He landed with a splash in knee-deep water.

Fabiola was in the narrow corridor between cabins, in front of Gage's door. "Ethan! The door won't open! I think Gage is hurt."

Ethan tried the door, but couldn't budge it. "Stand back!" he shouted. He propped himself against the opposite wall and kicked in the thin wooden door.

Gage lay on the floor, water up almost to his chest, stunned and barely conscious. Blood trickled down the side of his face from a gash on his forehead. Water spewed through the hull around the head of a coral encrusted boulder.

"We gotta get you outta here." Ethan grabbed Gage's arm to lift him. "No! My arm," Gage screamed, "I think my arm's broken."

Ethan slipped his hands under both armpits and dragged Gage of his cabin into the hallway. *Varuna* wobbled and shook, pinned against the rocks by the raging onslaught of the current.

"What happened?" Nils staggered out of his cabin, wearing a T-shirt and boxer shorts.

"We need to get out of here fast!" Ethan said. The boat listed further, the water now waist deep. "Let's move!" He dragged Gage to the ladder, then lifted him, draping him over one shoulder. With Fabiola pushing him from behind, Ethan carried Gage up the ladder. Addy met them at the top of the ladder and helped lift Gage onto the deck.

"There's a gaping hole in *Varuna*'s side, and we're taking on water," Ethan said. "Where's Richard?"

"With Talib. Sanjeev went to find Malik and Raj."

Suddenly, the deck jerked violently as more of *Varuna*'s hull caved in, knocking everyone off their feet.

Malik slid down the ladder from the bridge. He grabbed Addy's arm and helped her up. "We're wedged against the rocks and taking on water fast. We'll have to abandon ship." The words caught in his throat. Just uttering the words stabbed him like a knife. He took a breath to steel himself against his anguish. "Is everyone accounted for?"

"I haven't seen Raj," Addy said.

"Over here!" Raj called from beyond the stern.

He'd already climbed inside one of the Zodiacs and lowered the transom of the outboard into the water. Sanjeev ran over, grabbed the line to the other Zodiac, pulled it tight against *Varuna*'s stern rail and secured it.

Raj climbed out of the Zodiac and sprang up over the stern rail, onto the deck. "I'm going for the trunks," he shouted to Malik.

"What trunks?" Ethan grabbed Raj's arm. "You can't go down there; the hold's flooded!"

"Supplies. He's going for survival supplies," Malik answered.

Raj yanked his arm free and ran to the hatch leading down to the rear hold, opened it, and jumped down.

Malik called out to Sanjeev, "Keep the Zodiac tight against the stern while we load the passengers," Malik ordered. "Addy, get in the other and do the same."

"I'll get Richard," Ethan said. He laid Gage against the bulkhead and then ran toward the galley.

"The life jackets are in that cupboard," Malik shouted to Nils, pointing to the built-ins on the galley wall. "Grab them and hand them out. Make sure you get one to every person."

Nils grabbed a life vest from the cupboard, put it on, and secured the strap. He grabbed several more, ran to the stern rail, tossed them toward the Zodiac, and started climbing over the rail. Three of the vests landed in the Zodiac, two others missed completely, landing in the water.

Malik caught Nils before he could climb inside the Zodiac, grabbing the neck of the vest and pulling him back. "Go back and get the rest of the life vests and hand them out like I told you the first time." He shoved

Nils toward the galley.

Ethan and Talib came out of the galley carrying Richard. They brought him to the stern, lifted him over the rail, and down onto the platform. Addy helped Ethan lay him in the hull of her Zodiac as a wave sloshed across *Varuna*'s deck.

"*Varuna*'s going down," Malik shouted. "We have to hurry." He ran back to assist Sanjeev with Gage. He ducked under Gage's uninjured arm and helped walk him to the stern. They lifted Gage over the stern rail and across to Ethan in the Zodiac, now floating almost level to *Varuna*'s listing deck.

Nils returned with the last of the life vests. He tossed half in one Zodiac and the rest in the other, then climbed over the rail and jumped in the nearest one.

"Fab, put this on," Sanjeev said, grabbing one of the vests Nils tossed in. He helped her put it on, then picked up another and put it on.

"Talib, get in Sanjeev's boat," Malik shouted.

Talib put on a life vest, then stepped off the platform toward the Zodiac. Just then, a large swell pushed the Zodiac away, and Talib fell against the side, bouncing him off the rubber tubing, catapulting him into the water. Flailing wildly, Talib grabbed for the Zodiac, but the current quickly carried him out of reach.

Malik hurried across the listing deck and grabbed a life ring and tossed it toward Talib. It splashed in the water only a couple of feet from Talib, but in his panic, he didn't see it. Malik coiled it in to toss it again, but by the time he reared back to throw it again, Talib had disappeared into the night.

"We'll have to find him from the Zodiacs," Malik shouted as a wave sloshed over his feet.

Raj reappeared, dragging two large black trunks, soaking wet and breathless. "I could only get these two," he said. "The engine room is completely flooded."

Malik helped Raj tumble the two heavy trunks into a Zodiac. "Get in," Malik shouted. Raj jumped in and sat on one of the trunks. The last aboard *Varuna*, Malik stood on the aft deck, now listing at thirty degrees, gripping tight to her rail with both hands. He turned, in quiet despair, and stared at his doomed ship.

"Captain!" Sanjeev shouted. "You have to abandon ship."

Malik stood, unmoving, holding tightly to the rail. He thought about the endless hours he'd spent refurbishing her. Happy, contented hours. He thought about his family, and the fact he might never see them again. *Varuna*'s *all I have left. If I go down with her, I'll finally have peace.* Turning toward the bridge, something touched his arm.

"I know you can't bear to lose her, but we need you, Captain," Addy said. She'd climbed back aboard *Varuna* and held the rail with one arm; the other rested gently on his forearm. He met her gaze, managed a weary smile, and nodded. Addy jumped in the Zodiac on the right, and Malik untied the line to the other and jumped inside as water washed over *Varuna*'s deck.

Both Zodiacs motored away from *Varuna* as she listed further on her side. Her crew and passengers shivered in the cold night air, watching helplessly, as she succumbed to the sea. The swirling waters carried the two Zodiacs farther and farther away, until the tip of *Varuna's* main mast, still stalwart and unyielding to the raging current, faded in the darkness.

“We have to find Talib,” Malik shouted across to Sanjeev, in the other Zodiac. “We’ll make slow circles until we find him. Stay within sight.”

Malik twisted the throttle and headed down current to search for Talib. He stopped every few minutes, killed the engine, and shouted into the darkness. No response came. After an hour, Malik gestured to Sanjeev to steer his boat closer. “We have to give up,” Malik said. “If we use all our gasoline before we find a safe place to go ashore, we risk being swept past the islands. He has a life vest on. I hope God will save him; I’m afraid we can’t.” He yanked the cord, restarting the Zodiac’s outboard.

The two Zodiacs motored toward the coastline of an island Malik could see in the distance, visible in the dark by the white line of surf rolling onto its shore. Approaching closer, the ominous sound of rollers smashing against the rocks grew louder until they reverberated with, loud thunderous claps. The two Zodiacs motored along slowly, Malik’s in the lead, while the passengers scoured the darkness for a break in the surf where they might safely go ashore. Besides the white foam of the crashing waves, all they could make out were tall, foreboding cliffs and jagged rocks exposed by the retreating swells.

The temperature dropped, and what little clothing the passengers had on was soaked. They huddled inside the boats to protect themselves from the wind.

“Do you have any idea what island that is?” Ethan shouted over to Malik.

“One of the Lesser Sunda Islands, but I can’t tell which one. I’m not sure how long we were off course.”

“Off course?” Ethan shouted back. “Why were we

off course?"

Malik didn't answer.

"It doesn't look like there's any safe place to go ashore," Sanjeev shouted to Malik. "Maybe we should get out of here and try to find another island."

"We don't know which way to head," Malik responded. "We can't afford to be at the mercy of these currents in the dark. We need to conserve our fuel. We'll continue searching. There's bound to be a break in these bluffs where we can land."

"That looks like a cape," Addy said, pointing ahead. "Maybe there's a break on the other side."

Rounding the cape, a narrow white strip of beach appeared in view. It lay at the bottom of a steep ravine cleft in the steep bluffs. On the near side, the surf crashed over jumbled rocks broken off from the cliffs. On the far side, it thundered against the bare cliff face. In between lay a rocky beach, barely fifty yards wide.

"It's too narrow. This surf looks treacherous, Captain. Maybe we should wait till daylight," Sanjeev shouted.

"I'm concerned about Richard and Gage," Ethan said. "The sooner we get them ashore and find shelter, the better."

"I agree," Addy said. "Don't you think we can time the waves and run the Zodiacs right up on the beach ahead of the breakers? This is the only place we've seen that looks remotely possible to land."

"Maybe," Malik answered. He stood up, surveyed the crashing waves, then nodded. He idled his Zodiac and motioned for Sanjeev come alongside. "I'll go in first," Malik called out. "Hang back and watch where I go. Wait for the next big breaker to pass and follow it in. Stay out in front of the next one. These waves break close to shore, so gun your boat right up onto the beach."

Malik stood to make sure everyone in both boats could hear. "Everyone get down in the bottom of your boat and hold on."

Surfers from all over the world flock to Indonesia in search of the perfect wave off some remote island previously undiscovered by the surfing world. A swell that breaks close to shore, a sharply rising bottom, forcing the water up, creating the ideal tube. This spot had those characteristics. But the sweet spot here was too narrow for even the most experienced surfer. With the narrow strip of beach protected by sheer cliffs and jagged boulders on either side, any rider attempting it would almost certainly end up dashed against the rocks.

Malik counted the seconds between each swell passing under his boat. He waited until a large swell was directly underneath, then gunned the outboard, staying just behind it. Suddenly, the top of a reef appeared directly ahead, exposed by the trough of the large wave in front. Malik swerved hard left, barely skirting its outer edge, then jammed the steering lever sharply back right to maintain forward motion and avoid being swamped by the wave rushing in behind them. He continued at full throttle and rode the wash of the spent wave onto the sand. Malik leaped out of the boat and waved and shouted to Sanjeev to go farther left.

Sanjeev idled his Zodiac just beyond the surf break and watched the swells pass under his boat. Seeing the largest wave in a set sweep by underneath, he twisted the throttle wide open and followed it in. His attention focused on the surf; Sanjeev didn't see Malik onshore frantically waving to go farther left and saw the reef too late. He swerved hard left, and the hull of the Zodiac barely skirted it, but the transom of the outboard struck the rocks, shearing off the propeller. Without power and broadside to the next incoming wave, the wave broke over them. Caught in the roiling swell, the boat flipped over, spilling everyone into the foamy wash, sending them careening and tumbling across the jagged reef.

Ethan grabbed Richard's life vest as they capsized, then tucked his head and rolled into a ball. His back scraped across a rock, and he lost his grip on Richard. Tumbling across the sandy bottom, Ethan finally got his feet under him, and shoved off with both feet, launching himself to the surface. He took a breath just before another wave crashed down and spun him again. He surfaced again and caught a glimpse of an orange life vest and swam for it. It was Addy. He swam hard and grabbed her life vest. "Are you okay?"

"Yes. I'm fine," Addy said. She spat out a mouthful of water. "But I can't find Gage or Richard."

Ethan spotted a flash of orange beyond her. "I see someone else!"

They both swam toward it and found Gage, coughing and spitting out water. "My arm!" he moaned. "I think it got torn off."

"I've got you, buddy. Your arm's not gone." The white of Gage's exposed arm bone gleamed in the moonlight. "Let's get you out of this water." He held Gage tight against his body as another wave washed over them, then spat out a mouthful of water. "Can you take him to shore while I look for Richard and Sanjeev?" he asked Addy.

"Yes. I'll come back and help once I get Gage to shore." She grabbed the nape of Gage's vest and braced for the next wave.

Ethan ducked under the wash, surfaced and continued swimming, pausing only to bob up to shout and search for any sign of the others still missing. A few seconds later, he spotted someone and swam toward them. "Are you hurt?" he asked Sanjeev.

"No, but I can't—" They both ducked under the wash of another wave and then surfaced again. "—I can't find anyone else."

"Addy's taking Gage ashore," Ethan said. "But Richard's still missing."

"Let's spread out," Sanjeev said. "He had on a life vest, so we should be able to find him."

Ethan swam farther out into the surf and dove under a breaking wave, but it hurled him tumbling back. He struggled to the surface, but each time he tried to swim out farther, he was again thrown back, roiled in the turbulent wash like a rag doll. He surfaced gasping for breath and spitting seawater. Someone grabbed his vest.

"Ethan! We can't see a thing out here," Addy shouted over the deafening crash of the surf. She'd returned to the water after leaving Gage on shore with the others. "We'll have a better chance of spotting him from shore."

"I have to find Richard," Ethan shouted, his voice cracking.

"We will," she tugged on his vest, to pull him toward shore. "Come on. You'll get—" She ducked as another wave hit them, sending them rolling. Popping to the surface, she grabbed Ethan's vest again. "We have to get out of this surf."

"What about Sanjeev?" Ethan said. "Is he still out here looking for Richard."

"No," Addy responded. "I found him and told him to swim ashore."

Ethan followed her to shore, and they collapsed on the beach.

Malik ran over. "We've been searching all up and down the beach. We haven't seen any sign of Richard."

Ethan got up and looked out into the water. He couldn't see anything other than the white crests of the surf. To his right, Malik's Zodiac had been dragged high up the beach. Fabiola leaned against it, and Gage huddled next to her, shivering. The other Zodiac bobbed upside down in the spent wash of the surf.

"Richard was barely conscious and couldn't move his legs," Ethan said, shaking his head. "How could he survive this?"

"He was wearing a life vest. There's still hope," Malik answered. "We'll keep searching."

"Ethan," Fabiola called out to wave him over.

Ethan went over and knelt next to her and Gage. The makeshift bandage and sling they put on Gage in the Zodiac had been torn off, and the skin of his arm and shoulder shredded when he was thrown from the Zodiac and raked over the reef. The jagged bone poked through the flesh just below his shoulder.

"Can you see if there are bandages in those trunks Raj carried out of the hold?" Fabiola asked. "We need to do something about his arm, Ethan."

Ethan looked over at the Zodiac and then back out toward the water, momentarily unsure which emergency most needed his attention.

"Go ahead," Addy said. "We'll keep searching for Richard."

Ethan climbed inside the Zodiac and flipped over one of the trunks. "What the hell? They're locked," he said. A padlock held the zipper of each trunk. He stood up and shouted to Malik, still roaming up and down the shoreline searching for Richard, "Malik, these trunks are padlocked. We need the key."

Malik looked over at Raj and then back toward Ethan. "I'm sorry, but the keys were lost," Malik answered.

"Why would survival supplies be padlocked?" Ethan looked around inside the boat for something he could use to break the locks but found nothing.

"Ethan, Raj made a mistake," Malik told him. "He brought up the wrong trunks from the hold. There are no first-aid supplies in these trunks. I'll dress Gage's wounds. You can keep searching for Richard."

"I don't understand. If they're not supplies," Ethan answered, "then what's in them?"

Malik was already kneeling beside Gage, intent on examining his injuries, and didn't answer, so Ethan climbed out of the boat and waded back out into the surf to continue the search for Richard.

Malik carefully tore open the sleeve of Gage's cotton shirt. A piece of Gage's humerus poked through the torn flesh, just below his shoulder, and much of his skin was raked away down to his elbow. Gage also had a deep gash across his forehead above his left eye. Malik took off his shirt, then pulled out a pocketknife. He cut the sleeves off the shirt, then cut each sleeve into strips, laying each one across Gage's lap. He wrapped one of the strips around Gage's head to cover the gash on his forehead.

Studying Gage's shattered arm, Malik shook his head. "I'm going to try to set the bone." He glanced at Fabiola. "You'll have to help me hold him." Malik set both his feet against Gage's side, then picked up Gage's wrist and held it both hands. He looked at Fabiola, who had wrapped both arms around Gage's chest. "Ready?" he asked.

She nodded.

"I'm sorry, son, but this is going to hurt." Malik pulled hard, leaning back with all his strength.

The bone made a sickening, grinding sound as it was pulled back inside the gaping wound. Gage screamed and passed out. Malik tucked the arm into a sling he'd made with one of the strips of cloth, then used the remaining ones to hold the arm tight against Gage's chest to cover and immobilize the wound. "That will have to do for now," he said. He walked to the water's edge and washed the blood from his hands.

Shaking the water from his hands, he turned to survey the small beach. The dark outline of trees lined the back of the beach, about thirty meters from the shore. Beyond the tree line, a forested ravine climbed steeply from the shore. He considered traversing it to get their bearings but decided it would have to wait till daylight. He looked at his watch. Sunrise was still three hours away. Malik looked up at the sky, ablaze with stars, and cursed under his breath. *If I'd dared to stand up to Anand, Gage wouldn't have been injured. Talib and Richard would still be alive; and I wouldn't have lost Varuna. I didn't even have the courage to go down with my ship.*

Chapter 14

Ethan and Addy paced back and forth along the narrow strip of beach, scanning the water. The bluffs flanking both sides of the beach blocked the view of everything but the sea directly in front of the beach. Large boulders lined the base of the cliffs on the east end of the narrow strip of sand. Addy climbed one to get a better view. "Richard must have come out of his life vest. Otherwise, he would have floated to shore by now," she shouted down to Ethan from the rock.

"Then where's the life jacket?"

"I don't know. It's been almost an hour. I don't think he could've survived this long given his condition, Ethan. We're going to have to wait for daylight."

"I can't give up. I just can't," Ethan wrung his hands and paced back and forth along the beach.

"I know," she said. She stood atop the boulder and surveyed the area around them. "It looks like there's a cave over there. I'll go have a look." She climbed down and scrambled over several boulders to the opening. A small stream trickled out of it and down to the water's edge. "It's a crack in the cliff face," she shouted back to Ethan, her voice echoing against the rocks. "Maybe he was washed inside."

Addy walked into the dark opening, sliding one hand along the damp wall, carefully picking her way around large stones and driftwood. She saw light at the far end, so she continued several more feet to where it opened again to the sky, but surrounded on all sides by steep cliff face. The floor was littered with flotsam and driftwood, washed inside and trapped by the tide and surf. The sound of water trickling drew her attention. She continued toward the back, stepping over more driftwood logs and debris until she reached the cliff face. She held her hand under a tiny spring cascading down the cliff face and tasted it. *Good*, she thought. *At least we have fresh water*.

She made her way back out through the opening, found Ethan, and took his hand. "I think we should bring everyone over here," she said. "Everyone's exhausted, soaked, and cold. There's fresh water and we should get Gage out of the wind."

Ethan stood motionless, staring out at the surf.

Addy slid her arm around his waist. "You've done all you can. We need to take care of Gage and the others now."

"I had him, Addy," Ethan said. "I grabbed hold of Richard's vest when the wave hit us, but I lost my grip when we flipped over."

"We're all lucky to be alive. Come on. Let's get back to the others."

****

"I bandaged Gage's wounds and stabilized his arm as best I could," Malik said, once Ethan and Addy walked to where the others sat huddled against the Zodiac. "It's a compound fracture, Ethan, and he's got a concussion. I'm concerned he'll go into shock."

"Addy found an area out of the wind on the other side of the beach," Ethan said. "We'll carry him over there." He looked at the Zodiac. "I don't understand, Malik. Raj risked his life swimming into the flooded hold to recover those trunks, but now you're saying there's nothing of use in them?"

"Unfortunately, no."

"So what's in them, then?"

"It doesn't matter. There's nothing in them we can use."

Ethan shook his head and bent to pick up Gage. "That makes no sense."

Malik avoided eye contact with Ethan and instead leaned over to help him carry Gage across the beach to the cave. "Grab all the life jackets you can find," Malik said, turning toward Sanjeev. "We can use them to lay Gage on."

Addy led the group to the far side of the beach and pointed to the jumble of boulders. "We have to scramble over these and through that cleft in the rocks. There's an area on the other side protected from the wind." They followed her through the crack in the cliff face to where it opened up on the other side. The light from the moon and stars lit the small area just enough for them to see the jumble of driftwood against the back wall. "Take him over there," Addy said. "We can lean him against those logs."

Sanjeev put two of the life vests on the sand and propped one against a log. Ethan and Malik laid Gage on them.

Nils took his vest off, tossed it on the ground, and sat on it. "Is someone going to explain why we crashed?"

"It's my fault," Raj said. "I was at the helm. I never saw the rocks."

"Why was he at the helm?" Ethan demanded. "Does Raj even know how to pilot a boat?"

"I was distracted," Malik answered. "I don't know what to say. I'm sorry."

"You're sorry? We lost two lives."

"I don't need to be reminded of that."

"Do you have any idea where we are? What island this is?" Addy asked.

"It must be one the Lesser Sunda Islands, I'm just not certain which," Malik answered. "There are several small islands in this area. The currents must have swept us off course. I should be able to recognize the area once it's daylight."

"She led us to believe she'd hired an experienced captain," Nils said, angrily pointing at Addy. "He crashed us on the rocks and doesn't even know where we are," he added. "What if we're stuck here? That surf is huge. Can we even get back out through it?"

"Let's not do this now," Addy said. "We're all tired and cold, and we've been through a lot tonight. Let's get some rest. We'll be able to better assess our situation come morning."

"Yes," Sanjeev said. "Once it's daylight, things will be better."

Chapter 15

Ethan woke with a start. "What was that?"

Light bathed the tops of the cliffs surrounding them, but the rocky enclosure where the ex-passengers of *Varuna* spent the night was still in shadow.

"What was what?" Addy sat up and brushed away the sand caked on her arm and shoulder. She'd been lying next to Ethan, her head resting on his shoulder.

"I thought I heard something." Ethan got up and walked past the rest of the group, still sleeping, back out through the crack in the rocks to the beach. He stepped into the sunlight and stopped cold.

"Oh shit!" He backed up into the shadow of the rocks.

Addy followed. She put her hand on his shoulder and peeked around him. "Whoa! Komodo dragons."

"It looks like they're feeding on something. Can you see what it is?" Ethan whispered.

Addy squinted. "I can't tell. Probably a deer. Or maybe a pig."

Two large mottled brown lizards grunted loudly and tugged at a carcass lying in the sand on the far end of the beach. Each of the two looked to be over seven feet long. A few yards down the shore from the dragons, something bobbed in the spent surf on the shoreline.

An orange life vest. A wave of nausea engulfed

Ethan. His legs buckled, and he collapsed to his knees. "That's no deer." He buried his face in his palms. "That's Richard."

"Oh, dear lord, no," Addy said.

One of the dragons savagely shook the carcass, ripping away a mass of flesh. It lifted its head high in the air and gulped down the bloody mass. The other dragon bit down on Richard's midsection, its rows of inch long, razor-sharp teeth cutting deep into Richard's side. The dragon jerked its head, yanking back and forth, ripping away a chunk of flesh, then backed away, pulling a long strand of guts with it. It lifted its head and swallowed the stringy blob in three hulking gulps.

"We have to get him. What's left…" Ethan took a step.

Addy grabbed the back of his shirt. "I'm not sure that's a good idea. They're known to become aggressive defending a carcass."

"What's going on?" Malik walked up behind them and asked.

"See for yourself," Ethan said. He turned around and buried his face in the crook of Addy's neck.

"Oh my God," Malik said, recoiling in horror. He stumbled back and fell heavily onto the sand. "It's Richard, isn't it?"

"It was," Ethan answered.

"His body must have washed ashore overnight," Addy said. "Oh no, here comes another one." She pointed toward the tree line at the back of the beach. "Look at the size of that thing."

Malik stood again and looked around the rocks. Another Komodo dragon, at least three feet longer and a hundred pounds heavier than the two feeding on

Richard's body appeared at the tree line. It slid down the embankment and lumbered onto the beach, its torso moving laterally with each step, head swaying side to side. The dragon's two-foot long yellow tongue slithered out with each step, scenting the air

"Holy shit, that thing must be at least ten feet long," Ethan said, keeping his voice low.

"I've never seen one that large outside the national park," Addy said.

The dragon hissed loudly, announcing its presence, and charged. The other dragons quickly retreated, slinking out of the path of the charging behemoth. The dragon reached Richard's already partially dismembered body, lifted his body in its massive jaws, and shook it viciously.

Ethan turned away, unable to bear the gruesome scene. Nauseated, his shoulders slumped, in despair, he walked back through the cleft in the rocks to where they'd spent the night. Malik followed, then stopped, bent over, and retched.

"Everyone, wake up," Ethan said. He knelt on the sand. "Richard's body washed up on the beach last night."

"Oh no," Fabiola said. "I'm so sorry, Ethan."

"That's not the worst of it. There are three Komodo dragons on the beach. They're feeding on his corpse."

"Komodo dragons?" Nils said. He stood up and looked toward the opening. "Did you stop them?"

"No, we can't. Addy thinks it's too dangerous."

"I don't care what Addy says. It's your responsibility," Nils demanded. "Get out there and rescue his body."

"They're feeding. We risk attack if we try to drag a

corpse from them."

"Somebody needs to do something," Nils said. "It's disgusting."

"Now you're concerned?" Fabiola said. "You didn't show that much concern when Richard was alive."

"I'm afraid it's too late to do anything for him now," Addy said.

Ethan cast his gaze down to the sand. "I doubt there's much of anything left by now."

Several moments of uneasy silence passed as that reality set in.

"So we're on Komodo?" Fabiola asked. "There are people on this island, right? There'll be a doctor for Gage."

"We're not on Komodo," Malik answered. "We were well southeast of there and couldn't have traveled back that far. There are dragons on Rinca and some of the smaller surrounding islands."

"What do we do then? We need to get to the Zodiac, don't we? Can we go out while they're out there?"

"I don't think we should," Addy said. "One of them is the largest dragon I've ever seen. It must be at least four hundred pounds. I know it sounds awful, but I think we have to wait until after they've fed."

"Things just keep getting worse," Fabiola said. "I can't believe all this is happening."

"We've yet to hear your explanation, Captain," Ethan said. "You said we were off course and Raj was at the helm. Why was someone so inexperienced at the helm?"

"Wait," Addy said. "Now that I think about it, the

reef we struck was on our port side. If we'd been heading west, toward Bali, our port side would've been facing south. To the south was open sea. The only way we could've struck something on our port side would be if we were heading east again. How is that possible?"

"The currents must have turned us around," Malik fumbled to explain. "It's my fault. I sincerely apologize for the loss of your friend."

"I don't understand," Ethan said. "You were on the bridge. How could you not have noticed?"

Malik hesitated. "I don't have an explanation."

"Two people are dead, Gage has been seriously injured, all our equipment lost, and you don't have an explanation? Were you drinking?"

"No, I wasn't. I can't begin to express my sorrow or the shame I feel for what happened," Malik said. "All I can do now is get us out of here and find medical attention for Gage. Those lizards will retreat into the shade of the forest when the sun gets high. When they do, Raj and I will take a Zodiac and continue around the eastern shore. My guess is these bluffs fall away to a low shore on the eastern coast."

"Why only you and Raj?" Ethan asked.

"We can't all fit in one Zodiac. It would be overloaded and unstable and impossible to get out through the surf."

"The most commanding view will be from right up there." Ethan pointed to the top of the cliffs. "I'd think you'd want to check that out first."

Malik looked up at the cliffs surrounding them. "These are sheer walls. They don't look climbable to me."

“We might not have to climb here,” Ethan responded. “Once the dragons retreat, we can go up the ravine.”

“So you’re just going to sit there and do nothing while those beasts consume my partner?” Nils demanded.

“No one is making you wait, Nils,” Fabiola said. “Go on out there and chase them away.”

Nils glared at her. “It’s their responsibility.” He pointed at Ethan and Addy.

“What happened to Richard, happened on that dive,” Ethan said. “And I think you know exactly what.”

“Liar. You’re trying to shift the blame. That’s how your last cameraman got killed. Because of your wanton recklessness.”

“What?” Fabiola asked. “What’s he talking about?”

“You didn’t know?” Nils said. “He didn’t tell you Gage’s predecessor was killed in Afghanistan?”

“That has nothing to do with our current situation.” Ethan glared at Nils. “Don’t think for a minute I’m letting you get away with what you did to Richard. I believe Richard’s tank valve was intentionally closed, and you’re the only one who could have done it.”

“How are you going to prove that? The tanks are gone. Richard’s gone. The boat’s gone. The only thing to be uncovered is how you let all this happen.”

“Enough!” Addy demanded. “This won’t help Richard or Gage, and it won’t help us figure out what we need to do.”

“Listen to her, Ethan,” Gage said, awakened by the loud arguing. “I’m hurt bad. I need a doctor.”

“I know, and we’ll get you to one, I promise.” He

looked up again, scanning the cliff face. "I think I can climb this. Maybe I can get a sense of where we are from up there."

"You don't know the area," Malik said. "What good will that do?"

"I need to do something. I can go up and see whether this island's inhabited. Or if there is one nearby." Ethan walked along the wall, scouting for a route up. He grew up in the mountains and had climbed rock faces more difficult than this. But with boots. Now he was barefoot. About twenty feet up the cliff face, a narrow ledge was visible. Past the ledge, the cliff was less steep to the top of the bluffs, another twenty feet or so. "If I can make it to that ledge, I'm pretty sure I can make it to the top." He studied the cliff face for indentations, cracks, and nubbins he could use for handholds and footholds. He rubbed the sweat from his palms and reached a hand up on the wall.

Movement to his right caught his eye, and Ethan turned to see Raj already up on the rock. Raj had never climbed a mountain or rock face, but he grew up racing over fences and walls fleeing police and thugs on the streets of Jakarta. He moved nimbly up the rock face, jamming his fingers and toes in tiny crevices and smearing his insteps against the wall. In only a couple of minutes, both his hands gripped the ledge. He climbed up on the narrow ledge and pressed his back tight against the wall. "I can see the top from here." He turned, scampered up, and disappeared over the top.

Chapter 16

Raj stood atop the bluffs and surveyed the surroundings. To his right, the small rocky beach was sandwiched between rock outcroppings on either side. The largest of the three dragons rested on its belly in the sand. The only visible remains of Richard's body was a red stain on the sand. The other two dragons were milling around by the Zodiac, sniffing the spot where Gage had been propped up against the side while Malik dressed his wounds.

Past the embankment and tree line at the rear of the beach, the ravine rose to a high, heavily forested hill. Out to sea, beyond the sheer bluffs and the surf pounding against them, lay nothing but the blue expanse of the ocean. He walked a few feet to his left, where he could see past the ledge down to the others. He lay on his stomach and crawled to the edge.

"I don't see anything but forest," he shouted down. "No village or any other sign of people. I don't see any other islands either. There's a big hill. It looks like it could be the center of the island."

"How far is it?"

Raj looked back at the hill in the distance. "I don't know. Four or five kilometers to the summit, I'd guess."

"Does it look like we can climb up the ravine?" Ethan asked.

Raj nodded. "I think so."

"Can you see the beach from there?" Addy asked.

"Yes. The dragons are still there."

"Okay. Come on back down," Malik said.

Raj looked down at the sheer face. Going up, he could see the hand and footholds. Climbing down would be much more difficult. "I don't think I can climb back down here. I'll go around and come back down through the ravine. I'll scout around a bit." He crawled away from the ledge and disappeared.

Sanjeev, who had gone to the opening to keep an eye on the dragons, returned. "Good news, he said. "The dragons are moving back into the shade of the forest. I'm sorry, but there's virtually nothing left of Richard."

"Do we have anything of his?" Fabiola asked. "You know, to give his family. I wish I'd known him better. I don't even know if he was married."

"He was," Ethan said. "Barbara. I met her once. He has two grown boys and some grandkids. They're going to be devastated."

"Richard was suffering," Sanjeev said. "Even if we hadn't crashed, I don't think he would have made it to Bali. At least now he is at peace."

"Maybe not, but he didn't deserve to end up in the belly of a monster," Ethan said.

"Komodo dragons are not monsters, Ethan," Sanjeev insisted. "To us, they are Ora. Sacred, ancient creatures."

"What do you think, Addy? Is it safe for us to go out there now that those sacred creatures have stuffed their bellies with my friend?" Ethan said.

"Let's find out." She looked around at the

driftwood stacked up against the wall. Seeing a long, two-inch diameter branch, she picked it up, broke off the smaller branches, and hit it against the ground, testing its sturdiness.

"We'll head directly to the Zodiacs," Malik said. "We'll drag one to the water's edge. When Raj gets back, he and I will go out through the surf and find help, or at least determine where we are."

"Why Raj?" Ethan asked him again. "Sanjeev's your first mate."

"To leave the more experienced man behind to help you. It might take some time to find help and return."

"So we'll unload those two trunks first?"

Malik hesitated. "There's no need to take the time to do that."

"I see. It's time we talked about what's really in those trunks, Malik," Ethan said.

"Why does it matter?" Fabiola said. "They already said they're not supplies."

"It matters, Fab. I could see they were heavy when Raj dragged them from the hold. Why are they padlocked? There might be something in them we can use." Ethan stared at Malik. "So?"

"Spare parts, extra clothes, nothing in particular. Like I told you, Raj grabbed the wrong trunks. It was dark, and the hold had already flooded."

"We could've used those extra clothes last night when we were all soaked and cold. We can use them now for bandages for Gage."

Malik stayed silent.

"Okay, then," Ethan said. "We'll go out, break the locks, and see what's inside."

"I'm telling you there's nothing of use inside those trunks. We shouldn't waste time trying to open them."

"It's obvious you're lying, Captain." As a journalist, Ethan had learned to read body clues, and Malik's body language betrayed his discomfort.

"Come on, Ethan," Fabiola said. "Raj risked his life going for them."

"Exactly. He wouldn't have risked his life unless he knew what was in those trunks. Malik's being evasive. He's hiding something. Tell us the truth, Captain. What's in them? Are you carrying contraband?"

Malik stared, tight-lipped, at Ethan.

"That's not true!" Sanjeev protested. "Captain, tell him."

"Yes, Captain," Ethan said. "Tell me."

"As I said," Malik continued, "Raj and I will take the Zodiac. We'll send for help with the first person we see. We'll tell them where you are and that you need a doctor."

"You intend to take the Zodiac and strand the rest of us here? I don't think so, motherfucker. You're not going anywhere with that boat."

"Captain, please," Sanjeev implored. "This just can't be."

There was no point in denying it any longer—the truth at the root of all that had transpired. "Those trunks contain kilo-sized blocks of heroin," Malik admitted. 'Fifty kilos to be exact." He sighed. "There was a hundred, but Raj was only able to get two of the trunks off before *Varuna* sank. We were supposed to deliver them last night, but I agreed to change course to head for Bali to save Richard." He hesitated. "I loved my boat. *Varuna* was my ticket out of this nightmare. Raj wanted to wait until after we'd made the delivery, and we fought for control of the helm. I got knocked out, and Raj turned the boat around. That's how we ran up on the rocks. It's not his fault, though. It's mine. I'm to blame for all this."

"Raj was going to let Richard die?" Fabiola said. "Delivering those drugs was more important than Richard's life?"

Nils stood. "You hired drug smugglers to pilot our ship?" Nils said to Ethan. "I'll have your ass for this." He then pointed toward Addy. "How do we know she isn't in on this too?"

"Shut up, Nils," Ethan said, still glaring at Malik.

"Listen to me, all of you," Malik continued. "The people we were supposed to deliver those trunks to, as well as the man we work for, will be looking for us by now. These are dangerous people. They will kill me. All of you as well unless I can somehow return the remaining drugs to them and convince them we didn't try to steal them."

"Oh my God!" Fabiola said. "They're going to be looking for you here?"

"They don't know where we are…yet. The safest thing for all of you is for us to take those trunks and get far away from you."

"And strand us on this island? I don't think so," Ethan said. "We're not so stupid to believe you'd tell anyone about our being here."

"It's the best chance you have for rescue. You have my word we will send for help."

"The word of a drug smuggler. Right. If anyone's taking that boat," Ethan exclaimed, "it will be us."

"Yes, I am a smuggler. But not by choice. I can't let you take that Zodiac."

"Think you can drive that Zodiac out through the surf?" Ethan asked Addy.

"Yes, I can drive it," she answered, "but I'm afraid Malik's right. It will be too heavy and unstable to make it over the surf with all of us aboard."

"I'll stay behind," Ethan said.

"I'll stay as well, Sanjeev said. "The lighter you are, the better your odds for making it through the surf. But if you're going, you should go before Raj gets back."

"What about the dragons?" Fabiola asked.

"Their bellies are full, and they're probably sleeping," Addy replied.

Ethan nodded. "We'll head straight to the Zodiac and drag it down to the shoreline. Don't worry, Malik—we'll dump out your heroin first."

Chapter 17

The group walked cautiously out of the refuge in the rocks and over to the Zodiac on the far end of the beach. Malik followed along a few steps behind. Ethan climbed inside and tumbled the two heroin-filled trunks onto the sand, then jumped out and helped Sanjeev and Addy spin the Zodiac around and drag it down to the water. Fabiola and Nils lifted Gage inside while Sanjeev and Ethan held it in waist-deep water to keep it from being shoved back by the whitewash of the spent surf.

Addy jumped in and lowered the prop into the water. "We'll watch for the biggest wave in a set to break over the top of the reef and then head out at full throttle," she said. "Once I give it the gas, I want everyone sitting in the bottom and holding tight." She reached for the key on the front of the engine. It wasn't there. "Shit. The key is gone. I didn't check if it was here when we got in." She looked up at Malik, standing on the beach watching them. "He must have it."

"I'll get it," Ethan said. "Help Sanjeev hold the boat." Ethan waded to shore and up to Malik. "Hand over the key, Malik."

Malik shrugged. "Raj has it."

"You waited till now to tell us that? I don't believe you. Empty out your pockets."

"I don't have the key. Anyway, I told you before,

Raj and I are taking this boat."

"The hell you are." Ethan dove into Malik's midsection, tackling him to the ground, then began rifling through Malik's pockets.

"Ethan!" Addy shouted from the boat. She pointed toward the tree line. Appearing like a prehistoric dinosaur stepping through time from a primeval forest, the Komodo dragon, covered in armor-like scales, and with long strands of opaque saliva hanging from either side of its menacing jaws, slid down the embankment onto the beach.

"We better pull the boat back up on the beach," Addy said to Fabiola and Nils. She climbed out, and the three pushed the Zodiac up on the sand and out of the surf.

Nils pointed toward the trees. "Here comes another one." Nils swallowed hard and inched backward toward the water. "What do we do now?"

"Just keep calm," Addy said. She saw the look of growing panic on his face. "It'll be fine. Komodos are curious but not normally aggressive. Fishermen come ashore on these islands and give them food. The local people consider them sacred and give them offerings. They're probably expecting a handout. Give a little ground if they get too close. Whatever you do, don't run. These creatures can chase down deer in a short sprint. If you run, you're prey." She leaned inside the Zodiac, grabbed two boat paddles, and handed one to Ethan.

The two dragons hesitated at the spot where the Zodiac lay in the sand the night before. One clawed at the sand where Malik had redressed Gage's wounds. Then they continued toward the group standing near the waterline.

"What are they looking at?" Fabiola said.

"Gage," Malik said. "I think they've scented his blood."

Nils continued shuffling backward, farther into the water. He grabbed the line that ran along the side of the Zodiac. "Will they climb in the boat?"

"No. They won't do anything if we remain calm. Don't go into the water. Komodo dragons can swim."

Movement at the treeline caught Sanjeev's eye. He pointed toward the back of the beach. "Here comes the big one," he said.

"What do we do now?" Nils said. He gripped the line tighter. He squirmed like ants were crawling all over him.

"Just be still and calm down, Nils," Addy repeated. "I'm telling you it will be fine."

The nearest dragon's gaze appeared locked on something inside the boat. It continued its advance toward the Zodiac, so Addy jabbed on the nose with the stick she'd picked up. The dragon hesitated but lurched around her to the left and kept advancing until it was at the water's edge. Ethan punched it with the blade of the paddle he was carrying. The dragon hissed and stopped. The second dragon continued moving toward the boat and was now behind Ethan. He spun around and hit it on the nose. It recoiled, hissed, then plodded to his left and continued.

The largest Komodo drew closer. "Shit, this is making me nervous," Ethan said. "We need to keep moving steadily toward the protection of the rocks."

"Definitely," Addy said. She gestured to Sanjeev, Nils, and Fabiola. "You guys push the boat along the shore over to the rocks in front of our cave. We'll pull it back up onto the beach over there. It's too risky to try to take Gage out of the boat until we're nearer the entrance. Ethan and I will walk behind to keep the dragons back."

Malik helped them get the boat over to the rocks in front of the entrance to the cave. The three dragons followed, staying just out of reach of Addy and Ethan's jabs.

Malik took the bowline and looped it around a boulder while Fabiola and Sanjeev lifted Gage out of the boat. Seeing them carry the injured man, the largest of the three dragons advanced once again. Ethan hit it hard on the nose with the blade of the paddle. Addy walked beside Ethan, and they kept the dragon at bay poking and jabbing with the boat paddles while the others carried Gage over the rocks and into the cave opening.

Malik, Ethan, and Addy were the last to retreat over the low rocks to the cleft in the rock face. The Komodos didn't stop at the entrance.

"This is beginning to worry me," Addy said, glancing at Ethan, then Malik, her eyes widening.

Malik grabbed the end of a driftwood log. "Sanjeev, help me drag some of those logs over here to make a barricade."

Sanjeev and Fabiola laid Gage down on the sand, and then Sanjeev helped Malik construct a three-foot high barricade. Ethan and Addy jabbed repeatedly at the three dragons, but it only antagonized them, their attention focused on something beyond the wall. The largest of the three dragons, the apex predator on the island, climbed onto the barricade. It dug its long, sharp claws into the log at the top of the hastily constructed wall, and toppled it. Malik rushed forward and threw a large rock at the beast. It recoiled, then lumbered forward again.

"Shit," Malik said, looking down to search for another sizable stone to throw at the advancing beast, "they've got us trapped in here."

"Hey!" Raj suddenly appeared behind the dragons. He hurled a rock and hit one on its haunches. Raj shouted and waved his arms. Two of the dragons turned and started toward him. Raj spun and disappeared around the corner. Seeing him flee triggered the dragons' age-old instinct and they bolted after him.

Rounding the corner, Raj leaped up on the rock face and caught a ledge with his fingertips. He walked his feet up, extended his right hand, and clamped on another tiny feature. He walked his feet up the rock, stretched out his left hand, found another small crack, and quickly pulled his feet up the wall again. He was beyond their grasp when the dragons reached the wall.

The largest of the three dragons had stopped his advance when Raj appeared but now continued over the now-toppled wall. Malik hurled another fist-sized rock, hitting the dragon on the shoulder. Sanjeev and Fabiola followed suit, and the three hit the giant lizard with a withering barrage of rocks. Pelted with stone after stone, the dragon retreated, and lumbered out of the opening.

The group quickly rebuilt the barrier, stacking several large, heavy driftwood logs on the wall and filling in gaps with brush and stones.

"There's Raj," Sanjeev said, looking up at the cliff face. Raj descended, hand-over-hand down the rock wall, then jumped to the ground in front of the barrier.

"It's good to see you, my young friend," Malik said. "Things were getting intense."

"I had no idea those things could move so fast," Raj said excitedly. "Without a head start, they'd have caught me for sure. I wasn't sure I could climb that section of the wall, but I heard them coming, so I just jumped in hopes I'd find something to hang on to."

"You were gone a long time," Malik said." What could you see from up there?"

"The island's heavily forested. I didn't see any sign of a settlement or people. These bluffs appear to continue all the way to the west end. The cape blocked my view to the east, so I traveled inland about a kilometer. I found a huge tree with vines hanging from its branches and climbed it. From there I could see to the north shore."

"How far is it?" Ethan asked.

"Eight or ten kilometers, I'd guess. This is a small island. I could see a flat beach on the north shore."

"Could you see any other islands?" Malik asked.

"I could see the faint outline of land to the north. Nothing else."

"That makes sense. The island you saw to the north must be Rinca," Malik said.

"Did you see any more Ora up there?" Sanjeev asked.

"Ora? Oh, right. You mean the dragons. No. I came down the ravine all way to the beach. I thought they were gone till I rounded the corner. That was a hell of a surprise."

"We're glad you made it safely. Thanks for doing that, Raj," Ethan said. "Gage is in a bad way and needs medical attention ASAP. Malik says you have the key to the outboard. Is that right?"

"Yeah, I've got it. Why?"

"Give it to me, please. We need to take the boat to get Gage to a doctor."

Raj glanced at Malik.

Malik shook his head. "Sorry, Ethan, we'll send help to you."

"We know all about the drugs, Raj," Ethan said. "Give me the key."

"What happened while I was gone?" Raj asked, his gaze shifting back and forth between Malik and Ethan.

"Raj," Sanjeev said, uneasily. "Malik is no longer our captain, and we're not letting him abandon an injured person here on this island."

"He is still the captain," Raj asserted. "If he says he and I are taking the boat, then we're taking the boat."

"Give me the key, Raj," Ethan repeated, "or I'll take it from you."

Raj's body tensed and his gaze narrowed. "Then come take it."

Ethan clinched his fists and stepped toward Raj.

"Wait," Malik said. "We'll take Gage."

"What?" Ethan stopped. "Like hell, you will."

"Listen to me," Malik continued. "I have the best chance of making it out through the surf. Once I'm out beyond it, I'll recognize which way to head to find help. We'll take Gage with us and make sure he gets to a doctor. It's the best option to save his life."

"You're fucking criminals," Ethan said. "I'm not trusting you with his life."

"Why do you think those dragons are being so aggressive?" Malik said. "They want Gage. They've scented his blood. He's injured prey to them. He'll be safer with us."

"Is what he's saying true?" Gage overheard and struggled to sit up. "Those things are after me?"

"No, he's trying to scare us," Ethan said. "Addy's taking you in the boat and getting you to a doctor." He looked at Malik. "You're trying to sow discord among us. It won't work."

Ethan suddenly rushed at Raj. Quick as lightning, Raj pivoted and used Ethan's momentum to flip him. Ethan landed hard on his back on the sand with a thud. Continuing the motion, Raj drove his shoulder, and all his weight, into Ethan's chest. It knocked the breath out of Ethan who let out a whoosh and rolled into a ball gasping for breath. Raj quickly sprang to his feet.

Ethan struggled to his knees, but before he could stand, Raj delivered a spinning kick to the side of Ethan's head, sending him reeling again to the sand. Ethan made it to his hands and knees, and Raj kicked him in the gut knocking him over again.

"Stop!" Addy shouted. She turned to Malik, and implored, "Take the goddamn boat if you have to, but make him stop."

"That's enough, Raj," Malik said.

Raj, stopped, fists clenched, his eyes filled with rage and his gaze riveted on Ethan, ready to pounce again.

"We'll get Gage to a doctor; you have my word," Malik said. He looked down at Gage. "Come with us, son. It's your best chance."

"Should I go with him?" Gage said, looking toward Ethan, who'd managed to get to his feet. "Christ, I might die if don't. My arm hurts bad." He looked out past the barricade. "I don't want to get eaten by those monsters. L…like they ate Richard."

"Don't listen to him, Gage," Ethan implored. He spat, then wiped the blood from his mouth. "These two are drug smugglers, maybe even killers. I'm not risking your life with criminals. We'll find another way to get help."

"How?" Malik asked, pointing at Gage. "Those dragons smell his blood. How long will you be able to hold them off before they drag him away? He'll be safer with us."

"Maybe he's right, Ethan," Fabiola said. "If they're taking the boat anyway, maybe Gage will be safer with them."

"Don't take their side, dammit. He's trying to divide us."

"It's not about taking sides," Addy said. "It's about making the best choice in a bad situation."

"I don't want to die here," Gage said. His voice cracked. "I…I don't think I have a choice."

"Don't do it, Gage," Ethan said. "These are desperate men. They'll throw you overboard the minute they're beyond the surf."

"No, we won't," Malik insisted. "I'm truly sorry for what happened to Richard. If the men who own the heroin find us here, they'll kill all of us. Men like them don't leave witnesses."

"I'll come with you," Gage blurted out. "I'm sorry, Ethan." He looked at Malik. "You swear you'll get me to a doctor?"

"I swear." Malik looked back at the group. "We'll need someone else to go along to stay with him once we drop him off."

Raj looked at Fabiola. "Come with us, Fab."

"Fuck you. You can go to hell."

"I'll go," Nils said, stepping forward. "Take me with you, Captain."

"You traitorous coward," Ethan said. "You're already a murderer, right Nils? I guess abandoning your mates is nothing compared to that."

"Stop it, Ethan," Addy exclaimed. "We don't know that for sure."

"He's a liar," Nils said. "He's the one responsible. For all this." He turned to Malik again. "I have money. I can pay you. You'll need money to escape the criminals who own that heroin."

"Fab, you should go with them," Addy said, ignoring Nils' pleas. "Gage will need someone to take care of him."

"What are you doing?" Ethan exclaimed. "Jesus Christ, Addy."

"Gage will be more likely to survive if one of us goes with him."

"I already said I'll go," Nils insisted.

"Shut up, Nils." Ethan growled. "I don't want any of my crew going with those two criminals," he insisted.

"It's my life and my call to make, not yours," Gage said, weakly.

"Then let Nils go," Fabiola said. "I'm not going anywhere with those assholes."

Addy pulled her aside and looked her in the eye. "You know we can't trust Nils to take care of Gage. It has to be you, Fab. You have to go with them. Raj won't hurt you. They're more likely to get him to help if you're along."

Fabiola started to protest but didn't. She knew Addy was right. Avoiding any eye contact with Raj, she turned to Malik. "I'll go. But only to take care of Gage."

Malik nodded and looked at Ethan. "We'll need your help to get Gage in the boat. We'll need all your help."

"We're not helping you," Ethan said, tight-lipped.

Addy interjected, "Ethan, those dragons might attack when they try to board the boat unless we hold them back."

Ethan looked down at his feet and cursed. He reluctantly nodded.

Chapter 18

"They're still out there," Raj said, looking back from the opening in the rocks. "Over by the cliff face where I climbed to escape them. Now there's a fourth one. Lying in the shade, just inside the tree line."

"Damn. Nils, you go with Raj to help drag the trunks down to the boat," Malik ordered.

"Me?" Nils said. "No way. Not with those monsters out there."

"Do what he says, Nils," Ethan insisted.

"Now wait just a minute…"

"Shut up, and get moving," Ethan ordered. "Sanjeev, you and Fab go out and push the Zodiac back into the water. Addy and I will carry Gage to the boat." He glanced at Malik. "You know once you abandon us here, you'll become a wanted man. When we get out of here and notify the authorities, they'll be after you."

"You don't know the people we are dealing with," Malik replied. "My life is already ruined. The authorities are the least of my concern right now."

"Where are you heading?" Ethan asked.

"Sorry, I can't tell you. Once we're gone, I suggest you make your way to the other side of the island. You're more likely to be spotted by fishermen or passing boats on that side." He looked at the others. "Okay, let's go." Nils didn't move, so Malik shoved him ahead.

The group climbed over the barricade, scrambled over the jumbled boulders, and headed across the beach toward the two trunks lying on the sand. The dragons sensed the movement and started toward them.

Malik kept a tight grip on Nils, who never took his gaze off the approaching dragons. Once they'd arrived at the spot where Ethan had earlier tumbled the two heroin-filled trunks onto the sand, Malik grabbed the handle of one of them and put Nils's hand on it. "Drag this all the way to the boat. If you let go, I'll bust your head with this pole. Understand?"

"Yes." Nils grumbled and started dragging it toward the boat.

Raj grabbed the handle of the other trunk and walked along beside Nils, occasionally glancing back and forth between Nils and the approaching dragons.

The two smaller dragons approached first. Malik fell in behind the two men dragging the trunks to keep the lizards back, jabbing at them with one of the paddles. Nils picked up his pace, looking increasingly nervous the closer they followed.

"Slow down, Nils!" Malik commanded. "You're agitating them!"

"They're looking right at me," Nils said. He turned around and shuffled backward, dragging the trunk with both hands, his gaze locked on the largest of the three dragons following them. "Why is it looking at me?"

Malik again glanced back at Nils. "It's not. Don't make eye contact with them, you fool. They'll perceive it as a challenge."

"I can feel its eyes boring into me."

"Nils! Keep moving. Slow and easy. It's only a few more feet to the boat." Malik shoved him again.

Nils tore his glance away and looked toward the boat. He was almost there. *Only a few more steps*. He stared back toward the dragon, panic engulfing him.

The receptors in the dragon's long tongue picked up the electrical signals emitted by Nils' elevated heart rate and it quickened its pace. Malik jabbed at it with the boat paddle, but the behemoth barely flinched, forcing Malik to step out of its path. The dragon stepped on the trunk dragged by Nils, digging its four-inch claws into the canvas. The abrupt halt jerked the handle from Nils's hand.

Nils's eyes dilated, drawn into the black void of the dragon's gaze, swallowing the daylight like a train racing into a mountainside tunnel. A voice spoke from deep within his gut. *The boat's right behind you, Nils…Run for it.* The voice grew louder and louder until its din was all he could hear: *Run!*

Ethan saw the look of terror on Nils' face, "Oh shit! He's going to run."

The words barely left Ethan's mouth before Nils bolted in panic toward the boat. The dragon reacted with what millions of years of instinct had taught all pack hunters: attack the animal that strays from the safety of the herd. In the blink of an eye, the dragon was on him, catching Nils just as he jumped on the side of the Zodiac. It bit down on the back of Nils' thigh, its serrated teeth cutting deep into his hamstring. The dragon savagely yanked Nils off the boat and dragged him screaming and flailing, back onshore.

Malik rushed to rescue him. He swung the boat paddle, bringing the blade crashing down on the dragon's head. The force of the blow caused the dragon to release its grip and momentarily back away. It advanced again, but Raj rushed forward and hurled the fifty-pound trunk he'd been dragging. The trunk landed on the dragon's powerful neck causing it to recoil, It hissed loudly, but stopped in its tracks, its eyes still locked on its prey.

Ethan and Addy rushed Gage to the boat and lifted him inside. Addy grabbed the remaining paddle from the Zodiac, and they both ran over to Nils, writhing on the sand, clutching his leg and sobbing. Blood poured from the wound on his leg, pooling on the sand and billowing in the foamy water washed up from the surf. Sanjeev and Ethan picked up stones from the shoreline and heaved them at each of the dragons and kept them from advancing while Malik and Raj picked up the two trunks and carried them to the boat, then climbed inside. Fabiola grabbed Malik's extended hand and climbed inside.

"Take me with you!" Nils sobbed. "You can't leave me here." He crawled into the shallow water and grabbed the line on the top of the inflatable. "Take me with you," he blubbered. "Please!"

Raj pried Nils' fingers off the line, "You're already dead." He untied the bowline from the eyelet, coiled it up, and tossed it to Ethan. "Here. You might need this."

Malik inserted the key, gave the fuel bulb a couple squeezes, and yanked the starter cord. The engine roared to life with a belch of white smoke.

Sanjeev and Ethan shoved the Zodiac into deeper water and then helped the sobbing Nils back onshore.

"I'm sorry," Malik shouted from the Zodiac, a pained look on his face. "I…I had to. For everyone's sake." He twisted the throttle, and headed into the raging surf.

The group on the beach stole glances at the Zodiac heading into the thundering surf, but the advancing Komodo dragons kept their attention focused on the danger at hand. Sanjeev and Ethan carried Nils back toward the safety of the cave on the far side of the beach. Addy followed, chunking rocks and keeping the dragons at bay with the boat paddle. Blood oozed down Nils's leg from the savage bite, leaving a crimson trail on the sand.

Reaching the opening, Ethan turned and looked out to sea. The Zodiac climbed the vertical face of a huge wave, crested it, then disappeared from sight. Turning back to the task at hand, he motioned to Sanjeev to help him lift Nils over the barricade. They carried him to the back of the cave and propped him against a large driftwood log, then rushed to help Addy keep the dragons from climbing over the barrier.

Under the barrage of rocks hurled at them from behind it, the giant monitor lizards again retreated out of range. They lowered onto their bellies just outside the entrance to the enclosure and waited. Instinct told them it was only a matter of time until their prey sickened and bled to death. Then they would scatter the rest of the herd and feed on its carcass.

Sanjeev stayed to guard the barricade while Addy and Ethan rushed back over to the sobbing Nils to dress his wound and try to stop the bleeding. Ethan stripped off his shirt and handed it to Addy to use as a bandage. The bite had cut through muscle and tendon all way to the bone. Nils' lower leg was caked with blood and crusted with sand.

Addy closed the wound, folding in the flayed tissue, then she wrapped Ethan's shirt tightly around the wound, and tied it. Blood immediately soaked through the shirt. "There's a lot of blood, but I don't think the femoral artery was severed," she said. "Even so, with the size of this wound, he'll bleed out unless we can stop it. We need to put a tourniquet above the bite wound."

Nils was looking down at the wound and sobbing uncontrollably. Addy shook him and said, "Nils, listen to me. Lie back and be still. We have to stop the bleeding." She looked up at Ethan. "Keep steady pressure on the wound while I find something to make a tourniquet."

Ethan put both his palms on Nils's leg and pushed down. The wound made a sickening squishing sound. Blood was already pooling on the sand underneath the leg.

"What's going to happen to me?" Nils raised his head and stared, glossy-eyed toward the barricade. He grabbed Addy's arm, his eyes wide with terror. "Ethan wants to leave me to them, doesn't he? Please don't let him. Don't let him feed me to those beasts."

"He won't, Nils. We won't let them get you. Now sit back, and be quiet." She called to Sanjeev. "Can you find a short piece of branch or driftwood? Something about an inch in diameter. And we need your shirt. We're running out of things to use for bandages."

"Yes, ma'am." He took his shirt off and handed it to Addy. He searched the area until he found a driftwood branch and brought it over, then went back to guard the barrier.

Addy twisted the shirt lengthwise tightly and wrapped it around Nils's leg just below his butt, cinched it tight, and tied an overhand knot. She broke off a one-foot-long piece of the branch, placed it over the knot, and tied another over the top of it. "I'm sorry, Nils, but this will hurt." She twisted the stick around twice, then tucked a fold of the cloth over the end.

"Stop! You're cutting off my leg," Nils cried, in agony.

Ethan held Nils' arms while Addy tucked a piece of the sleeve over the end of the stick to hold it in place. "That should slow the bleeding," Addy said. "We'll loosen it for five seconds once every five minutes." She went to the trickle of water cascading down the cliff face and washed the blood and sand from her hands, then cupped her hands under the water and drank.

"A little different scenario than the last time we stood under a shower," she said, stepping aside so Ethan could wash and drink from the trickling waterfall.

"Yea, a little different." He looked toward the tops of the cliffs, then out past the barricade. "Malik was right, you know. We can't stay here," he said. "No one will see us or be able to come ashore through that surf. We have to get to the other side of the island."

Addy looked out through the narrow opening to the surf beyond. "I agree, but how?"

"I don't know. Do you think we can battle our way past those lizards and up the ravine?"

"With Nils?" Addy asked. "Once we take him beyond this barricade, they'll attack. I'm not sure how long we could hold them off. Someone else could get bitten."

"He brought this on himself."

"You're not telling me you'd just let them have him, are you?"

"He killed Richard. The person I admired most in this world. Then he wanted to desert us. He's the one who panicked and ran. I don't want to risk your life or anyone else's to save his."

"Come on, Ethan. I've come to know you well enough to know you wouldn't abandon anyone. Not even Nils."

Ethan glanced toward Nils. "Isn't the bite from one of those things poisonous?"

"That's a myth. Their mouths are full of bacteria from eating rotting carrion, though. The wound will become infected. Plus, their saliva contains anti-clotting agents. The tourniquet will slow the bleeding, but likely won't stop it. He won't survive unless we get him to a hospital. And soon."

Ethan sighed. "If we can't get past them, that's our only other way out," he said, pointing toward the top of the cliffs.

Addy looked up at the sheer cliff face and shook her head. "Raj may have been able to climb that, but I'm not sure we can. Even if we could, how would we get Nils up it?"

"We'll use the rope Raj left us." He walked over and studied the cliff face. "If I can make it up to that ledge, I can use the rope from the Zodiac to belay everyone else."

Addy looked at the cliff face. "I don't know. If you fall, you could break your leg, or worse."

"If Raj made it, I can make it."

"I don't care about Raj. I care about you. He's thirty pounds lighter and climbs like a spider. Plus, you're barefoot. We're all barefoot."

Ethan looked again at the rock face. "I think I can

do it."

"Let's ask Sanjeev what he thinks." She motioned for Ethan to follow her to the barricade "We think we need to get to the other side of the island," Addy said to Sanjeev. "Ethan thinks we have to climb this cliff, like Raj. What do you think we should do?"

"Maybe we should wait till morning," he suggested. "The Ora might leave by then. We could go out onto the beach and walk up the ravine."

"Even if they leave, I doubt they'll go far," Addy said. "I'm worried they'd ambush us. Besides, if we have any chance of saving his life," she glanced toward Nils, "I don't think we can afford to wait."

"We don't know how much longer Nils will be awake and lucid," Ethan said. "We won't be able to lift him if he's dead weight. I say we've got to climb that cliff, and I think we need to do it now."

"What if Malik and Raj send help and we're not here?" Sanjeev asked.

"The longer we wait, the more our chances for survival decrease," Ethan insisted. "We have no food, no blankets, and no lights. We'd have to post someone on watch tonight. The longer we stay, the weaker we'll get. I say we climb out, and we do it now."

"Even if we get to the top, how do we know there aren't more of those Ora in the forest?" Sanjeev asked.

"There certainly could be," Addy answered. "But we know for certain there are three or four right outside."

Sanjeev nodded. "Okay. How can I help?"

"Once I reach the ledge, I'll make a loop on one end and drop it down," Ethan said. "Put it around Nils's chest. I'll secure myself and pull up on the rope. You'll have to lift him from below. Nils will have to help with his hands and his good leg. Once I get him up to the ledge, I'll belay Addy. She can hold him while I climb the rest of the way up. Once we get Nils to the top, I'll climb back down to the ledge and belay up Sanjeev."

Addy took a deep breath. "Okay, let's do it. Let's get the hell out of here."

Ethan crouched beside Nils. "Tell me what you did to Richard." Ethan grabbed Nils's shirt with both fists. "If you lie to me, I swear to God I'll leave you behind."

"I didn't do anything. I swear." Nils lifted his head from the sand and looked toward the barrier. "Please, don't leave me to those beasts!" Nils broke down into sobs again.

"You fucking liar. I'm going to let them rip your guts out, just like they did to Richard. Except you'll be alive to see them coming."

Nils laid his head back in the sand and covered his face with his hands. "I didn't mean for him to die. I was so angry. I…I didn't mean to kill him. I swear I didn't."

Ethan let go of Nils's shirt and wiped his hands on his shorts. "I should leave you to die." He stood up, picked up the coil of rope Raj left him, and draped it over his shoulders.

Chapter 19

Ethan stepped his right foot up to a small ledge, barely a half inch wide. He ran his hand along the wall till he found a tiny crack and crammed two fingers in it. He shifted his weight to his right foot and stepped up. Feeling farther up with his other hand, he found another and held on with his fingertips. Keeping his face and chest plastered against the wall, Ethan hoisted his left foot and scraped it along the wall until he found a slight indentation, shifted his weight, and pushed himself up higher again.

Bit by bit, he inched his way up the rock face until he was just below the two-foot-wide ledge, thirty feet off the ground, halfway up the cliff. The shelf just beyond his grasp and the cliff face had become featureless. Daring not lean away for fear of losing his balance and falling to the jumble of logs and boulders at the base of the cliff, he scraped his right foot up and down along the rock, finally finding an indentation he hoped would support his weight.

Ethan fixed his gaze on the ledge above him, took three deep breaths, shifted his weight to his right foot, and jumped, extending his arms and reaching for the rim of the ledge. He caught it, dug in his fingertips, and held on for dear life. Taking a deep breath, he mustered his strength, swung his right heel up, hooked it on the ledge, and with a surge of adrenaline, rolled up onto the narrow shelf.

He caught his breath and peered over the ledge. “Whew, that was sketchy.”

“Nice job, Spiderman,” Addy called up, finally taking a breath.

Ethan dangled his legs over the ledge. He took the coil from his shoulders, tied a bowline loop on one end, and tossed it down.

Addy helped Nils over to the cliff wall. She slipped the loop over his arms and under both armpits.

Ethan put the rope around his shoulders for leverage and lay back against the cliff face. He found an indentation in the rock face and lodged his foot against it. “Okay, Nils, start climbing.”

“You’re too heavy to lift without help, Nils,” Addy said. “You’ll have to use your hands and your uninjured leg. Do you understand?”

“I can’t. I can’t feel my leg.”

She grabbed Nils face and turned it toward the barricade. “Your alternative’s right over there. If you can’t help, you get left behind.”

“I’ll climb. Don’t leave me, I’ll climb.” Nils turned facing the cliff and ran his hands along it to feel for handholds.

Ethan winched Nils upward, while Addy got under him and pushed. Every time Nils’s injured leg bumped into the wall, he cried out in anguish, but the fear of Ethan dropping him kept him grabbing for any tiny hold he could get his fingers on and pushing with his uninjured leg. Once they got him above her head, Addy put her hands under the foot of his uninjured leg and pressed up to her full extension, but Nils was still several feet below the shelf.

The line bit into Ethan's hands and shoulder as he struggled to keep the line from slipping through his grasp. Nils dead weight on the line dragged him, inching toward the edge. "I'm slipping," he shouted. "I can't hold him."

"Sanjeev," Addy called out, "you'll have to come help."

Sanjeev backed steadily toward the cliff, keeping his gaze focused on the dragons on the other side of the barricade.

"Climb up a little way," Addy told Sanjeev, "and see if you can get under his foot and push him up farther. I'll steady you," Addy said.

With Addy bracing him from below, Sanjeev climbed a few feet up the wall. He got a hand under Nils's uninjured leg and pressed. Ethan took up the slack and winched him up a few feet higher. Addy leaned against the rock face and braced Sanjeev's foot, allowing him to climb a couple of feet higher. Precariously balanced on one leg, Sanjeev pushed up on Nils's instep, turning his face aside from the blood dripping on his face. They finally got Nils high enough for him to get a hand up high enough for Ethan to grab. With furious effort, Ethan dragged him over the lip and onto the rock shelf beside him.

"Oh shit!" Addy said, glancing toward the barricade. "Ethan, toss the loop down to Sanjeev. Hurry!" She jumped away from the wall and ran toward the barricade.

Ethan saw the dragons scaling the barricade and dropped the loop to Sanjeev.

Nils's groans while being dragged and shoved up the cliff attracted the attention of the dragons. One had climbed the makeshift wall, its claws, then its head appearing at the top. Addy grabbed the boat paddle on the run, tucked it under her arm like a jousting lance, and rammed the dragon's shoulder, toppling it over backward. She spun the paddle, then swung it like an axe, smacking the second Komodo on the snout. It hissed at her loudly, but slunk back in retreat.

The biggest of the three had hung back but now plodded slowly and steadily toward them. While standing at the barricade earlier, Sanjeev had built a pile of stones behind it. Addy hurled one, then another, and another, until it too halted its advance.

Strong and agile, Sanjeev quickly made his way up the cliff face and squeezed in beside Nils and took the loop from around his chest.

"There's not enough room on this ledge for all four of us," Ethan said, trying to swallow a creeping panic due to Addy being left alone to fend off the dragons. *This wasn't how I planned it,* he thought. "We've got to get Nils to the top before we can get Addy up." He handed Sanjeev the length of rope. "Get to the top as fast as you can. You'll have to belay Nils."

Sanjeev draped the rope over his shoulder, maneuvered around to face the wall and stood on the narrow ledge. "It looks easier from here up." He started up the wall.

"For God's sake, hurry!" Ethan glanced down at Addy and the dragons just beyond. "We need to get Addy up here fast."

Sanjeev quickly reached the top and found a eucalyptus tree near the edge that appeared sturdy enough to use as an anchor to belay Nils. He wrapped the line around the trunk, tossed the loop down to

Ethan. "Ready," He shouted.

Ethan slipped the loop under Nils' arms, then cinched it tight. "Wake up, Nils." Ethan slapped him back and forth across his face." Get it together. Just a little farther." Ethan pulled him up and helped him stand. Nils teetered unsteadily on his uninjured leg. Ethan glanced again at Addy, his anxiety growing, worrying how he would get her up the cliff face with no one to keep the dragons from attacking. Ethan maneuvered Nils around to face the wall. "One more section to climb, Nils. We've no time to waste; now get going." Ethan grabbed Nils right hand and put it on a sturdy feature on the rock face and gave him a shove, then signaled up to Sanjeev to pull.

Using the tree trunk for friction, Sanjeev ratcheted Nils up the slope. Ethan climbed alongside the rapidly fading Nils, keeping him upright, lifting, shoving, and prodding him step by step until they struggled over the rim. He quickly took the loop from around Nils' chest, recoiled it, draped it around his own shoulders, stole a quick glance toward Addy, then descended to the ledge. Reaching it, Ethan situated himself securely on the ledge and then tossed the loop over the side. "Ready, Addy, come on."

With a rock in one hand and the boat paddle in the other, Addy backed steadily toward the cliff face. She hadn't gone ten feet before dragon claws appeared at the top of the barricade. Addy hurled the rock, turned, and sprinted for the cliff. She slipped the loop over her arms, shoved the blade of the paddle into the sand, and lodged the handle against the cliff. She stepped up on it. "Pull me up!" She shouted. She glanced back. The barricade toppled under the weight of the dragons.

Terrified that razor-sharp teeth would clamp down on her legs at any moment. Addy stretched up and clawed at the wall searching for a nub or indentation that would hold her weight. The rope cut into her chest and armpits. She dug her fingertips into a small feature and pulled up her legs, but the tiny hold she clutched proved too thin, and her fingers scraped down the wall. "I'm falling!"

Ethan gritted his teeth and leaned back against the cliff face. He arrested her fall, but it dragged him closer to the edge. "Grab something," he cried out in panic. "I'm about to go over!"

Addy's fingers again probed the wall. Finding a small crack, she crammed two fingers of her right hand into it. This time able to hold on, she quickly walked her legs up underneath her. Claws scraped the rock face below her. "Pull me up!" she screamed, reaching high with her left hand and grabbing the line. Glancing down, the forelegs of the largest of the three dragons were on the wall. His neck craned upward, his massive jaws agape. She pulled her legs up in a ball, and clung for dear life, two fingers of one hand pinched in a tiny crack on the wall, the other holding precariously to the thin nylon rope.

Ethan shuffled his butt away from the edge and once again leaned against the back of the ledge, took a breath, and pulled with all his might, lifting Addy another two feet higher. She found another handhold, then a solid foothold, then another, until she was high enough to grip the ledge. Ethan grabbed her hand and pulled her up.

"That was too close," Addy said, her voice quaking. She threw her arms around Ethan's neck. "I thought it would get me," she said, still trying to catch her breath. "I imagined its teeth tearing into my legs and dragging me down. I've never been so terrified."

Fighting back his own tears, Ethan said, "I didn't mean for you to be the last on the wall."

"I know. It's just the way it worked out." Addy looked down at Ethan's hands. The rope had carved deep rope burns on the palms of both. She lifted one of his hands and kissed it. She glanced one last time at the dragons milling below at the base of the cliff. "Let's get the hell out of here."

Once at the top, Ethan and Addy stood next to Sanjeev and the three looked out at the wide, empty expanse of sea. To their left was the long line of bluffs; to the right, the sheer wall of the cape with the surf rolling in and smashing against it. No other islands were in view. They turned and focused their attention on the interior, and the dark forest beyond.

Chapter 20

Malik steered into the cresting wave and cranked the throttle wide open. He'd sent Raj to the bow with Fabiola and Gage to tilt the center of gravity as far forward as possible. The small boat climbed the water until almost vertical on the face of the rising wave. Malik leaned as far forward as he could while still holding the steering throttle, to try to keep them from being swept over by the advancing wave. Malik timed it perfectly and topped the wave just before it crested. The bow crashed down on the backside as it swept past.

"We made it!" Malik breathed a sigh of relief. "We're beyond the breakers. I told you we'd make it," he exclaimed.

"Thank you, Captain," Gage said. He struggled to get up on a bench but lacked the strength. He craned his neck, trying to look past the captain toward the beach, and caught a brief glimpse of his compatriots before a rolling swell rose up and hid them from sight. A sudden panic struck him; the image of Nils writhing in the sand, etched on his mind. "You will get me to a doctor, won't you?" Gage asked Malik.

"I'll keep my word."

"Where are we going?" Fabiola asked.

"Toward the eastern shore. Once we round the southeast corner, we'll turn north, and I'll have a better idea where we are." Malik hoped they would come across local fishermen on the way, intending to drop Gage and Fabiola with them, but only if the fishermen couldn't speak English. He knew Gage and Fabiola would tell their story to whomever they met, and he needed a head start. Once he off-loaded his passengers, he would turn northeast toward the small harbor at Golo Mori village on Flores. But first, he needed to stash the heroin.

They rounded the southeastern coast of the small island, and turned north. Motoring along the eastern shore, the water calmed, and Malik slowed the Zodiac, easing off the throttle to conserve fuel. The tall bluffs gave way to a low, boulder-strewn shoreline. Two hours later, they reached the northern coast of the island, arriving at a long, thin finger of rocky shore at the northeast corner of the island. Inside the rocky point lay a protected white sand beach with shallow, turquoise water lapping the shore. He steered around the point and ran the Zodiac up onto the beach He and Raj jumped out and hauled the Zodiac up onto the sand.

"Why are we stopping here? I don't see anyone," Gage said, looking out across the deserted beach.

"We'll be back in a few minutes." Malik signaled Raj to follow him to the line of palm trees at the rear of the beach.

"Go ahead. I'll be along in a minute," Raj said. He held out his hand to Fabiola. "You want to get out and stretch your legs?"

"Fuck off, asshole. I thought you were someone special. You're just a common criminal."

Stung by her rebuke, Raj backed away from the Zodiac and ran after Malik. He caught up and the two walked into the palm grove. Malik stopped and turned to look northward, past the boat resting at the water's edge. "I hoped we'd have run across some fishermen by now. Since we haven't, we'll need to head toward that island in the distance." He pointed toward the east. "I'm pretty sure that's Flores Island. There's a village on the western shore called Golo Mori."

"With the heroin onboard? Don't you think that's risky?"

"Definitely. We should bury it here. Once we get to Golo Mori, you can call Anand and let him know what happened and where it is."

"You want me to call him? You'll be with me, right?"

"No. When we get there, we'll find a medical clinic where we can leave Gage. Then I intend to disappear."

"I'm the one who caused the crash, Malik, not you." Raj said. "I'll take responsibility for what happened. You shouldn't have to do that. He'll listen to me."

"No, he won't, Raj. Anand's a psychopath. He doesn't let mistakes go unpunished. Blame what happened on me. Tell him I didn't notice the currents run us off course. Tell him after we crashed onto the rocks, you salvaged two of the trunks, and made me bring you here. Say right after we arrived in Golo Mori, I left to use the phone and disappeared."

"I'm not letting you take all the blame, Malik."

"If I stay, I'm dead. It won't matter which of us takes the blame." He placed his hand on Raj's shoulder. "Listen to me and do what I say, son. Blame what happened on me. Don't put yourself in danger."

"Anand won't hurt me," Raj said. "If you run, he'll hunt you down. He'll find you."

"I'll take my chances. I've known for a while, my only escape from Anand's twisted world was to disappear. Losing *Varuna* has made it more complicated. Nevertheless, I'm going through with it."

Raj nodded. "If he orders me to go after you, I'll refuse. You have my word."

"Thank you." He glanced at the sun, already low on the horizon. "I'm not certain we have enough fuel to make the crossing to Golo Mori. I'd rather do it early in the day when it's more likely we'll be spotted if we do run out. We should stay here for the night and take Gage and Fab with us to Golo Mori in the morning."

Raj nodded. "I'll look for a spot to bury the trunks."

"You're going to abandon us here, aren't you?" Fabiola said, when Malik returned to the boat.

"No. I said we're taking Gage to a doctor, and that's what we intend to do," Malik reassured her. "First, however, we have to unload those trunks. Then we'll have to come to an understanding."

"What kind of understanding?"

He lifted out one of the trunks and set it on the sand. Raj grabbed the handle and dragged it toward the tree line.

"We're facing a dilemma," Malik said. "There's a village on that island across the strait." He pointed toward the outline of an island to the east. "There's a doctor, and you'll be able to get transport to a hospital.

"What's the dilemma?" Fabiola asked.

"If you tell the authorities Raj and I are smugglers, they'll arrest us. Our best option is to leave you here, go across ourselves, and notify them you're here and in need of rescue."

"But you just said you wouldn't do that," Fabiola said.

"We need time to get away." Malik climbed inside the Zodiac and sat across from her. "I need to believe you'll give us that time. A full day. I'd be foolish to believe you won't tell anyone about the heroin, but if we're not convinced you'll delay telling the authorities about us, we'll have no choice but to leave you here."

"If you take us to that village, we won't mention anything about the heroin for one full day," Fabiola said. "I swear it."

Malik smiled wearily. "Thank you. I don't want to risk running out of fuel in the dark, so we'll spend the night here and head for Golo Mori first thing in the morning." He lifted the other trunk out of the boat and dragged it up the beach into the trees.

Raj found a spot to bury the trunks next to a sandy swale surrounded by palm trees. He and Malik dug a pit in the sand with their hands, tumbled the trunks into it, and covered them. Raj swept the area around where they buried them with a palm frond to erase the footprints and drag lines in the sand, and then took a mental picture of the area.

Chapter 21

"Let's head inland here, toward the summit," Ethan suggested, pointing northwest. "Raj said we would come to the ravine and dry creek bed he said looked like the easiest route inland. Hopefully, we'll come across the tree he climbed from where he said he could see the other side."

A forest of tall, fragrant eucalyptus trees lay before them. Below the canopy, the forest was thick with scrub brush, and the ground covered with fallen leaves. Addy knelt beside Nils and loosened the tourniquet around his leg. Blood immediately oozed from the wound. She counted to five, then retightened it.

"Stop! I'll lose my leg," Nils begged.

"I'm sorry, Nils. Unless we stop the bleeding, you'll lose your life," Addy said. She re-secured the end of the stick with the wrap. She went over to Ethan and spoke to him in a hushed tone, "He's lost too much blood. We shouldn't loosen the tourniquet again." She looked inland. "Raj estimated it was eight to ten kilometers to the other side. Nils is too heavy to carry that far."

"You're right," Ethan said. "We'll make a litter to carry him on. Let's find some sturdy saplings. We can use the rope to lash them together."

They found two long saplings and uprooted them, stripped off the branches and wove the line from the

Zodiac between them. Once they'd laid Nils onto it, the group started inland with Ethan carrying the front, Sanjeev and Addy the rear.

After going a couple hundred yards through the trees, they found the ravine that snaked down from the interior of the island to the beach. A dry creek bed led uphill toward the center of the island. Scrambling down into the ravine, they came to a well-worn game trail running through the middle of it and followed it uphill. The trail was mostly free of brush, making carrying the litter a little easier.

After another half mile, they spotted a large tree towering above the surrounding canopy. They laid the litter down to rest, while Sanjeev scrambled up the ravine to check it out. The tree had long buttressing roots extending above ground in each direction, cantilevering the forest giant in the thin soil. Long vines hung from high up in the tree's branches, some reaching all the way to the ground.

"It's a Tualang," Sanjeev said. "This must be the one Raj said he climbed to see the north shore." He grabbed one of the vines and tested his weight. Confident it would hold, Sanjeev climbed up, hand over hand, using his bare feet to grip the vine each time he reached for a higher grip. He made it to a large branch halfway up the tree and stood atop it. The tops of the surrounding trees still blocked his view, so he kept climbing, going branch to branch until he was a hundred feet off the ground.

After taking in all he could see in every direction, Sanjeev climbed back down. Dropping to the ground, he slid down the ridge to where the others awaited his report.

"We can continue following this ridge up the hill. About halfway up it, it looks like there's a ridge running along the eastern slope. From the top of the ridge, we can cut to the right and skirt around the summit at the center of the island. I could see a wide flat beach on the northern shore. Beyond that, I saw the faint outline of a larger island across the channel to the north."

The group resumed up the trail. The farther inland they traveled, the steeper it became. After another couple of kilometers, they were forced to stop to rest. The trees cast long shadows, giving the group a respite from the stifling heat of the afternoon. After a few minutes, they started again. The trail continued to steepen, and their pace slowed. Stepping wearily into a small clearing, they stopped again to rest.

"The trail leading to the ridgetop can't be much farther ahead," Sanjeev said. "I'll scout ahead to find it." He continued up the trail and disappeared.

Addy knelt to examine Nils' leg. He was semiconscious and mumbling incoherently. His foot and lower leg had turned black. Red streaks appeared on his skin above the wound. She waved Ethan over.

"See these red streaks?"

"Infection?"

She nodded. "He's lost too much blood. Between that and the infection, I'm not sure he'll make it much longer. I don't think we'll reach the other side before dark, and it's not a good idea to be stumbling around this forest after dark."

"Agreed," Ethan said. "But I don't like the idea of stopping for the night in the middle of a game trail either."

Addy nodded, “Copy that. Let’s see what Sanjeev found, then we can decide what to do.”

A half hour later, Sanjeev reappeared. “I found a spring,” he said excitedly. “It’s at the base of the ridge, about a kilometer ahead. Once we reach it, it’s only a short climb to the top, then its downhill to the north side.”

With renewed energy, they picked up Nils and started up the trail again. It took a half hour to make it the next quarter mile up the steep ravine. Dragging Nils, every step became more difficult. Their progress slowed to a crawl. The sun had long since dipped below the trees, and their long shadows faded in the dusky light.

“Hold it a second,” Ethan said, setting the litter on the ground. “I stepped on a thorn.” He sat down and carefully pulled it from the heel of his foot. Climbing the cliff face, then trekking through the forest in bare feet left his feet cut, bruised, and swollen. “How much farther to the spring?” he asked.

“Not far,” Sanjeev said. “Maybe another half hour.”

Addy knelt beside Nils and patted his face. “Nils. Nils, wake up.” He didn’t respond. She shook him. Still no response. His breathing was shallow. Addy lifted one of his eyelids. His pupil was rolled back and unresponsive, his skin, pallid and clammy. “He won’t make it much longer,” she said.

“We can’t make it to the spring with Nils,” Ethan said. “You two go on. He won’t survive the night. I’ll stay with him till he passes, and then I’ll catch up.”

“If you stay, we all stay,” Sanjeev said. “I won’t abandon a shipmate.” He looked up at the sky. Dusk had fallen and stars began to fill the night sky. "It's a clear night. I can lead us there in the dark. We'll all wait."

"I'm worried the dragons may have picked up Nils' scent," Addy said. "We should at least get off this game trail."

"This far away?" Sanjeev said.

"They can scent prey for miles," Addy replied.

"If they can scent prey that far away," Ethan said, "I doubt it will matter whether we're on the trail."

"I suppose that's true. Still," She shook Nils again, this time more vigorously. "Nils, wake up. Nils!" Nils didn't respond. Addy got up, then went over and sat next to Ethan and put her arm on his shoulder. "I'm sorry for all this. I checked Malik's references. I guess I didn't dig deep enough."

"It's not your fault," Ethan said. "If Nils hadn't done what he did to Richard, none of this would've happened. We probably never would have even known about the heroin."

"I guess. Of all the things I thought might go wrong, I never would've imagined something like this."

"No one could have imagined this," Sanjeev said. "I've known Malik for years. He was a good and honest man. I think he still is. I'm sure he'll send for help." Sanjeev walked around the edge of the small clearing. "There's nothing but thick brush off this trail," he said.

"Looks like we're staying here, then," Addy said. "I guess I'd rather be able to see what's around me than be blind in that thorny scrub," She laid back and looked up at the sky. "It's going to be a beautiful night."

****

Sanjeev tapped Ethan on the shoulder, and he

awoke with a start. The forest was alive with the croaking tree frogs, the rhythm of insects, and the calls of night birds. It was pitch dark, the sky ablaze with stars. Sanjeev nodded toward Nils and shook his head.

Ethan carefully unhinged his arm from around Addy's neck and crept over to where Nils lay. Ethan felt his forehead, then for his carotid artery. Nils' forehead was cold as clay and he had no pulse. Ethan looked back toward Addy. Seeing she'd also awakened, he shook his head and said, "He's gone."

Addy sat up and nodded. "I wish I had some kind words to say…but I don't."

Sanjeev began quietly gathering stones and brush and laid them over Nils' body. Ethan and Addy helped until his body was covered.

Placing the last stone, Sanjeev said, "Whether he deserved it or not, I admire you both for trying to save him in spite of what he did to Richard. You risked your lives. It's good karma we stayed with him to the end and gave him the best burial we could."

"We're due for some good karma." Ethan glanced around the clearing, searching for a landmark he might remember, figuring they'd have to come back to retrieve Nils' body. Ethan couldn't pick out anything remarkable about the area in the dark, however, so after a final glance toward the pile of stones and brush, he turned and followed Addy and Sanjeev toward the spring.

Chapter 22

"There's a boat heading toward us," Raj said, standing in the bow of the Zodiac and shielding his eyes from the glare of the morning sun. They'd spent the night on the beach to avoid the risk of a night crossing, awakened with the sun, and were headed east toward Golo Mori. They'd been on the water for an hour when they spotted the boat. "It's coming fast. Do you think it's a patrol boat?"

"I don't think so," Malik said, seeing the tall sport-fishing poles extending from each side of the approaching boat. As it neared, he could discern more detail. A large bearded man stood at the helm. The sudden recognition sent a chill up Malik's spine. Hope turned to despair. He collapsed on the bench and cut back on the throttle. *This can't be happening.*

The fast-approaching boat was on a collision course with the Zodiac.

"Watch out!" Raj shouted.

Just before colliding with the Zodiac, it veered sharply and passed to the starboard side. The wake of the boat washed over the Zodiac, drenching its four passengers. The Zodiac rocked wildly and sent Gage reeling against the side. He cried out in anguish as the jagged bone again gouged his wound. The big powerboat made a wide turn and bore down on them again, veering at the last moment, once more rocking the Zodiac and sending a wake washing over it.

The boat was a gleaming twenty-five-foot Boston Whaler-type sport-fishing boat, powered by twin jet-black two-hundred-fifty horsepower outboard engines. It made another loop, then slowed and idled toward the nearly inundated Zodiac.

"What do you know?" Anand Priya said, standing with his arms resting atop the windshield. "It's my good friend Malik and my trusted young protégé Raj. What a coincidence running into you two out here in the middle of nowhere."

Eko maneuvered the powerboat up alongside the Zodiac. A third man, another of Anand's henchmen, called Nur, grabbed the line running along the top of Zodiac's tube with a gaff hook and pulled it alongside the powerboat. Eko killed the engines, picked up a Kalashnikov and pointed it at Raj.

"Lucky for you, though. It appears you're lost. The ship you were supposed to make my delivery to was in that direction," Anand said mockingly, pointing southwest.

"*Varuna* hit a reef and sank, Anand," Malik said. "This man was injured, and we're taking him to a doctor." He pointed toward Gage.

Anand craned his neck to look down in the Zodiac. Gage sat in the hull, leaning against the side, water sloshing almost to his neck. Fabiola sat near him, on the inflatable tube, drenched, seawater dripping from her hair. "And the merchandise I entrusted to you?" Anand said. "I don't see it."

"We—"

Anand cut him off, "I already know you were near the drop-off point and left without delivering it."

How could Anand possibly have known where we were? Malik's mind raced. "Listen, Anand, and I'll explain. There was a diving accident the night we were to make the delivery. We were forced to turn around to get the injured man to the compression chamber on Bali."

Anand laughed out loud. "You're as bad a liar as you are a navigator. Bali is that way," he said, pointing in the direction from which they were coming. "Is that him?"

"No," Malik fumbled to explain, "that was another man. He died. This man was injured when *Varuna* hit the reef.

"Hmm, seems like a lot of people around you were getting hurt. Is that it, or is there more?"

"You can plainly see this man is injured. We're taking him to a doctor. At the village at Golo Mori. On Flores Island."

"Bali, Golo Mori, get your stories straight, Captain." Anand turned his attention to Raj. "You," he pointed a long, thin finger, "of all the people I suspected might betray me, I never imagined it would be you. I treated you like a son."

Raj glared back but said nothing.

"Listen, Anand," Malik said. "No one's betrayed you. We were stranded on an island. We took the Zodiac to get this man to a doctor and secure your merchandise."

Anand ignored him, keeping his attention on Raj. "I'm waiting. Let's hear your lies."

"You've already closed your mind," Raj shot back. "I'll say nothing while you allow that fat monkey to point a gun at me."

"It's the truth," Malik insisted. "We intended to call you once we got to a phone."

"I bet you did. It's a good thing I had a moment of doubt when you said you wanted out. Do you know how I know you're lying, *Captain*? I put a homing device in one of the bags. Guess you didn't count on that when you hatched your plot, did you?"

"Goddammit, Anand, there's no plot," Malik said.

"Imagine my surprise when my customer said you never showed up. I called the satellite phone on your boat. It rang and rang. Sure enough, when I turned my tracking device on, it showed my merchandise moving away from the rendezvous point. Eko and I flew to an airstrip on Flores. I got this boat to track it, *and you*, down." Anand pointed in the direction from which they'd just come. "Its last location, before it stopped transmitting, was somewhere on that island. If you already sold it, *Captain*, you're a dead man."

"I haven't sold it to anybody," Malik insisted. "If you'd just listen—"

"Shut the fuck up. Both of you, get aboard this boat," Anand ordered. He turned to Eko. "Keep your rifle trained on Raj, and this time, don't let him get the jump on you."

Malik climbed out of the Zodiac and onto the gunwale of Anand's boat. Before he could step down, Eko grabbed him and slung him onto the deck, making sure he never took his gaze, or the rifle he held, off Raj.

Raj climbed aboard and turned to Anand. "Listen—"

Eko blindsided him with the butt of the Kalashnikov, sending Raj reeling to the deck of the boat. Jealous of the attention Anand paid Raj, Eko relished the change in circumstances. "That was just a little taste of what's to come," Eko sneered. He motioned to Nur and barked an order, "Tie them up."

Nur wrenched Raj's hands behind his back, tied them with a zip tie, and shoved him down on the bench. He then tied Malik's arms in the same manner.

"I'm gonna kill you for that, fat monkey," Raj glared up at Eko, then spat blood at Eko's feet.

Eko raised the butt of the rifle again, but Anand stopped him. "That's enough. You leave him to me. Roll up my trousers. I'm going over to the Zodiac to talk to our other guests."

Eko handed the rifle to Nur, then bent down on one knee, pulled the brand-new Top-Siders off Anand's feet, and rolled up the hem of Anand's linen trousers to just below the knees.

Anand climbed into the Zodiac and sat on the bench across from Gage. He pulled the bandage aside to look at the gash on Gage's forehead, then gripped Gage's bandaged shoulder and squeezed. Gage cried out in anguish and struggled to pull away, but Anand pinned him against the side of the boat.

"Leave him alone," Fabiola shouted, grabbing Anand's arm.

Anand reacted instantly. He slapped Fabiola across the face with such force it knocked her over. She splashed down into the hull of the boat. Dazed from the blow, her face stinging, and ear ringing, Fabiola got back up on the bench and stared in silent defiance at Anand.

From the corner of his eye, Anand noticed Raj's flash of anger when he slapped the young girl, and he made a mental note of it. "Don't ever put your hand on me again," Anand told Fabiola with a thin, menacing smile. "Now tell me, who the fuck are you?"

"My name's Fabiola Martinez. He's Gage Tucker. We're part of a film crew that was on that man's boat."

"What happened to him?" Anand said, glancing toward Gage.

"We hit some rocks. The hull buckled, and it broke his arm. Later, when the Zodiac he was riding in capsized, he was raked across the reef."

Anand, leered, staring at her chest. Fabiola's T-shirt was soaked, her nipples showing through. "Where's the rest of your party?" he demanded.

Fabiola crossed her arms, covering her breasts. "Stranded on an island, back that direction."

"Do you know anything about my merchandise?"

She shook her head. "All I know is, Raj took two trunks out of the hold of the ship as it was going down and loaded them into one of the Zodiacs. They buried them on that island." She pointed in the direction they'd traveled."

"Raj, huh? You two are on a first-name basis?"

"That's his name, isn't it?"

Anand smirked. He stood up and looked over at Malik. "Where exactly on the island did they bury them?"

"I was in the Zodiac and couldn't see exactly. They dragged them into the trees behind the beach."

"How many trunks did you say?"

"Two."

Anand nodded smugly and climbed back into the fishing boat. "Hit him," Anand ordered Eko.

Eko grabbed Malik, yanked him to his feet, and punched him in the stomach. The blow lifted Malik off the ground. Malik doubled over and fell to his knees, gasping for breath. Eko grabbed a shock of his hair and yanked him to his feet, then back-fisted him across the face, sending Malik reeling to the deck.

Anand stood over Malik. "We're all going to that island to recover my merchandise. If we get there and find only two of my trunks, we'll continue this conversation until you tell me where you've hidden the other two." He turned to Eko. "Tie a line to the bow of the Zodiac. We'll tow it."

"What about them two?" Eko gestured toward Gage and Fabiola. "You want I should dump them out?"

"Not yet. They might still be useful."

Chapter 23

"Listen." Sanjeev hesitated. He was in the lead, as he, Addy and Ethan made their way in the dark. "Can you hear that?"

Addy craned her ears. "Trickling water." She smiled and squeezed Ethan's hand. "The spring must be just ahead."

"Yes," Sanjeev said. "Follow me. There's fresh water and a place we can rest."

Ethan and Addy followed him up a short slope to a large boulder at the base of a hill. A tiny spring bubbled from underneath it, forming a small pool. The water trickled from the pool and over another ledge a few feet away. Soft grass covered the area around the spring.

"Come. Drink. It's cool and clear," Sanjeev said, waving them over. The light from the crescent moon sparkled on the surface of the small pool.

"You first," Ethan said.

"I drank some earlier, so you two first, please," Sanjeev said, graciously.

Addy dropped to her stomach and drank her fill. "Sweetest water I ever tasted." She wiped her chin with the back of her arm and rolled aside for Ethan.

After drinking, Ethan cupped his hands in the water and splashed his face. He crawled over beside Addy and rolled to his back, looking up at the stars. The forest had become quiet except for the occasional call of a nightjar and the gurgling of the spring.

"Did Nils ever say why he did it?" Sanjeev asked after he'd taken a drink.

"No," Addy replied. "He never actually admitted how or why he did it."

"Too bad. I hoped he'd want to clear his conscience."

"He did it because he wanted the grant money for himself," Ethan said. "And because he was jealous of Richard. I don't think the man had a conscience."

"It was *Varuna* who exacted his punishment on Nils."

"What are you talking about?" Ethan said.

"*Varuna*, the god with a thousand eyes. He exacted his judgment for what Nils did to Richard. *Varuna* can change shapes, and become other creatures. He became Ora. He became the Komodo dragon that attacked Nils."

"I do like the thought of that," Ethan said. "But what about Richard? He didn't do anything to deserve what happened."

"Richard was already dead when the Ora consumed him," Sanjeev said.

"Maybe we're all being punished," Addy said.

"It's because of me," Ethan said, sullenly. "We're all here because of me. Once again I've led people into danger. All this is my fault."

"None of this is your fault. Enough of this morose talk, we need to cheer up. We've made it through some long odds. We'll make it to the north coast tomorrow morning and flag down a boat. We'll alert the authorities, and put out a search for Gage and Fab. I get the feeling Malik is a good guy trapped in a bad circumstance. I'm sure he won't harm either of them."

"I don't think so either," Sanjeev said. "Before all this happened, Malik was the person I most respected. He taught me everything I know about sailing."

"We are talking about the guy who left us stranded to face those dragons, or Ora, whatever in the hell you want to call them."

"Even so, I don't think he'll harm them," Addy said again. "Anyway, rest is what we need right now. I'll take the first watch. I'll wake you in a few hours."

****

The sun was well above the horizon when the three started once again toward the north coast of the island. They continued up the trail to a point where another trail diverged off it to the right, and followed it up the ridge Sanjeev spotted the afternoon before. After a short hike along the tree-covered ridge, patches of blue appeared through the canopy.

They entered a small clearing at the edge of a steep embankment. Standing at the precipice, they looked northward across a green carpet of treetops as the land fell away toward the coast. Beyond the beach lay the turquoise waters of a calm sea. Across the strait, they could make out the hazy outline of a larger island.

"Beautiful!" Addy said. "It can't be much more than a quarter mile to the shore."

"I see boats," Ethan said, pointing toward the right side of the beach. "Over there, near that long spit of rocks."

Their hearts leaped at the sight of two boats resting in the calm water on the right side of the beach, just inside a rocky finger-like outcropping that extended from the eastern shore of the island.

"There are people as well," Sanjeev said. "To the left of the boats."

"Awesome!" Addy said. "Let's find a trail off this ridge and get the hell off this island!"

"Wait," Sanjeev said. He shielded his eyes from the sun with one hand and squinted toward the shore below.

"What is it?" Ethan asked.

"One of those men is huge. He's standing over someone lying on the sand. Oh no, he's kicking him." Sanjeev had the practiced eyes of a sailor and took pride in his ability to identify far-off objects at sea. "Look over there," he pointed. "See that person to the left of the others? He has something wrapped around his head. Is that Gage? Yes, it must be. The one being kicked is Malik. The one on his knees must be Raj."

"Are you sure?" Ethan said, shading his eyes and straining to see what Sanjeev described.

"He's right," Addy said. "It's them."

Sanjeev surveyed every detail of the scene below. "There's a guy with a rifle," he said. "The smaller boat on the right must be our Zodiac."

"Oh my God, Ethan. Look over there," Addy pointed toward a slender man in a white shirt. The man shoved Gage over with his foot, then stepped on his shoulder.

"Motherfuckers," Ethan said. "We have to do something."

"I agree, but what? They have guns." Sanjeev said.

"They could be the men who own the drugs Malik was carrying," Addy said.

Sanjeev pointed again. "Look. At the back edge of the beach. Those two black things on the sand."

"Must be the heroin. We need to back away from this ledge," Ethan said. "The last thing we need is for them to see us up here."

They backed away from the edge of the clearing and knelt.

"Gage and Fab are in trouble because of me," Ethan said. "I have to go down there."

"Wait a minute." Addy took hold of his hand. "We all want to save Gage, but it won't help if you end up captured as well. Or worse. We need a plan."

"I'm the one that got him into this mess," Ethan said. "I can't sit idle while he's being hurt."

"We won't," Addy said, keeping hold of his arm. "But we need to think this through."

"We need to think fast. Those men might kill them at any moment."

"What if we had something to bargain with?" Addy asked. "Sanjeev, do you think we could drag those trunks away without being seen?"

Sanjeev crawled over to the ledge again. He surveyed the area around the trunks and then crept back. He shook his head. "No. They're in plain view."

"What if I tell them I have the other fifty kilos?" Ethan said. "Malik said there was a hundred kilos in the hold, but Raj only salvaged two of the trunks before it flooded. I'll say I can lead them to where the rest is hidden in exchange for releasing Gage and Fab."

"We don't know that's what they want," Addy said. "Even if it is, you don't have the rest of the drugs." She crept over to the ledge and looked up and down the beach. Just to the right of the boats, on the other side of the spit, was the eastern shore of the island. She motioned to Ethan to come over. "What if we could steal the boats?" she said. "We may be able to sneak over from those rocks along the shore on the right and get away before they could get to us. We could bargain them for Gage."

"The boats are in plain sight. They'd shoot us before we could get away," Ethan said.

"Yeah, you're right," she said. Another idea popped into her head. "But maybe we could take the keys."

"How?"

She pointed to the area to the right of the beach. "The area behind the beach is hidden from their view by the trees. I can go down through the forest and swim out to the point at the end of the spit. Once there, I can swim inside the bay to the boats. If I can make it without being spotted, I can take the keys to both boats. Then we'd have something to bargain with to get them to release Fab and Gage."

"They'd see you as soon as you rounded that point. Even if you could, what if the keys aren't in them? I'm going down there."

Sanjeev stepped in front of Ethan, "Being reckless won't help, Ethan. We must have a plan."

"I won't sit by while my friends are in danger. Too many people have been hurt following my lead. I won't let either of you risk your lives as well."

"It's suicide, Ethan," Addy said, "and it won't get them rescued. Listen to me. I think this plan can work. I can swim underwater from the point to the boats. They won't see me if I'm underwater."

Ethan looked again down toward the beach. "It's at least a hundred yards from the end of the spit to the beach. Even you can't hold your breath that long. Even if you make it, they'd see you as soon as you try to get keys."

"Not if you distract them. I can make it most of the way underwater. If you can hold their attention, they won't see me in the water or when I get to the boats."

"What if the keys aren't even inside? What if they're in their pockets?"

"I'll find a way to disable the boats. I'll swim back around the point, and we'll have our bargaining chip to use to free Gage."

Ethan considered her idea. Addy was the better swimmer, but it was too much of a long shot. "I don't want to put you in that kind of danger. I'd never forgive myself if something happened to you."

"I don't want to lose you either," she said. "But I won't let you do this alone."

"She's right Ethan. We're all in this together," Sanjeev said.

They all crawled back over to the ledge to survey the scene on the beach again. Ethan nodded. "It just might work. Okay, I'll give you time to swim on the ocean side of the spit out to the point. Once I see you're at the end, I'll walk out on the beach and draw their attention. When I do, you can round the point and swim underwater to the boats."

"What are you going to say?" Sanjeev asked.

"I don't know, but I'll think of something. I'm a journalist—that's what I do. I'll keep their attention focused on me as long as I can. Hopefully, it'll be long enough for you to take the keys and swim back around the point. Then I'll tell them we have something we want to trade."

"I'll go down to those rocks where I can see you

both," Sanjeev said. "If something goes wrong, I'll draw their attention. Maybe it will scare or confuse them. I can at least try to improve the odds for you."

"Good. I hope your sea god will be watching after us," Ethan said.

"I'm sure he will," Sanjeev said.

Chapter 24

Eko picked up a handful of sand, grabbed Malik by the hair, and jerked his head back. He clasped the sand over Malik's nose and mouth and held it while Malik struggled to breathe. Eko let go and laughed as Malik rolled over on his side, coughing furiously, trying to spit out the sand coating his mouth and tongue. Malik's hands were zip-tied behind his back and his face bruised and swollen from the beating Eko had given him.

"Damnit, Eko," Anand said in mock annoyance. "How do you expect him to talk with a mouthful of sand?" He knelt beside Malik, rolled him up to a seated position and brushed away some of the sand from his face. "I must admit, Captain," Anand said, gazing out at the idyllic beach and turquoise waters beyond. "You chose a lovely spot to hide the drugs you stole from me. I could stay and enjoy this sunshine all day." He looked once again at Malik. "You don't look so good, my friend. Would you like some water?" He shouted to his henchman, "Nur, fetch some water."

Nur hurried to their boat, grabbed a bottle of water from the cooler, and brought it to Anand.

Anand uncapped the bottle and took a long swig, draining half. "Ahh, refreshing." He wiped his mouth with the back of his forearm. "Oh, sorry. How rude of me. Did you want some?"

Malik spat out more sand. "Fuck you, Anand."

"I regret all this ugliness, my old friend. Really I do. Abandon this ridiculous story and tell me where the rest of my merchandise is. I'll give you some water and let you go. Hell, I'll even let you take the Zodiac. All will be forgiven. Just tell me where you've hidden the other two trunks."

"Okay, Anand, you've got a deal. I'll take you right to the spot where *Varuna* went down. You can swim down and carry them up yourself."

Anand smacked him across the face with the back of his hand, then stood and rubbed his knuckles. "You know what disappoints me the most?" He said, glancing toward Raj, kneeling on the sand a few feet away. Raj's hands were also bound behind his back with plastic zip-ties. "Except for Raj's betrayal, that is. It's that you think I'm stupid enough to believe you. I caught you red-handed, yet you cling to this charade. You two must have been plotting this heist since the day I told you about it."

"Why would I sink my own boat? It's all I had left I cared about."

"I can think of five million reasons why."

"Why would they lie?" Malik gestured toward Gage and Fabiola. "They've told you the same as I."

"Oh, I don't think they're lying. You probably fooled them as well. You thought they'd provide you cover."

"You're fucking psychotic."

Anand drew the 9mm from the holster in the small of his back, pressed it against Malik's cheek, and cocked the hammer. Malik gazed ahead with an emotionless, blank stare. Anand recovered his composure and holstered the gun. “I’m not psychotic,” he said defensively. “I’m just angry, like the victim of any theft would be.”

Malik laughed out loud. “I’m the one with my hands tied, yet you’re the victim.”

Anand stood up and looked over at Raj. “I think Raj is jealous you’re getting all my attention,” he said, patting Malik on the shoulder. “But don’t fret, my friend. I’ll be back.”

“Why are you doing this?” Raj said, when Anand knelt beside him. “I almost drowned swimming into the flooded hold of that ship to rescue your fucking heroin.”

“Even if what you say is true, you still failed me. You knew these Macao Chinese were important customers. We were opening a whole new trade route using my fishing trawlers and processing ships. They showed trust by paying me half in advance for this first shipment. If I don’t deliver all their merchandise, they’ll expect their money back. And then some.”

“Then give them their goddamn money back. You stole the heroin in the first place.”

“Give the money back?” Anand’s face contorted in disbelief. “I thought I taught you better. We have to deliver. And since we missed the delivery, not just the merchandise. They’ll want blood.” He pointed to Malik. “Oh, sure, I can deliver Malik’s head, but he’s a fucking nobody. They know you’re my protégé. Like my own son.” Anand’s voice cracked. “If we don’t deliver all the merchandise, someone will have to be held to account. It breaks my heart, but that someone will have to be you.”

“You sick bastard.” Raj struggled in vain to free

his arms. “You’d sacrifice me just for money?”

Anand looked down at him quizzically. “Yes. But it’s not just the money. You betrayed me, or failed me. One is as unacceptable as the other.”

“Let me kill this little traitor,” Eko pleaded, “and let’s get out of here.” Eko wore a dark suit, and in the midday heat and humidity, sweat streamed down his face.

“No. You are not to kill Raj. Do you understand, Eko? He’s my responsibility. I have to do it myself.”

Eko smiled at the thought of it. As much as he wanted to kill Raj himself, he relished the thought of Anand putting a bullet in Raj’s head. “What about Malik?” Eko asked. “You believe his story?”

“Hell no. Malik’s story is concocted. Think about it. A seasoned captain and the best smuggler I have, crashing his precious boat on the rocks? He told us they were heading for Bali, but we found him going in the opposite direction. To top it off, he buried two of the trunks here on this deserted island in the middle of nowhere.”

“Where’d they hide the other two?” Eko asked.

“That’s what we’re trying to find out, idiot.”

“Okay, boss. Let me work on Malik some more. I’ll make him talk.”

“Remember, we need him alive. For now.” He looked over at Gage. “Maybe *he* knows something. But just doesn’t know he knows it.”

“Huh?”

“Never mind. Go work on Malik,” Anand said. Eko started toward Malik, but Anand grabbed his massive arm. “I’m serious, Eko. Don’t kill him.”

“I won’t, boss. Yet.”

Anand walked over and knelt on the sand beside Gage and Fabiola. Barely conscious and severely dehydrated, Gage leaned against Fabiola, and her hand shielded his face from the midday sun.

Anand patted Gage's face. "Wake up, Gage Tucker. Let's go over this again."

"We've told you everything we know," Fabiola said. "He needs a doctor."

"Yes, yes, of course. I'll take him to one myself. I just need some information first." Anand slapped Gage's face harder.

Gage groaned and opened his eyes.

"Tell me, Gage Tucker, did you actually ever see any other trunks, like those?"

Gage stared glassy-eyed at Anand for a couple of seconds, then closed his eyes again, and his head rolled back.

Anand grabbed his face and turned it toward the two black trunks lying in the sand a few feet away. "Did you see any others?" he said again.

Gage opened his eyes, then shook his head. "No."

Anand slapped him again, "tell me once more what happened."

Gage licked his dry lips and took a breath. "The captain's boat hit some rocks. It was taking on water. We had to abandon it. In the two Zodiacs."

"Where were those two when it happened?" Anand gestured toward Malik and Raj.

"Up on the bridge maybe. I don't know. Raj might have been with the girl."

"Girl? What girl?" He poked Gage's injured shoulder.

"Stop it," Fabiola said. "Me. He meant me."

"Why would he have been with you?"

Fabiola stared back in a defiant silence, so Anand patted Gage's injured arm to wake him up again. "Why would he have been with the *girl*?"

"They had a thing, I guess," Gage said, weakly. "All I know is"—he licked his lips again—"after we hit the reef, Raj dragged two large trunks from the hold. He and Malik loaded them into one of the Zodiacs."

"They told us they were survival supplies," Fabiola said.

"A thing, huh?" He raised an eyebrow. "You saw the boat sink?"

"No," Gage answered. "I must have passed out."

"I did," Fabiola said. "I saw it sink."

"Where are the others in your party?"

"I already told you," she said. "Stranded on an island. I think it might be this one. The other side. It has tall bluffs battered by surf."

"Did you ever see either of those two leave in one of the Zodiacs before the boat supposedly sank?"

"Several times," Fabiola answered. They used the Zodiacs to ferry us back and forth to dive sites every day. Raj sometimes drove one of the Zodiacs."

"Now we're getting somewhere. Are you in on their plot to steal my heroin?"

"No," Fabiola said.

"Maybe he told you he'd share some of the money with you? That you two would run off and live like a little prince and princess."

"Like hell, I would."

Anand grabbed her arm. "You see that big guy over there? If I find out you're lying to me, I'll tell him to drag you to the water and drown you. Understand?"

"I'm not lying. We've told you everything we know," Fabiola said. "We're of no value to you. Please let us go."

"Oh, you'll be of value to me, I assure you, pretty little lady." Anand's smile made Fabiola shudder. "You come from money," he said. "I can tell. I bet your daddy's rich and will pay a pretty sum to get his little girl back." He looked over at Raj. "Besides, you don't want to leave now things are beginning to get interesting."

Chapter 25

Ethan, Addy, and Sanjeev made their way down from the ridge toward the eastern shore of the island. They emerged from the trees well south and out of sight of the beach and made their way across the rocks down to the water's edge. Addy studied the rocky finger of land jutting out from the island along the eastern edge of the island. It appeared to be about a quarter mile out to the point at the end of the spit. She tossed a twig into the water. The current carried it southward. "Damn," she said. "I'll have to swim against the current."

"How long do you think it will take you to swim to the point?" Ethan asked.

"Against this current, I'd guess twenty minutes."

"Once you get to that far rock at the point, you should have a clear view of the beach," Ethan said. "With any luck, you'll be able to see me come out of the trees. If you can, wait to start your underwater swim until you see I have their attention." He looked at his watch. "If you can't see me, start your swim at eleven sharp. That should give me plenty of time to get over to the tree line and walk out onto the beach.

Addy looked at her dive watch and nodded. "That's twenty-five minutes from now," she said.

"I'll be in those rocks right over there," Sanjeev said as he pointed to a jumble of boulders. He shook Ethan's hand, then Addy's. "Good luck to you both."

"Thanks, Sanjeev," Ethan said.

"You be careful," Addy told Ethan. "I'll never forgive you if you get yourself killed."

Ethan squeezed her hand. "I won't forgive me either. If you see things going awry, get the hell out of there."

Addy stripped down to her swimsuit, handed her T-shirt and shorts to Sanjeev, and slipped into the water. She shoved off, took a breath, and started swimming toward the point. With no swim goggles or facemask, the salt water stung her eyes and blurred her vision. She took a breath with every other stroke, each time looking to her left, judging her distance, staying close to the rocks to remain out of sight of the men on the beach.

After swimming only a hundred feet, she became winded. She switched to breaststroke to catch her breath. Not able to make forward progress in the strong current, she took a few deep breaths to calm herself, and switched back to the crawl. She dug deep and kicked hard with each stroke, and again began to inch out forward progress. At each gap between rocks, she dove and swam underwater to the next one, keeping out of sight of the beach on the other side of the spit. She caught her second wind, and feeling stronger with each stroke, made a final push to reach the end of the spit. Diving under, she made four long body strokes and surfaced behind the lone rock at the end of the point. She looked at her watch, five to eleven.

Addy inched around the rock and peered toward the beach, a hundred yards away. The men on the beach were about thirty feet to the right of the boats. The bow of the Zodiac was pulled up onto the beach. A few feet to its right, the stern of the fishing boat was anchored in shallow water just offshore. A bowline extended onto the beach, held by a stick driven into the sand. The boat's two large outboard engines were tilted forward, their propellers just above the waterline.

Addy visualized the underwater swim she had to make, hoping the water behind the fishing boat was deep enough to swim submerged to its stern. She took several long, slow breaths to ventilate her lungs—in through her nose, out through her mouth. *You can do this, Addy. Skim along the bottom, count fifty long strokes and kicks. Leave yourself enough breath to surface slow and quiet. Take a breath, drop down again and keep going.* She scanned the beach. *Where are you, Ethan?*

Even though the water was crystal clear, Addy knew everything would be a blur with no face mask. The seafloor appeared to be nothing but white sand, no features to keep her on course. She knew she'd have to stay left, within sight of the rocks. Straying to the right meant she would surface in plain view of the men. Anything just under the surface might be seen from the beach, so she knew she'd have to skim along the bottom the entire distance.

There he is! Ethan appeared at the tree line at the back of the beach. He looked in her direction, paused, then walked out onto the beach. *Now or never, Addy!* She focused on relaxing her body and emptied her mind of all thoughts except her breath. She took a final deep breath, dropped below the surface, and shoved off with both feet. She swam to the bottom. It was deeper than she hoped. Thirty feet, she estimated. She counted her strokes. Her arms shot forward like a spear, then came together at her sides, followed by a frog kick with her long legs. She skimmed along, counting her strokes, torpedoing just above the sandy bottom.

Can't see shit! Damn, if only I had goggles. She counted each stroke, *twenty-five, twenty-six, twenty-seven...Goddammit! I can't make fifty strokes. What was I thinking? You're not a twenty-year-old anymore.* The swim against the current had taken more out of her than she expected; her lungs burned, demanding she surface for air. She arched her back and rose slowly toward the surface. Suppressing the urge to take a deep, gasping breath, Addy surfaced just enough to bring her eyes above the water line. She blinked to clear her vision. Ethan stood facing the men; his arms held high above his head. One of the men pointed a rifle.

She exhaled and rose enough to take three deep breaths, holding the last one in and swam to the bottom again. *Calm your mind. Too much adrenaline. Slow your heart rate. A third of the way. You can do it.* The bottom was now only about twenty feet deep and rising with each stroke. *Thirty-five, thirty-six, thirty-seven...Have to surface!* Addy rose to the surface, again raising only her eyes above the waterline and looked toward the shore. Ethan knelt on the sand; his arms behind his head. *Shit!* She'd drifted too far right. She ducked under the surface without taking a breath and swam left. Unable to suppress her need for air any longer, she exhaled, rose slowly to the surface and took a quick breath, then ducked under again. The water was only ten feet deep and getting shallower with each stroke.

I must be close! Where are those fucking boats? She hugged the bottom, her chest brushing over the sand. She let out precious air to keep from bobbing to the surface, and her need for air became more urgent with each stroke. The water was now three feet deep and the back of the fishing boat nowhere in sight. She focused on controlling her growing panic. Surfacing in plain view meant they could all be killed.

Don't think about that! She turned her thoughts to Ethan's deep blue eyes, the shape of his lips when he smiled, his shaggy brown hair, his long legs. *Oh, those muscular legs. Where's the goddamn boat? Shit. I must still be too far left.* She swam to the right, and after a few strokes, a dark shape appeared. *Concentrate. Almost there. Hold it. Three more strokes. Two, one...* She let out all her breath and surfaced. The twin props of the two outboard engines were right above her.

Safely hidden from view between the two outboard motor props, Addy rested for several moments, and caught her breath. *Don't make a sound, or even the slightest ripple in the water*, she told herself. She inched to the right edge of the stern and peeked around. No one ran her direction. *I did it!* Feeling a surge of pride, she told herself; *stay focused, so far, so good.* Addy surveyed the scene: Gage and Fabiola were the nearest to her. Farther up the beach were the three men with Ethan. Twenty feet from them was Malik. A few feet to his left was Raj. Both sat on the sand with their hands tied behind their backs.

She backed away from the right edge of the stern and pulled herself through the shallow water to the Zodiac, partially obscured from view of the people of the beach by the higher profile of the fishing boat. She crept behind the Zodiac and spotted the orange key fob hanging from the faceplate of the Zodiac's outboard engine. She grabbed the key and slipped it into the back of her bathing suit bottom, then slipped back into the water.

Addy pulled herself through the shallow water around again to the stern of the fishing boat and once more peeked around it. Ethan's face was turned toward her, and everyone else on the beach had their back to her, facing Ethan. Addy tilted her head from behind the boat, and Ethan's gaze immediately shifted toward her. Addy quickly ducked back. *He saw me!*

"The Indonesian navy is on their way here right now," Addy heard Ethan say loudly. *Way to go, Ethan. It's go time, Addy.* She slipped back around to the side of the fishing boat, climbed up and over the boat's gunwale, and slid down into the hull. Feeling the boat rock, she froze. *Easy, boat...Calm down...Please stop rocking. That's it, easy now.*

She closed her eyes and listened for sounds of men running her way. Hearing nothing, she peeked over the gunwale. No one was coming her way, but Ethan was sprawled face down on the sand. The huge man knelt over him, his knee on Ethan's back. *Must hurry.* She ducked back down and crept to the captain's seat. She found the throttle where the key would be. *Shit! No key. What now? Think, Addy, think! Pull the spark plug wires? Can't do that without opening both breastplates. Battery? No, too big. Fuse? Do outboards even have them?*

She looked around the boat, desperate for an idea. A long rubber hose led from a gas tank up to the two outboard engines. *Fuel line!* She disconnected the hose in front of the splitter, then pulled the other end loose from the top of the gas tank and looped the four-foot rubber hose around her waist and tied it in an overhand knot.

She peeked over the side one more time and, seeing the men still distracted by Ethan, crept back to the port side and slid out into the waist-deep water. She held the side of the boat long enough to keep it from rocking. Addy's heart pounded, distraught by the image of Ethan face down in the sand. *Can't think about that. Focus on the plan!* She ventilated her lungs with several long breaths. *Fifty long strokes, Addy.* She felt for the key in her bathing suit bottom, then tightened the fuel line wrapped around her hips. She took in a deep breath and held it, and slipped beneath the surface.

Chapter 26

Ethan quickened his pace through the thinning forest. Nearing the tree line, he slowed and crouched. He crept up behind a large palm and peeked around it, looked past the boats and the water beyond toward the point, but didn't have a clear view of it. *No sign of Addy.* He looked at his watch. *Five to eleven.*

He waited five minutes. S*howtime.* He took a deep breath and stepped out of the forest onto the beach. He raised his arms over his head and shouted. "Don't shoot. I'm unarmed."

"What the…" Anand spun toward the sound of the voice. Quick as lightning, he drew his 9mm semiautomatic and pointed it. In the same instant, Nur dropped to one knee and aimed his Kalashnikov at Ethan.

Ethan raised his arms higher, "Don't shoot," he said again, taking another tentative step.

"Who are you?" Anand called out.

"My name's Dayne. Ethan Dayne." Ethan continued toward the men, taking slow, deliberate steps.

"What do you want?" Anand motioned to Nur, who got up from his crouched position and strode briskly toward Ethan, keeping his rifle aimed as he approached.

Ethan stopped and did a slow, deliberate 360-degree turn to show he had no weapon. "I'm a documentary filmmaker, and those two are part of my crew." He lowered one arm enough to point toward Gage and Fabiola. Nur circled behind Ethan and poked him in the ribs with the barrel of his assault rifle, shoving him forward toward Anand.

"How'd you get here?" Anand scanned the tree line looking for signs of anyone else.

"I walked from the other side of the island."

"Where's the rest of your crew?" Anand demanded.

"Back on the other side. The ship we were on, the one belonging to that other man over there, hit a reef." He pointed toward Malik. "They took that Zodiac and left us stranded. I walked here to look for help. Who are you?"

"I'm the one with the gun, so I'll ask the questions. So, Mr. Ethan Dayne. It took a lot of balls to walk out here like that. What the fuck do you want?"

"My cameraman needs medical attention. I'm going to take that Zodiac, get him to a doctor, and alert someone to rescue the rest of my crew."

Anand laughed. "Just like that? You walk out here like you own the fucking beach and tell me you're taking my boat?"

"Listen, mister. We have nothing to do with whatever business you have with those other two gentlemen. I only intend to take my friends and leave." There was something familiar about the man's face. Ethan was sure he'd seen it somewhere before.

"Like hell you are. Search him," Anand ordered.

Nur, a thin, pockmarked man, kept his assault rifle pointed with one hand while he rummaged through the pockets of Ethan's board shorts with his free hand. Ethan had no shirt on, so it was a quick search.

"Nuthin."

"Have you radioed for help?" Anand asked.

"Yes. The authorities are on their way. There's no place to land safely on the other side, so I told them to meet me here."

"I know who you are," Anand said. "You're that fucking war correspondent. For a guy who lies for a living, you're not very good at it. If they're coming here, why do you need the Zodiac?"

"You can see he's been gravely injured and needs medical attention right away. I'd prefer not to wait." Ethan remembered where he'd seen the man's face: in photos he'd studied of organized crime members involved in the illegal fishing trade.

Eko turned and scanned the waters of the strait. "If someone's coming, we better get out of here, boss."

"He's bluffing," Anand said. "No one's coming." He paused for a few seconds. "Tell you what, Dayne. We'll take you and your friend to a doctor." Anand motioned Eko over and leaned in close to his ear. "Tie this jackass up and put him in the Zodiac. Put Malik and the hurt guy in with him, but I want the girl in the boat with us. Once we're well offshore, kill the three of them and put enough holes in the Zodiac to make sure it sinks."

"What about them other trunks?"

"They probably sank as they all claim, or maybe Malik hid them, but we can't wait here all day. Load the two we have in the boat, and let's get the fuck out of here."

"Yes, sir," Eko said. He turned toward Nur. "Gimme one of those zip ties and then go load them two trunks in our boat."

With Eko heading toward him with the zip tie, Ethan started backing away. "Why are you going to tie me up if you're taking us to a doctor?" Just then, Ethan caught notice of movement at the stern of the fishing boat. *Addy!* He took a quick step back to make sure he kept the men's attention. "The Indonesian navy is on its way here right now. I'm a journalist and reporter. Kidnapping me will rain down more trouble on you than you can imagine."

Anand laughed. "Nice try, Dayne. Now, shut the fuck up."

Eko lowered his .45 and grabbed Ethan by the throat. Ethan punched him with a hard right, square on the jaw. Unfazed, Eko smirked and swung his .45, whipping Ethan across the face with the barrel and knocking him down. Dazed and bleeding from the pistol whipping, Ethan stumbled to his knees, but Eko kicked him down again, then drove his knee between Ethan's shoulder blades, crushing him face down in the sand. Eko grabbed Ethan's arms and wrenched them back to put on the zip tie.

"I have your drugs," Ethan coughed out.

"Hold it!" Anand yanked his 9mm out of its holster and was over Ethan in a flash, pressing the barrel against the back of his head. "What did you say?"

"Can't breathe," Ethan gasped.

Anand nodded, and Eko let off a little pressure.

Ethan gasped. "Your heroin. I have the rest of your heroin."

Anand cocked the hammer. "You have only seconds to live. What heroin?"

Ethan fought for breath; Eko's knee smashing him down even harder. "Can't breathe." He gasped. "Let me up…I'll tell you."

"Let him up."

Eko grabbed Ethan by the neck and dragged him to his feet. Ethan's cheek was cut, and blood dripped from his nose. Ethan wiped the blood and crusted sand off his face and glanced again toward the boats. *Must stall for more time.* He leaned over, hands on his knees, and spat on the ground. "Gimme a second."

"I'm done waiting, asshole," Anand demanded.

Ethan's mind raced. He didn't know whether Addy still was inside one of the boats or had gotten what she needed and was back in the water. *Time to go all in.* He stood up. "I have your other two trunks. The ones filled with heroin. Malik and I are partners."

Anand's placid face contorted into an angry scowl and turned red as a beet. He turned toward Malik, his rage like a volcano set to erupt. "You thieving motherfucker," he said under his breath. Anand took a breath to regain his composure and then gave Eko a slight nod. Eko cuffed Ethan's face back and forth with his open hand, then slugged him in the belly.

Ethan crumpled to his knees and rolled to the sand, clutching his stomach, again gasping for breath.

"Wow. I bet that hurt," Anand said. He knelt beside Ethan. "Take your time…Catch your breath. That's it. Breathe."

It took Ethan several breaths to recover.

"Let's take this from the top," Anand said. "So you and Malik are partners. And the two of you conspired to steal my drugs. Is that what you're telling me?"

"Yes."

"So where is it? Where's the other half of my merchandise?"

"Hidden on the other side of this island."

"I was told the other trunks were lost when the boat sank. Your friends over there confirmed it."

"The other two were already off the boat when it sank. That's why Raj only came up with two. I'd already taken my half."

"So why did he take your friends?"

"After the boat sank, the Zodiac I was in capsized in the surf. Raj and I fought over the other one. I lost. They took my crewmates hostage to make sure I lived up to my end of the bargain."

"What bargain?"

"He had the buyer. To make sure I delivered my half."

"So you walked out here to make a bargain with me? Okay, then. What the fuck do you want?"

"If you agree to let my friends and I leave in the Zodiac, I'll tell you where to find it."

"Sure, no problem. You got a deal. Tell me."

"You can follow me. I'll take you to where it's buried."

"You insult me, Dayne. A minute ago, you said you were a journalist and reporter. Now you want me to believe you're a drug thief who's going to lead me on some wild-goose chase? I'm tired of your games. I think I'll just shoot you and get the fuck off this island." Anand pointed his gun at Ethan's face.

Ethan's story was full of holes and wouldn't hold up much longer. He was running out of time. Hoping Addy already made it in and out of the boats; it was time to play his last card. "I have something else of yours."

Anand lowered his gun and looked up at the sky.

"What else of mine could you possibly have?"

"I have the keys to your boats."

"What?" Anand looked over at Nur.

Nur smiled. He took the key to the fishing boat from his pocket, held the keychain with two fingers, and dangled it. "You mean this key?"

"You're full of shit." Anand raised his 9mm and pulled the trigger. The sound of the shot reverberated across the bay. Ethan cried out in anguish, cradled his right arm, and fell to his knees. Blood dripped from the wound in his hand where the bullet passed through it and fell onto the sand in long rivulets.

"Did you see that?" Anand said to Eko.

"Yeah, boss. You missed and hit his hand.

"I didn't miss, dumbass. I meant to hit his hand." Anand shoved Ethan with his foot, tumbling him over on his side, then glanced back at Eko. "I do like these steel-jacketed shells you gave me," he said, matter of factly. "They make a nice clean wound." He turned back toward Ethan, and scowled, "Get up, you piece of shit. I think I'll put the next one through your knee cap."

"Wait!" Ethan grimaced. He tucked his throbbing hand under his left armpit and struggled again to his knees. "One of my crew disabled your boats."

"Anand glanced toward the boats. Seeing nothing unusual, he turned back toward Ethan. "Bullshit."

"Go check them. You'll see it's the truth." Ethan prayed he'd given Addy enough time to get in and out of the boats. He struggled to keep his nerve and think clearly over the searing pain and surging adrenaline.

Anand waved his gun toward the boats. "Nur, go check them," he said with an exasperated sigh. He cast a sarcastic smile at Ethan, "I'll go along with your bullshit a few more seconds, asshole, then I'm going to shoot you in the face."

Nur trotted over to the boats. He looked inside the Zodiac first. "The key's not here," he shouted.

A look of concern replaced Anand's smug smile. He scanned the beach up and down. Nothing but the rocks, sand, and water. "Check the other boat," he barked.

Nur waded out and climbed inside the fishing boat. He took the key from his pocket and put it in the ignition. He put the shifter in neutral and turned the key. The engine started right up.

"Looks like your plot failed," Anand sneered, the smugness returning to his face. "You're about to die."

Ethan wondered if he would feel the bullet. Then came the sweet sound of salvation. The engine sputtered; then it died.

Nur turned the key again. The engine fired up but again sputtered and died. He turned the ignition again. This time it didn't catch. Nur stepped to the back of the boat to check the outboards and saw the problem. "The fuel line's gone!"

"Goddammit," Anand shouted. "Find them! They can't have got far!" He shoved Eko. "You too. Go search those rocks." He turned back toward Ethan. "You are a tricky bastard. I'll give you that. All that talk to keep our attention diverted from the boats." He put the barrel of his gun against Ethan's forehead, "Where are they?"

"Let my friends go, and I'll lead you to the trunks and give you the fuel line."

"I'm going to count to three," Anand shouted. "If

whoever took the key and fuel line doesn't come out, I'm blowing his head off. One…two…" Anand cursed something in Indonesian, then lowered his gun.

"I don't see nobody," Nur shouted from the boat.

"Nothing over here, either," Eko yelled from the rocky spit on the right-hand side of the beach.

She did it! She really did it! Ethan breathed a sigh of relief.

"All right, motherfucker," Anand said. "I'll play your game. What now?"

"By now, the fuel line is being taken to a hiding place up that hill behind us. Only the person who has it and I know where. You and I will go up unarmed. When we get there, my friend will come down with the key to the Zodiac. She'll take my crewmates and leave. You'll order your men not to stop them. Once I see they're safely away in the Zodiac, I'll show you where the fuel line's hidden."

"Her? So it's a she who stole my key and fuel line."

Ethan cursed himself for revealing too much. "That doesn't matter. If you want your boat, you'll do as I say."

"What about the rest of my merchandise?"

"I'll take you to where I buried it."

"How far up the hill is the fuel line hidden?"

"About a twenty-minute walk."

"Can you make it?"

"Give me something to wrap my hand. I'll make it."

"Eko, give him a handkerchief," Anand ordered.

Eko handed Ethan one of the supply of silk handkerchiefs Anand made him carry.

"All right," Anand said, "but Nur's coming with me; and I'll have this," he waved his 9mm at Ethan's face.

Ethan held one end of the handkerchief with his teeth and wrapped the other around his hand. The bullet passed through his hand, nicking the bone of his index finger. He pulled the cloth as tight as the pain would allow, then tucked under the end. He put the hand under his left armpit and held pressure against it to immobilize it and slow the bleeding. He took a breath, looked Anand in the eye, and said, "Follow me."

Anand glanced at Eko, "Keep the others alive for now," he ordered. "But if his friend doesn't show, or if I'm not back in an hour, kill the injured guy." Anand reiterated, "Only the hurt guy, Eko. Don't kill the girl." He looked at Ethan and shrugged. "Sorry, I find I have to be extremely explicit with Eko. He gets excited about killing. Now, lead on, asshole."

"That's not enough time," Ethan protested.

"Then you better get moving up that hill. My sense of compassion, and my patience, is wearing thin. Any tricks and the next bullet will be to your brain. Understand?"

"Understood." Ethan said. He glanced toward Gage and Fabiola and tried to give them a reassuring look. "I'll get you out of this," he shouted.

Chapter 27

Addy swam deeper with each stroke to keep her outline from being spotted in the crystal-clear water, skimming along the bottom as it fell away out from the beach. The sight of Ethan getting beat up by those thugs and the adrenaline of sneaking in and out of the boats had her heart racing. She suppressed the urge to surface. *Relax, Addy. Keep going, nice long strokes.* The din in her head telling her to surface became louder. *A little farther...five more strokes...They might already be looking for you.*

The urge to burst up through the water and take a breath engulfed her. *Don't think about it! Another five strokes!*

Her need for air overwhelmed her. She swam for the surface, turning her body to face the beach when she came up. Fearing she would black out at any moment, she tilted her head, exhaled and brought only her nose and mouth above water. She took a quick breath, ducked back under, expelled it, and surfaced for another. The third time, she rose up a little higher to steal a look toward the beach. The man in white raised his gun and pointed it at Ethan. The crack of the shot reverberated across the water and Ethan crumpled to the ground.

Addy's heart leaped into her throat. She ducked under the water and screamed, the bubbles erupting from her mouth and boiling to the surface. She surfaced again. Ethan was up his knees, cradling his right hand under his armpit. *He's alive! Continue with the plan.* She took a deep breath and sank below the surface. *He must have told them about the boats. They'll be looking for me now.* She swam to the bottom and veered right until the blurry outline of the rocks along the spit appeared. She kept the blurry rocks in sight on her right, and made for the end of the spit. *Too risky to surface before you reach the cover of the rocks. You were a champion once—you can do it. Calm your mind.*

Try as she may to will away her urge to surface, her need to breathe became more and more urgent and the last rock at the tip of the point was still nowhere in sight. She'd trained to recognize the signs of shallow-water blackout, when a free diver pushes beyond their limit, and levels of oxygen in the blood dip too low. A feeling of euphoria means blackout is imminent.

Two eagle rays soared passed her, their spotted wings undulating gracefully in the crystalline water. Addy reached to touch one, but it swam just out of reach. She kicked harder, taking long, powerful strokes, and again extended her hand, but the rays glided just beyond her fingertips, and then banked right in perfect unison. Desperate to keep up, Addy followed, mesmerized by the beauty of their arching wings. The two rays sailed farther and farther ahead, until they were a dark blur, then they disappeared.

Addy's urge to breathe suddenly returned with a vengeance. She burst to the surface and gasped for breath. Terrified she'd exposed herself, she spun around toward the beach. She was past the last rock at the end of the spit and safely out of view from the beach. *I made it!*

She swam to the rock, held tight, and took several recovery breaths. Once her breathing slowed, she pulled herself to the edge and peeked toward the beach. One of the men was inside the fishing boat, standing at the helm. The twin outboards roared to life and revved. Then they sputtered and died. A satisfying smile spread across her face. *That's right, motherfucker. They ain't gonna start.* The man in white barked orders; and the huge man with the braided beard immediately reacted and charged toward the rocks. *They're looking for you now, Addy. You've got the current running with you. Swim deep and fast.*

She took several cleansing breaths, then drifted around the rock to the ocean side of the spit. She took in one last breath and held it, brought both feet against the rock, and shoved off. She needed to swim deep enough not to be seen by the man running toward the spit, so she dove at a steep angle. After four strokes, she held her dive watch up close to her left eye. Through the blur, she read thirty feet. She leveled out and made long, deliberate strokes. Swimming with the current, she sliced through the water like a dolphin. *Break your record, Addy: more than a hundred yards. You've got to reach the cover of the low cliffs.*

After what seemed an eternity, her lungs screaming for air, Addy swam close to the ledge. She'd memorized the indentation along the bank of rock ledges where she'd entered the water to start her swim, but they were a blur with no goggles. *Did I already pass it?*

She hugged her chest to the rocks, exhaled, slowly surfaced, and took a breath. She was still short of her starting point, but the jumble of rocks along the shore hid her from view of anyone standing on the spit. Careful not to stray away from the edge and be spotted by the men searching for her, she pulled herself along till she spotted the narrow break in the rocks where she'd started her swim.

Sanjeev was hunkered down, waiting for her. He put his finger to his lips, "Quiet. They're not far." He helped Addy out of the water. "Follow me," he whispered. "We must hurry." He took her hand and led her past the jumble of boulders and into the trees.

They hiked swiftly up through the forest, Sanjeev pulled Addy along with one hand, and carrying her T-shirt and shorts with the other. After another hundred yards, Addy slowed, so he stopped to let her catch her breath. "That guy, their leader, shot Ethan in the hand," Sanjeev said, crouching next to her. "He appears to be okay though," Sanjeev continued, "because he's leading those men up the hill. We need to stay ahead of them." He smiled broadly, pointed to the fuel line wrapped around her waist, then hugged her. "You did it, Addy. You really did it!"

Addy took the key from inside her bathing suit bottom and showed it to him before slipping it back. "I got the key to the Zodiac too," she said, smiling. "I bet they're pissed."

"No doubt. Take a few more seconds to rest and recover," Sanjeev told her. He handed her the shirt and shorts. "We've got a bit of head start but need to get moving to keep ahead of them."

Addy pulled on her T-shirt and shorts. "Okay, let's go."

Exhausted from her swim, Addy struggled to keep

up, but Sanjeev kept her going, pulling her along up the steep hill. Stumbling into a clearing at the top of the hill, Addy paused again to catch her breath. "Find a place to hide," she said between breaths. "I'll stash this fuel line where Ethan and I agreed. Stay of sight and don't come out until you hear the all-clear from Ethan or me."

"I should stay with you," Sanjeev said.

"Just go. Hurry," Addy said. "And thank you, Sanjeev. I wouldn't have made it up here in time without your help." She waited for Sanjeev to disappear up the trail and then went to the bush at the edge of the clearing where she and Ethan agreed she would stash whatever she took to disable the fishing boat. Addy unwrapped the rubber fuel line from around her waist, re-coiled it, dropped to her stomach, and shoved it under the bush and covered it with dry leaves.

Brushing herself off, she walked to a tree just past the edge of the opposite side of the clearing, and set the key and fob in the crook of the tree. Then she walked to the center of the clearing, crossed her legs, and sat down. *Here we go.*

Chapter 28

Eko stood over Raj, raised one of his massive legs, and stomped his gut. Raj let out a whoosh, groaned, and rolled over on the sand. He'd learned how to take a body punch in his muay thai training. But his training didn't consider getting stomped on by someone with Eko's strength and bulk. "Anand won't let me kill you, little rat," he taunted Raj. "But he didn't say I couldn't have a little fun." He stepped back and kicked Raj in the side.

"Do you want to be a rich man, Eko?" Malik called out. He wanted to divert the big man's attention. Raj was tough, but no one could survive that kind of a beating for long. "Anand lives in a mansion," Malik continued baiting Eko, "but you still live in that shithole in Maura Angke. I've got a buyer for all that heroin, and I'll split it with you. Come on, big guy. What does Anand ever give you? Look at you. It's hot out here, yet he makes you wear a black suit. On a beach. You look like his monkey. We'll give you half. Raj and I will split the other half. You can live like a king."

Eko paused his assault on Raj. "I told you to shut up," he said. "When Anand returns, we'll tie a rope around your feet and drag you behind the boat. Let's see how much you talk then."

"When Anand returns? Ha. You can't do anything without his permission, can you, lapdog?" Malik said, continuing to needle Eko. "That's what you are: A fat, hairy, boot-licking lapdog."

Eko peeled off his black suit coat and tossed it aside. His long-sleeved white shirt was soaked through with sweat and stuck to his massive chest. His sunburned face grew even redder with rage. "Let's hear you talk after I shove a bucket of sand down your gullet." Eko started toward Malik.

At that moment, Gage suddenly woke up. Dehydrated, delirious, and burning with thirst, he crawled toward the boats on his one good arm and knees. "Water. I need water."

Eko looked over at Gage, "Where do you think you're going?" He kicked Malik in the gut, knocking him to the sand. "Don't go anywhere," he said, sarcastically. "That was just a taste of what's to come." He headed toward Gage to drag him back.

With Eko distracted, Raj rocked back and forth in the sand, working his zip-tied hands around his butt and then past the back of his legs. He got one leg out, and then the other. His hands were still tied, but now they were in front of his body. He crouched and nodded to Malik.

His back turned and distracted by Gage, Eko didn't see Malik struggle to his feet, lower his head, and rush him. Malik dove into the back of his knees. Eko's knees buckled, and he toppled forward to the sand. Cursing, he delivered a savage kick to Malik's face with the bottom of his foot, sending Malik rolling in the sand. Eko rolled to his knees just as Raj raced over and leaped on his back. Raj looped his wrists over Eko's massive neck and yanked the zip-tie against Eko's throat with all his strength.

Eko rolled to his back, burying Raj under his three hundred fifty pounds of bulk. Gasping for air, Eko grabbed Raj's wrists, and with brute strength, pulled them off his throat, and began bashing the back of his head against Raj's. Trapped underneath the huge man, Raj could only turn his head to protect his face.

Suddenly Fabiola appeared and clasped two handfuls of sand over Eko's face. "Let's see how you like it, you fucking monster." She covered his nose and mouth and held tight.

Forced to let go of Raj's arms, Eko slapped Fabiola's hands away, but not before inhaling a lungful of sand. Coughing violently, he rolled over and got up onto his hands and knees.

Still clinging to his back, Raj slipped his zip-tied wrists over Eko's head again, but Eko grabbed them before Raj got them down over his throat. Raj pulled with all his might. Choking from a mouthful of sand, enraged, and desperate to relieve the searing pain of the plastic zip-tie cutting into his lips and cheeks, Eko stood, pulled Raj's arms off his face, and flung him from his back. Coughing furiously, he reached for the .45 automatic in his shoulder holster. Just as his hand closed on the grip, Malik rammed into the back of his legs again. Eko toppled forward just short of the water's edge. He again struggled to his feet just as Raj launched himself, and delivered a flying kick to Eko's chest with both feet.

The force sent Eko stumbling backward, splashing into the water on his back. Before Eko could turn and get to his feet in the shallow water, Raj pounced again, driving Eko face down on the sandy bottom. In a panic, the .45 already in his hand, Eko shoved himself off the bottom, driving the gun barrel deep in the sand. He stood, coughed out a mouthful of seawater and blinked repeatedly to clear the saltwater from his eyes. Raj was splashing through the water toward him again. He raised the gun and fired.

The .45 exploded. Eko let out a bloodcurdling cry as the smoking remains of the gun plopped into the water. The sand-plugged barrel blew apart the breech and blew off two of Eko's fingers. Raj rammed into Eko, knocking him into deeper water. Raj quickly grabbed the back of Eko's collar with both hands, and dragged him farther from shore. Eko yanked free of Raj's grasp, but now his legs found nothing but water beneath them. Eko kicked and flailed in a growing panic, his short, thick arms plopping like a dog tossed into deep water for the first time. "*Tolong saya!*" Eko begged, choking on mouthfuls of water between panicked cries for help. "*Tolong saya!*"

Raj swam beyond his flailing grasp. He treaded water and watched Eko struggle in frantic, wide-eyed terror until he went under. The water churned for a few more seconds, then stilled. Raj swam a wide berth around where Eko went under, waded ashore, and stood next to Malik. "I told you I'd kill him one day."

"How'd you know he couldn't swim?" Malik asked.

"Water was the one thing he was afraid of," Raj answered. He looked at Fabiola. "Thank you. If not for your help, he'd have murdered me for sure."

"I couldn't just stand by and let him kill you." She glanced toward Gage. He was struggling to climb into the fishing boat to get water. "I'll get it, Gage." She ran over and grabbed a bottle of water from the ice chest, and helped Gage take a drink. "Let's get you under some shade." She motioned for Raj and Malik to help.

Raj went to the back of the fishing boat and worked the zip tie back and forth along the blade of the propeller until he managed to cut it, then helped Malik do the same. They lifted Gage into the fishing boat and laid him on the bench under the sunshade. They gave him more water, and Malik cleaned his wounds again, ripping a towel into strips to re-dress them.

"Can we get out of here before the others come back?" Gage asked, weakly.

"I'm afraid not," Malik answered. "You were in and out of consciousness, so I'm not sure how much you heard. Addy must have come down and disabled these boats while Ethan distracted them. Ethan struck a deal to give them what they need to operate this boat in exchange for releasing you two."

"What do we do now?" Fabiola asked.

"They must have a plan, but I don't know what it is." Malik grabbed more bottles of water. He handed one to Fabiola and tossed another to Raj. "Ethan and Addy risked their lives to save the two of you, and we're still alive because of it. I have to go help them."

"I'm going with you," Raj said. "Anand will kill Ethan as soon as he gets what he wants."

"Not if you kill that sadistic bastard first," Fabiola said in a menacing tone.

Chapter 29

Anand and Nur followed Ethan up through the forest. The palm trees thinned as they moved inland, replaced by tall eucalyptus and thorny undergrowth. A few minutes into their trek, Ethan stopped to tighten the wrapping on his hand. He wanted to make sure Addy had time to arrive at the clearing before they did.

Anand motioned to Nur. He responded by shoving Ethan in the back with his assault rifle. "Move it," Nur ordered.

"How much farther?" Anand demanded.

"See that rise up there?" Ethan said, pointing through the trees toward the hilltop, partially visible through the canopy. "We'll veer left up ahead to skirt the steepest part of the slope and then traverse back to the right near the top." Ethan talked loudly and stepped on every twig he came across to alert Addy of their approach.

"Remember, I'll put another bullet in you at the first sign of trickery," Anand said, growing increasingly wary.

"No tricks." Ethan continued up the hillside, grabbing saplings and branches along the way with his left hand to pull himself up the hill. The loose soil and dry leaves covering the forest floor made finding secure footing more difficult as their trek steepened.

After a few more minutes, they scrambled to the

top of the ridge. Ethan stopped to catch his breath and adjusted his bandage again. Breathing heavily, he pointed to his right. "This way. It's not much farther," he said, this time even louder.

Ethan found the game trail and followed it for fifty yards. He stepped into the clearing and stopped cold. Addy sat cross-legged in the middle. *This wasn't in the plan.* They'd agreed she would hide the fuel line, then stay out of sight.

"You must be the ghost who disabled our boats," Anand said, walking past Ethan into the clearing. He'd drawn his 9mm and held it at his side. "Tell me, pretty lady, how did you do it without us seeing you?"

"I swam underwater," Addy said.

"Ah. Impressive. You must be one hell of a swimmer. And thief. I could use someone like you. As it turns out, I'm suddenly short-staffed. Want a job? It pays well."

"I already have a job."

"Too bad." He waved his handgun toward the blood-soaked handkerchief around Ethan's hand. Still tucked under his left armpit, Ethan's torso below it was wet with blood. "As you can see, I'm not someone to be trifled with. Do I need to shoot you too?"

"Not if you want to get off this island."

Anand looked up at the trees. "It is quite lovely here. But I am tiring of it. So, here we all are, just like you wanted. What now?"

Ethan answered, "You and I will stay here while she goes down to the beach. As soon as I see her and my other two compatriots safely away in the Zodiac, I'll give you the fuel line."

"Stand up," Anand ordered, pointing his 9mm at

Addy's face.

Addy stood up.

"Where's the key to the Zodiac?"

"Hidden," she said.

"Empty your pockets and turn around. Slowly."

Addy pulled out the linings of her pockets and did a slow 360-degree turn.

"Were you in on the conspiracy with him and that fat captain to steal my merchandise?"

"I don't know what you're talking about, scumbag. Do we have a deal or not?"

"You steal my merchandise, sneak in and disable my boats, then have the nerve to call me a scumbag? Listen, bitch, give me the key and fuel line, or I'll kill you both. Right here and now."

"Fuck you, asshole. I hope you like your new island home," Addy said, staring back.

"Grab her," Anand ordered.

Nur lowered his Kalashnikov and grabbed for Addy's arm. She wrenched it away and punched him in the face, took a quick step back, and kicked him in the balls. He dropped his rifle and fell to the ground, grasping his crotch.

"Worthless moron," Anand said, looking down at Nur, rolling in the dirt and moaning. Anand kept his pistol trained on Addy and picked up the rifle.

"Live up to the deal," Ethan said. "It's the only way you'll get the fuel line and recover your precious heroin."

Anand shook his head and chuckled. He tossed the rifle to Nur, who'd recovered enough to stand. Anand lowered his 9mm and slid it back in its holster. "All right, you and your tough lady friend win…for now."

He made a waving motion, “You better get that pretty ass moving.” He looked at his watch. “If you don’t show up in the next half hour, Eko will kill your friends.”

“Go, Addy,” Ethan said. “Get them and get out of here. I’ll be okay.”

Addy squeezed Ethan’s hand. She looked back at Anand. “You harm him, and I’ll kill you.”

“Yeah, yeah, sure you will.” Anand motioned toward the trail. “Get along, now, before I change my mind.”

Addy disappeared into the trees.

“Wow. I bet she’s a tiger in bed. What’s she like?”

“It’s easy to talk tough when you’re holding a gun,” Ethan said.

“I’m the most dangerous man you’ll ever know, Dayne, with or without a gun. Keep testing me, and you’ll join the rest of my enemies in the dirt.”

****

Addy grabbed the Zodiac key from the crook of the tree where she’d hidden it and hurried downhill toward the beach. Making it off the steepest part of the hill, she picked up her pace, breaking into a run, hurdling brush and dodging limbs.

A blur appeared out of the corner of her eye. Before she could react, something hit her hard and dragged her to the ground. Stunned, she fought to get up, but an arm circled her throat, and legs entangled and held hers. A hand clamped down on her mouth like a vise. She couldn’t move.

“Addy, it’s me, Raj.”

Malik crouched next to her, “Sorry,” he said. “We weren’t sure who was running down the trail.”

Raj loosened his grip and let her up.

"How did you escape?" Addy asked. "What about Fab and Gage? Are they all right?"

"They're fine," Malik assured her. "They're inside the fishing boat. The man Anand left to guard us is dead. It must have been you who stole the keys, right?"

Addy nodded, uneasily. "Is that why you tackled me? To take the key?"

"No. We've come to help."

"Wait…That big man is dead?" She looked up the hill in the direction of Ethan and Anand. "He'll see!" She panicked. "The ledge. Ethan will lead him to the ledge. He'll know you've escaped. Oh my God, they'll see the body."

"Not unless he floats to the surface," Raj said.

"They'll know you escaped."

"Does Anand already have the key or the fuel line you took?" Malik asked.

"I have the key to the Zodiac. I hid the fuel line. The plan is for Ethan to lead them to it once I've taken the Zodiac."

Suddenly three gunshots rang down from up on the hill, followed seconds later by two bursts from an automatic weapon.

"Oh no, they've killed him!" Addy started to run back up the hill.

"Addy, wait!" Raj grabbed her. "Two different weapons fired. He might've grabbed one or, he could've run. There's a chance he's still alive."

"Let's go then!" Addy struggled to free herself.

"No, wait," Malik said. "Ethan risked his life to rescue Gage and Fab. You should take the Zodiac and get them out of here. It's what he'd want. Raj and I will go after Ethan."

Addy looked from the hilltop to the beach. She nodded reluctantly. "You're right," she said, taking a deep breath and expelling it with a heavy sigh. "Please save him." She took off toward the beach.

****

"Hey, I can see the beach from here," Nur said. He'd walked over the ledge. "Where'd they all go?"

Anand stood next to him and looked over the edge. "What the fuck?"

"I don't see them other two neither."

Anand raised his palm to shade his eyes. "I can see the girl and the hurt guy inside the boat, but I don't see Eko. Or Malik and Raj."

"Where do you think they are?"

"Eko might've dragged them off into the trees. He's wanted to kill them both for a long time. Or maybe Raj killed him and escaped and is coming up here after us."

"Then where's Eko's body? He's too big to carry. I don't believe he's dead. He's Eko. Besides, how could they have gotten free? Their hands were tied. Even if they did, they ain't got no guns."

"Shut the fuck up," Anand said. "Raj is dangerous. I taught him myself." He turned and faced Ethan. "This changes the deal, Dayne. Give me the fuel line now."

"Not until I see my friends away from the beach in the Zodiac," Ethan said.

"Nur, the moment you see that bitch come out on the beach, shoot her," Anand ordered. He pointed his gun at Ethan's head. "This isn't a bluff, Dayne. Nur will kill her, and I'll put a tidy little hole right between your eyes. Give me the fuel line right now, and I'll spare you both."

Ethan swallowed hard. "Nothing's changed," he said. "You'll get it when I see the Zodiac leave."

Anand put the barrel against Ethan's forehead and cocked the hammer. "Your friend is going to step out onto that beach any second now, and my man is going to open fire on her. You're running out of time, and I'm running out of patience. What's it going to be?"

"It's over there," Ethan said, pointing toward the brush to his right at the edge of the clearing. "I'll show you. Tell him not to shoot her."

Anand waved Nur off. He shoved Ethan toward the brush. Ethan walked to the edge of the clearing and pointed to a thick, thorny shrub. "It's hidden under that bush."

Anand stepped forward and knelt, but then hesitated. The branches were covered in inch-long thorns. "I'm not sticking my hand under there. How do I know you don't have some other trick up your sleeve?"

"There's no trick. Just reach in and get it."

"I don't trust you. You get it." Anand stepped back and motioned to Ethan with his gun.

Once he has it, he'll shoot me. Then they'll kill Addy. Guarding his injured hand, Ethan dropped down to his elbows and reached under the bush. He ran his fingers through the dead leaves until he found the coiled rubber hose. His hand gripped the primer bulb in the middle of the coil, and a plan materialized. He gently squeezed the bulb and immediately smelled gasoline. Ethan dragged the fuel line out and stood up. He held the coil in his left hand, and gritting his teeth to stand the pain, raised the end with his bandaged right hand. “Here it is,” he said.

“Smart move, Dayne,” Anand said, a look of relief on his face. He lowered his gun and reached for the hose.

Ethan pointed the nozzle at Anand’s face and squeezed the primer bulb as hard as he could. A stream of gasoline squirted out, spraying Anand in the eyes.

“Argh!” Anand recoiled and stumbled back, ducking his face away from the spray.

Still holding the hose, Ethan pivoted and dove into the bushes. The thorns tore into him as he crashed through it, landing on the other side. He held his injured hand to his chest, rolled to his feet and took off at a dead run, tearing through the bushes and zigzagging around the trees.

Pop! Pop! Pop! Anand fired blindly. He yanked out a handkerchief and wiped his eyes. “Get him!” he screamed. “Shoot that motherfucker!”

Nur, dumbfounded at what he’d just witnessed, suddenly snapped to and opened fire on the bushes with his Kalashnikov. He ran over to the edge of the clearing where Ethan disappeared and squeezed off another burst.

“Quit firing, you idiot!” Anand shouted. “Save your ammo.” Anand cursed and blinked repeatedly. “Get over to that ledge, and shoot that woman the moment you see her come out onto the beach. Do not let her get away with that boat. Do you hear me, you fucking moron? Do not let her get away!”

“Yes, sir,” Nur ran over to the rim overlooking the beach and looked down. “It looks like half a kilometer down to that beach. I don’t think I can hit her from up here, boss. Maybe I should go after her.”

"She'll be gone by then. You've got a fucking machine gun, so you damn well better not miss." Anand holstered his 9mm. He spat into his handkerchief and wiped his eyes again, blinked several more times, then stuffed the handkerchief back into his pocket. He turned sideways and squeezed through the thorny brush. The thorns ripped his silk shirt and gouged his skin. "Goddammit," he said, carefully extracting a thorn from his side. He gritted his teeth and pushed his way through.

Anand spent years fighting in the jungle and built his reputation leading ambushes and tracking adversaries. Confident Ethan wouldn't get far with a bullet wound, Anand muttered, "I'm going to enjoy killing that sneaky bastard." A short way past the clearing, the thorny undergrowth thinned. Jogging through the trees, he spotted a splotch of blood on the ground. He knelt and rubbed it between his finger and thumb, looked up the trail and smiled. *I'm on your track, Dayne. No tricks can save you now.*

Chapter 30

Ethan stopped to listen for the sound of someone following, but his own labored breathing was the only sound. He hoped both men were following him so Addy could make it safely to the boat. *At least one of them must be,* he told himself. He had the fuel line, and that boat was their only way off the island. Ethan resumed running up the trail. His hand throbbed, and a sticky mix of blood and dirt covered his torso down to his thigh. The adrenaline which had given him the stamina to push onward was flagging, and every step became more difficult.

Ethan slid down an embankment and then clambered up the rocky swale to the little glade where they'd spent the night. He dropped to his stomach, plunged his face in the cold, clear water, and drank. Getting up, he glanced back down the trail. A flash of white appeared through the trees up on the ridge. *Shit! He's close behind.*

****

"Where do you think they are?" Malik asked, struggling to catch his breath.

"I don't know," Raj said. He paused to let Malik rest. "But since they're armed and we aren't, our best chance will be to surprise them. We should split up. You continue up this trail. I'll cut right here and climb up from the other side of that ledge. It's the steepest part, so they won't be expecting it. Once you get to the top, maybe you can create a distraction." Then he added, "But don't get yourself shot."

"I'll do my best," Malik answered. He started once again up the steep trail.

"You're a good man, Malik. Thank you."

Malik looked back. "For what?"

"For showing me how it feels to do the right thing." Raj turned and headed up through the rocky scrub leading to the summit.

****

Addy hid behind a large palm tree and looked out onto the beach. It appeared deserted except for the two boats. She couldn't see Gage or Fabiola in either one. "Fab," she called out.

Fabiola raised her head and looked over the bow of the fishing boat. "Addy?"

"Yes. I'm going to make a run for your boat. I've got the key to the Zodiac. We need to get Gage over to it and launch it."

"Okay. Come on."

Addy burst from the tree line and ran toward the boats. She'd made it halfway when the sand around her exploded. The sound of gunfire echoed down from the ridge. Addy hit the ground, rolled, and sprang to her feet. She sprinted back toward the cover of the trees. The sand in front of her feet erupted again as the sound of another burst of gunfire reverberated through the trees. Addy hit the dirt, then rose to her hands and feet, and scampered to the nearest palm tree. She leaned back against the trunk and pulled her knees tight against her chest.

****

Nur sat cross-legged on the ledge, his Kalashnikov resting across his knees. *What happened down there,* he wondered. *Could Eko really be dead? No way.* Nur had seen him shot before, cut with a knife, hit by a club. *Eko's invincible. And them other two were tied up. Maybe Eko killed them both and dragged their bodies off somewhere. I hope so.* Raj scared him too. Raj was a different kind of killer, cunning, and quick with a knife. *Could Raj be coming after me now?* He shuddered and gripped the smooth wooden stock of the rifle.

Suddenly a woman sprinted toward the Zodiac. Nur sprang to his feet, fumbled to aim the gun, and pulled the trigger. The woman fell to the ground. He smiled, thinking he'd somehow hit her, but she got up and ran back toward the trees. He squeezed off another burst. She hit the ground but again quickly sprang to her feet. Certain he had the angle right this time, Nur aimed again and squeezed the trigger. Nothing. He popped out the magazine. *Empty.*

Nur looked down at the beach. The girl was nowhere in sight. *What do I do now?* Anand had disappeared into the forest chasing the guy with the fuel hose. *If she gets to the boat, there's nothing I can do to stop them from taking it and leaving.* Anand was already furious at him for letting the woman get the best of him. *He might just be mad enough to shoot me.* Deciding that going after the woman was better than waiting to suffer Anand's wrath if she got away, Nur headed down toward the beach.

****

"Come on, Dayne," Anand's voice echoed through the forest. He'd followed Ethan's trail for a quarter hour, periodically seeing traces of blood. He was gaining on him. Ethan couldn't be too far ahead. "All I want is that fuel line. Drop it on the trail, and no one gets hurt." Silence. Anand started jogging again. He kept up a constant pace for another few minutes. He was in his element. *I'm like one of my pets, chasing wounded prey through the jungle.* A twig snapped somewhere ahead, and he paused to listen. He caught a glimpse of Ethan, running, thirty yards ahead. Anand drew his 9mm and aimed through an opening in the trees. *I've got you now.* He squeezed off a shot. Missed. He brought his other hand up to steady the gun, aimed, and fired again.

****

Ethan slowed, his entire body seizing up. He pushed through the pain, willing himself forward, knowing death awaited if he stopped. Just as he burst into a clearing, a shot rang out, and a bullet whizzed past his ear. *Run!* Ethan's brain relayed the command to his legs just before the second bullet hit his back just inside the scapula. It tore through flesh and exited his chest below his collarbone. The shock sent Ethan sprawling face-first to the ground. He struggled to his feet, ran a few more steps, stumbled, and fell.

"Well, well. You led me on a merry chase, you tricky motherfucker," Anand said as he walked into the clearing. He picked up the coil of rubber hose from the ground where Ethan dropped it when the bullet hit.

Ethan attempted to stand but collapsed back on his haunches.

"That was one hell of a shot, if I do say so myself." Anand looked back to where he'd stood when he squeezed off the shot that brought down Ethan. "I hit you on a dead run from thirty meters."

“Excuse me if I don’t congratulate you,” Ethan grimaced.

Anand laughed. “You got balls, Dayne; I’ll say that for you. Your lady friend too. It’s a shame to have to kill you both.”

Ethan recognized the small clearing. He looked over to where Nils’s body had been. The rocks and brush they’d piled on it the night before were scattered and the ground torn up. There was no sign of Nils body. Ethan looked up at Anand. “If you kill me, you’ll never find your missing heroin.”

“For fuck’s sake, give it up. How does that saying go? Fool me once, shame on me. Fool me twice, I kill you.”

“I don’t think that’s how it goes,” Ethan said. He made a slight nod toward the far side of the clearing. “It’s buried just ahead. Not much farther. If you shoot me, you’ll never find it.”

Anand sighed. “That’s an inconvenience I’ll just have to deal with. Besides, I’m not going to shoot you. Thanks to your little stunt, I only have one bullet left. I’ll need that in case Raj is still alive.” Anand returned his 9mm to its holster in the small of his back. “I don’t like getting my hands dirty, so please don’t struggle too much. A quick snap of the neck, and it’ll all be over. If you insist on struggling, it’ll just piss me off more than I already am, and I’ll have to choke you to death.”

****

Malik paused at the top of the slope and leaned against a tree to catch his breath and survey the surroundings. Hearing the crunch of a footstep, he looked up to see Nur step from out behind another tree and aim the Kalashnikov at him.

“Hands over your head,” Nur ordered. “Where’s the other one? Where’s Raj?” he looked around nervously.

“Down by the boats,” Malik raised his hands.

“I didn’t see him.” Nur glanced down the hill. You spent all that energy climbing up here, now turn around and head back down.”

Malik dropped back on his haunches. “I can’t. I’m exhausted. I need to rest.”

“You can rest when you’re dead. Which will be right now if you don’t get up and get moving.”

“Okay, okay,” Malik said. He struggled to one knee while holding his hands over his head, panting heavily. “Please, give me just a few more seconds.”

“I said now,” Nur ordered. He pointed the rifle menacingly at Malik’s face.

A twig snapped. Nur spun around, too late. Crack! Sanjeev swung a thick branch, smacking Nur across the side of his head, sending him sprawling to the ground. Dazed, Nur made it up to his hands and knees just before Sanjeev brought the branch down on the back of his head with a sickening thud. Nur crumpled to the ground.

Malik grabbed the rifle and tipped Nur faceup with his foot. The man’s eyes were wide open and his mouth agape. He bent over and felt Nur’s carotid artery. “He’s dead,” Malik said. “Thank you, Sanjeev.”

Sanjeev looked down at the man lying in the dirt and shuddered. “I didn’t mean to kill him.”

“It’s a good thing you did because he certainly intended to kill me.”

Raj ran into the clearing. “Nice job, Sanjeev,” he said, looking down at Nur’s body.

Malik handed Raj the Kalashnikov. Raj ejected the magazine and looked at it. He started to say the clip was empty but stopped, seeing Sanjeev stare down in horror at what he'd just done. Just then, a shot reverberated through the forest. Then another. Raj popped the clip back into the rifle and took off on a dead run in the direction of the shots. Malik and Sanjeev followed, zigzagging through the trees.

****

Ethan pretended to cower when Anand walked toward him and then launched himself into Anand's midsection, tackling him to the ground. Ethan cocked his left arm and swung it, slamming his elbow into Anand's face, splitting his lip and bloodying his nose. Anand reacted in an instant, slugging Ethan's shoulder wound. He shoved Ethan over, and they grappled for control, rolling over and over in the dirt. Anand overpowered Ethan, by now too weakened to put up much of a fight. Anand straddled Ethan's chest, his knees locked on either side, the weight of his haunches sitting back on Ethan's chest and stomach. With murderous rage, Anand pummeled him, raining blows on his face and the exit wound on his shoulder. Blood splattered everywhere and coated Anand's knuckles as he hammered away at Ethan. Then Anand clamped his long, thin fingers around Ethan's throat.

Ethan struggled to free himself, but he was pinned hopelessly on his back. His energy used up, he couldn't pry loose Anand's vice-like grip on his throat. Desperate for air, Ethan clawed at Anand's hands and punched him futilely. Blood from Ethan's hand and the wound on his shoulder splattered across Anand's hands, face, and neck.

Feeling himself slipping away, Ethan closed his eyes and focused his mind on Addy. Knowing he was about to die, he wanted her to be his last lucid thought before losing consciousness. He stopped struggling. *This is it.* Suddenly, Anand's grip on his throat loosened, and the weight on his chest lightened. Ethan gasped and opened his eyes. He gasped another breath and blinked several times to make sure he wasn't hallucinating. Anand levitated above him, his head cocked at an odd angle, looking down at Ethan with a strange, almost quixotic stare. Anand began to shake back and forth, then jerked backward.

Ethan sat up, still locked on Anand's wide-eyed stare, watching the man's limp body dragged away, his neck grasped in the jaws of a huge Komodo dragon. Suddenly, two more dragons rushed in from the side. One grabbed a leg, the other an arm. Grunting and jerking, the three giant monitors tore Anand apart. Ethan shuffled backward in horror when something grabbed his arm.

"It's okay, we've got you," Malik quietly reassured him. He slid his hands under Ethan's armpits and pulled him a few feet away, then helped him stand. He draped Ethan's uninjured arm over his shoulder. Sanjeev carefully lifted his other arm and ducked under it, and the two carried Ethan, backing away slowly, out of the clearing. Raj appeared, crouched, and picked up the coil of rubber hose, then paused, mesmerized at the sight of the dragons grunting and tearing at Anand's dismembered body.

Chapter 31

"Addy, look!" Fabiola pointed back toward the beach. "It's them. It's Ethan and the others."

Addy stood in the stern of the Zodiac and looked back across the bay toward shore. With Gage and Fabiola resting safely in the bow, she'd motored a couple hundred yards offshore and stopped. Ethan limped out of the trees, his arms draped over Malik and Sanjeev's shoulders. Elated, Addy fired up the engine, headed toward shore, and ran the Zodiac up onto the beach. She leaped out and ran to meet them.

"Oh my God, Ethan, what did they do to you?" She asked. His face was cut and bruised, his torso caked with blood and dirt.

"That asshole shot me again, then he tried to strangle me," Ethan rasped. "He almost succeeded."

"Are those men still up there?" Fabiola asked. "Are they following you?"

"They're up there," Raj answered. "But they won't be following us."

"They're dead?"

He nodded.

"Good," Addy said. "How? What happened?"

"Sanjeev took care of one," Raj said. "The dragons got Anand."

"Anand loved to feed his enemies to exotic animals," Malik said. "It's only fitting that one got him."

"Now that's some good karma," Ethan said, weakly.

"Yes, Ethan. That is definitely some good karma," Sanjeev agreed.

"How's Gage?" Ethan asked Fabiola.

"He's still in a bad way, but I think a little better now he's had water and knows everyone is safe. He'll be glad to see you."

Malik and Sanjeev helped Ethan over to the fishing boat, then carried Gage over from the Zodiac and laid him next to Ethan. Malik started cleaning and dressing Ethan's wounds.

"You're getting to be a real pro at this, Malik," Ethan said. "Maybe your next career could be as a medic."

"Treating my friend's wounds is not the kind of thing I want to get into the habit of."

Gage struggled to lift his head. "Damn. What happened to you? You look beat to shit, boss. Hell, you look worse than me."

"Seems like beating me up has become a popular pastime."

"Well, here we are again," Dayne," Gage joked. "Gettin' patched up."

"Yeah, here we are again." He squeezed Gage's hand. "I'm sorry, Gage. I almost got you killed."

"Hell, boss," Gage said, trying not to laugh, as any movement caused shooting pain in his shoulder. "You're the one who got shot."

Ethan looked up. Raj and Fabiola were dragging the two black trunks across the sand. "What do you and Raj intend to do with the heroin?" Ethan asked Malik.

"You are a smuggler, after all. Right, Captain?"

"I used to be," Malik said. "Just watch, and you'll find out." He climbed out of the boat and went to the Zodiac. He lifted out the gas tank and carried it up the beach to where Raj and Fabiola were tossing blocks of heroin on top of palm fronds.

Malik doused the pile with gasoline, then returned it to the Zodiac. He walked over to the fishing boat. "We're gonna have ourselves a bonfire," he said. "Would you like to come watch?"

"You guys go ahead," Ethan answered. "Gage and I will watch from here."

Malik took a red flare gun out from under the steering transom of the fishing boat. He popped open the canister and looked to see it was loaded, then snapped it shut. "I'm sorry for what happened to Richard," he said. "And Talib. Even Nils. I betrayed all of you. If I'd dared to stand up to Anand years earlier, none of this would've happened."

"It took courage to decide Richard's life was more important than making your delivery," Addy said. "And it took courage to go up that hill after Anand."

"I'm sorry it took such extraordinary circumstances to find it."

"Won't men still be coming after you?" she asked. "Won't they be after their drugs?"

"Not if they think Raj and I went down with *Varuna*."

Ethan glanced at Addy, and they both nodded. "When we tell our story to the authorities," he said, "we'll say you both died when *Varuna* sank. We'll leave out the part about the drugs. We'll say Anand and his men were kidnappers who captured us after the shipwreck."

"Thank you," Malik said. What about you and Addy? Will you finish your research project and film now?"

"Yes," Ethan said, squeezing Addy's hand. "After I get a little R & R, that is. Addy's invited me to come stay with her in Ubud."

"Richard left some big shoes to fill," Addy said. "But I'm going to give being a biologist another shot. You should come visit sometime."

"Maybe I will," Malik said. "In the meantime, expect an envelope delivered to your dive shop in Denpasar in a couple of weeks."

"What might it contain?" Addy asked.

"Information identifying Anand's pirate fishing fleet. You see, I had a plan to disappear after I made Anand's delivery. Over the past several months, I recorded all the information I could on his criminal organization, including his pirate fishing fleet. I intended to use it as insurance against him coming after me. It won't make up for all that happened, but you should have quite a story to tell. You've discovered one of the biggest illegal fishing operations in this part of the world, and you've rid the world of a notorious gangster, poacher, and hijacker in the process."

"Thank you, Malik," Ethan said.

"What will you do now?" Addy asked Malik.

"First, we'll make sure you get Ethan and Gage to Golo Mori. If Sanjeev and Raj are still willing to serve with me, we'll take the Zodiac and see if we can salvage *Varuna*. I came across her in the same condition a few years ago. It's a long shot, but maybe she'll still be where we left her, foundered on the rocks.

Then I'll go in search of my wife and son."

"I'm sure they are waiting for you to come find them," Addy said. "I hope you do." She glanced up the beach where Sanjeev, Fabiola, and Raj were waiting.

Malik offered her the flare gun. "Care to do the honors?"

"I think it'll be more meaningful if you do it."

Malik and Addy walked over to the pile of white blocks and palm fronds.

"What are you waiting for, Captain?" Raj said. "Light em up."

Malik took aim and fired.

A word about the author...

Phil is a writer living in Portland, Oregon. Taking a break from a career recovering assets from the wreckage of failed financial institutions, Phil plumbed his experiences in the seedier realms of international finance, along with his lifelong passion exploring and diving the world's oceans, to write his debut thriller, *Varuna*, the first in a series.

http://philvincentbooks.com